PRAISE FOR *ALL THE GOOD PARTS*

"Deceptively lighthearted and delightfully written, *All the Good Parts* is the story of a woman of a certain age, pondering a dream with a time stamp: that of becoming a mother. Should she or shouldn't she? What's best for her? Who should the father be? Everyone weighs in on the question: her sister, her brother-in-law, her niece. Even her home health care clients. But the hilarity of choosing among some mighty unusual suspects is tempered with compassion and wisdom that speaks to the very heart of what matters—of what makes us matter to ourselves and each other. And the clincher? What takes *All the Good Parts* over the top into must-read territory? There's a twist near the end that will leave you breathless."

—Barbara Taylor Sissel, author of *Crooked Little Lies*

"*All the Good Parts* by Loretta Nyhan is a tender, warmhearted, and fast-paced story of a family finding its way through an uncertain time for everyone. Nyhan's writing delicately balances the stress and love felt between sisters Leona and Carly. Nyhan also examines the intricate dynamics of Leona's unusual friendships. These pivotal relationships are the story's backdrop as Leona decides if she's going to have a baby on her own at thirty-nine. I laughed, I cried, and I cheered as Leona fought herself and others, stumbled, and in the end became a better version of herself—which is always a good thing, baby or not. I read this book way past my bedtime."

—Amy Sue Nathan, author of *The Good Neighbor*

"Leona Accorsi, thirty-nine, suddenly decides she wants a baby, simply to love. The decision leads her on a journey of self-discovery and puts a unique twist on the idea of looking for love in all the wrong places. Her funny, tender, and heartfelt interactions with each of the not necessarily appropriate people on her short list of potential daddy donors all ultimately bring her to new insights about herself. The story kept me smiling and wondering, *What's going to happen next?!* from the first scene to the very satisfying finish."

—Jackie Bouchard, author of *House Trained* and *Rescue Me, Maybe*

"Quirky and laugh-out-loud funny, we loved *All the Good Parts*! Nyhan had us at page 1 with this unique yet relatable story of the deep bonds between sisters and family and the yearning for motherhood. Readers who want to be swept up and taken on an emotional roller coaster will love *All the Good Parts*!"

—Liz Fenton and Lisa Steinke, authors of *The Year We Turned Forty* and *The Status of All Things*

"*All the Good Parts* is wildly original and features a mixture of heartfelt and laugh-out-loud moments. The main character's quest for motherhood is poignant and relatable . . . [but] it's the ensuing complexities that arise as the main character tries to find a suitable daddy donor from a varied potential list that make this story hard to put down."

—RT Book Reviews (4 stars)

"[Nyhan] creates an original and endearing contemporary heroine in Leona Accorsi . . . [Her] novel tells a surprising, sweet, and unconventional story about family and friendship."

—*Booklist*

Digging In

ALSO BY LORETTA NYHAN

All the Good Parts
Empire Girls
I'll Be Seeing You

Digging In

LORETTA NYHAN

LAKE UNION
PUBLISHING

Text copyright © 2018 by Loretta Nyhan
All rights reserved.

Published by Lake Union Publishing, Seattle

www.apub.com

Amazon, the Amazon logo, and Lake Union Publishing are trademarks of Amazon.com, Inc., or its affiliates.

ISBN-13: 9781542047296 (paperback)
ISBN-10: 1542047293 (paperback
ISBN 13: 9781503951709 (hardcover)
ISBN 10: 1503951707 (hardcover)

Cover design by David Drummond

Printed in the United States of America

To those who know the worst that life can bring, and still hope for the best . . .

CHAPTER 1

We had a system in the morning. The alarm squawked at 6:08, and I switched it off, no snoozes allowed. I ran a hand through Jesse's adorably pillow-flat hair to wake him, and he nuzzled me a little, stubbly chin tickling my jaw, then swung his long legs over the side of the bed, sighed, and headed downstairs to make coffee. I jumped in the shower, and ten minutes later Jesse got in while I slid past him, pretending to be outraged as he copped a feel. My outfit, chosen carefully the night before, lay across our reading chair. I dressed quickly, dried my hair upside down for volume, and carefully applied a layer of makeup using the closet mirror. Jesse donned a suit and dress shirt, pausing only to ask my opinion on his choice of tie. Together, we pounded on Trey's door until we heard a moan and the heavy thud of bare feet hitting the hardwood floors. Once downstairs, we shared a cup of coffee, split a bowl of yogurt, and hugged Trey goodbye when he slunk into the kitchen. We walked out the French patio doors hip to hip, shouted overzealous "Good mornings!" to Mr. Eckhardt next door, and laughed when our cranky neighbor ducked his head, pretending he hadn't heard us. Then we kissed, a real one, somewhere between perfunctory and embarrassing, got into our cars, and began our days.

Our shared life was perfect.

Until two years ago, on a bright, clear summer morning, when Jesse's Volvo tapped the median on the Kennedy Expressway. If he'd been driving during the aching crawl of rush hour, it would have amounted to a fender bender, but traffic was sparse that Sunday, and a mere brush with concrete at sixty-five miles per hour sent him spinning off across all four lanes, slamming into a few cars on his way over to the guardrail, where his car flipped once, twice, and hit the concrete bottom with such force it flattened the top of Jesse's car.

People said I should be thankful no one else was seriously injured. I wouldn't wish pain on anyone, but I had to admit I did wish the universe had disbursed it more fairly—a broken leg here, a fractured clavicle there. Jesse took it all, his body crumpled and broken, and he wouldn't have had it any other way.

I would, though. I'd have had it *any* other way.

Because now? That perfection? That safety? That comfort?

All gone.

Our perfect system.

All. Gone.

～

I jabbed the snooze bar for the third time, settling in for another dip into the dark underworld of sleep, when Trey pounded on the wall between us, shouting, "Just get up already!"

"You can shower first!" I said, trying to sound chipper from beneath the duvet. Our elderly hot water heater was in its last throes, crackling and popping ominously every time we tried to take two showers at once. Trey said something that sounded vaguely like a curse word, but then I heard the groan of the pipes and the light rain of our weak water pressure.

I tucked my nose under my arm and sniffed. Not terrible. If I skipped a shower, I could close my eyes awhile longer, and push the start of morning to the side until after Trey left for school.

What felt like a few moments later, the jolt of an almost-man scream tore through my veil of sleep. "Mom! MOM! It's freezing!"

Wincing as the sun's bright rays bullied their way through my tightly shut blinds, I hauled myself out of bed. "I'll call the guy," I said, though I wasn't quite sure which guy. The plumber with no sense of humor? The heating guy who always smelled like sauerkraut? Jesse would have known. The first phone call should have been to him.

Trey flung open the bedroom door, a towel around his waist. He shook his head like an angry dog, longish dark hair slapping wetly against goose-bumped skin. "This has got to be fixed, like, now."

I managed a half smile. "How about later? Tools are required. And possibly mechanical equipment. And . . . a brain. I don't think I have any of those right now."

Shivering, he ran a hand through his sopping hair. "I could take a look at it."

He looked apprehensive. Both of us knew he wouldn't know what he was doing. Jesse hadn't quite gotten around to teaching him basic fix-it skills. I put my hands on his frigid shoulders. At seventeen, he was taller than Jesse ever was, and more solidly built, and I brought myself up on tiptoe to kiss his cheek. "Taking a shower in cold water is energizing. Look at the bright side."

He eyed me suspiciously. "Since when are you into bright sides?"

"I have a good feeling about today."

"Whatever," he said. "But if we don't have hot water later, I'm sleeping at Colin's."

I mentally Rolodexed through his friends, as he'd begun hanging with a new crowd this year. "I don't know his family. I'll need to speak to his mother before you spend the night."

Laughing, Trey turned back toward his bedroom. "Yeah, good luck with that."

"His mother isn't home?"

"His mother doesn't treat him like a child."

But you are still a child, I thought. *A scared, lonely child.* "Text me her number anyway."

~

When Jesse and I planned our wedding ceremony, the priest offered to let us write our own vows, but like we did in every other aspect of our lives, we played by the rules and went with the conventional wording, the litany that ended with "Till death do us part." Though we'd seen young people die at each other's hands in the gang-infested neighborhood we grew up in, a tiny square just northwest of the city's center, we felt untouched by it. We were too young, too new, with a future bright enough to blind the grim reaper.

So I gave no thought to what "parted" really meant. How unfair it was, how permanent, how out of our control. At his service, everyone said he was still with me, but the truth was that not only was he gone, parts of me went with him. I missed them, too, and like Jesse, they weren't coming back.

We had a good courtship story because it started with friendship—we found each other in eighth grade, in a rough city school in an even rougher neighborhood. Now the place boasted a Starbucks on every corner, but in the '80s and '90s, gangs ran the area—Polish and Puerto Rican, and they weren't like the carousers in *West Side Story*. If Jesse and I hadn't teamed up, our options would have been death, jail, or getting hooked on drugs. Instead, we did our homework together while Jesse's mom and my grandmother played bingo. We walked home from school, shoulders touching, heads down, minding our own business.

Somehow we managed to make ourselves invisible. But I could always see Jesse, and he could always see me.

We were careful with our friendship, because we knew it was the key to our survival. We didn't hug or hold hands or experiment with each other, and when others sparked our interest, we didn't talk about it or offer advice. Those infatuations never lasted longer than it took for us to realize relationships threatened our trajectory toward success. Success was all that mattered.

So we remained careful, and we remained together. Junior college to save money, then a state school. I majored in graphic design with a minor in business. He became an actuary. We lived together as friends to save funds, and then, during our senior year, we decided to stay living together. As more than friends.

Forever. Till death do us part.

The thing is, no one tells you what to do when the parting happens. And they forget to explain that when death is sudden, the parting is actually a ragged tear, not a clean separation. It leaves all the ends unfinished, and they just unravel and unravel and . . .

CHAPTER 2

I got to work at eight forty-five, a miracle given that I couldn't find a single clean item of clothing to wear. Just as I was about to pluck something from the laundry basket and throw it into the dryer for ten minutes, I spotted an old suit still in the cleaner's plastic hanging around the back of my closet. Sure, I bought it sometime during the Bush administration (the old guy, not his son), but it wasn't wrinkled, and the gauzy pink scarf I threw around my neck looked nice with the light gray wool. A little heavy for mid-May, but the spring mornings still held a chill in Illinois. It would do.

My employer, Giacomo Advertising and Design, was the newest tenant of Gossamer Space, an old factory converted into open, airy lofts. Our previous address did not hold the same allure. Frank Giacomo hired me seventeen years ago, when I was both a recent grad with no experience and a new mom (also with no experience). He took me on anyway. Short and round, always chomping on a cigar and wearing more gold around his neck than a rap star, Frank was a secret feminist, and he filled his office with smart, talented women. The vast majority of our clients were local, as Frank wasn't ambitious in the traditional sense. Frank appealed to me because he liked stability, and he appealed to his clients because he had an old-school method of holding their interest—he wined and dined them, asked about their spouses and kids and tennis games, sent them gift baskets at Christmas, and paid his respects when one of them passed on. Everybody liked Frank, because Frank had that one quality no one could resist—he knew who he was and still liked himself.

Our office used to sit above a dental office on Wright Street, beige and bland, nine cubicles in a row, and a cramped, windowless room for Frank. It didn't matter. Every year I got a raise, and I never worried about losing my job. When I needed a vacation, I took one. When Trey got sick, I stayed home with him. Frank usually called midday to see how he was doing.

Last Christmas, at our annual company party in the back room of Marinetti's Chop House, Frank excused himself and never came back. He was found slumped in a bathroom stall, cigar still lit. They had to unclench his jaw to get it out. Frank's heart, as big as the rest of him, had simply worked too hard.

Jesse had only been gone a year, and I'd never had to grieve a father—my own was gone long before tangible memories—so Frank's death sucker punched me. I felt Jesse's absence more acutely. Most of Frank's employees drifted as the company slid into uncertainty, but I stayed on. With both Jesse and Frank gone, even the spare remains of Frank's company offered some bit of stability.

So Giacomo Advertising and Design survived, helmed by Frank's only son, Frank, Jr., a graduate of a small, private university on the East Coast who'd worked a series of vague internships in New York. He carried the city in with him when he walked into the Giacomo offices two weeks after Big Frank's death—skinny jeans and a black leather jacket, expensive sunglasses, and a disdainful expression. Big Frank's genes came through in ways Frank, Jr. tried to hide, his hair carefully disheveled to disguise a premature bald spot, silver rings to dress up Sicilian workingman's hands, a laugh that seemed too hearty for his body. These ghosts of Big Frank had me nodding my head in agreement when Frank, Jr. enthusiastically vowed to make the changes his father had only dreamed of. I never thought Big Frank was much of a dreamer; he was a doer. But if his son had both qualities, Giacomo might survive.

I'd met Frank, Jr. a few times over the years, and it was hard to see him as something other than a kid, until he held a staff meeting with his nervous employees: me; Jackie, the shy, acid-washed-jeans-wearing designer who had been at Giacomo even longer than I had, and a random collection of young designers Big Frank hired when he decided to expand the company after we had a good run—Rhiannon, Seth, Byron, and the timid, newest hire, Glynnis.

On Frank, Jr.'s first day, we had assembled in Big Frank's office, where the walls still exuded cigar smoke. Frank, Jr. held his hands in a namaste style and seemed at a loss for words. He motioned for us to come closer.

"You'll do a good job, Frank," I said, putting a hand on his shoulder.

He eyed my hand distastefully. "I prefer Lukas."

"What?"

"It's my middle name," he said quickly.

His middle name was George, same as his father's, but I didn't disagree. "Okay, *Lukas*. I think I speak for everyone when I say we want the best for Giacomo Advertising and Design, and we will work just as hard, even with Big Frank gone. Actually, even harder."

Frank, Jr./Lukas drew us tighter, our spines awkwardly bending forward to form a group huddle. "You're here because you believe in me. I'm grateful for your trust, and I promise you this," he said, voice solemn and full of emotion. "I not only want to carry on my father's legacy, I want to surpass it by doing right by our clients, new and old, just as he did."

Jackie sniffled, and I admit my eyes stung with tears. We managed an awkward group hug, and then Lukas (after that speech, I figured he was now deserving of whatever name he wanted) sent us back to work, renewed and energized. But I couldn't shake a nagging feeling that somewhere out there, Big Frank was chomping on a cigar, growling, "Never shit a shitter." My bullshit detector, honed to perfection by my former boss, quivered like a flagpole in the wind.

My reservations aside, Lukas jumped into action and, in a move of complete optimism, leased a new space with a conference room and parking lot, hoping to bring in some bigger clients. It worked. In addition to beefing up our local roster, we scored an Italian gelato company eager to break into the American market, a nationally distributed brand of caramel-cheese popcorn, a company dedicated to 100 percent eco-friendly paint, and an ancient cast-iron cookware company looking to ditch their stodgy image. I smiled to think of Big Frank's reaction to our success. He would have been proud.

It wasn't until a few weeks later that I was able to identify why my bullshit detector had gone off. Jackie and I sat on the fire escape silently sharing a sleeve of Girl Scout Thin Mints. Lost in thought, I remembered Lukas's first afternoon. With all the talk of honoring Big Frank and his vision and keeping clients happy, Lukas hadn't said a thing about doing right by us.

~

When I arrived at work, sweating through my gray suit, the first sign that something was awry was an actual sign. The scripted *Giacomo Advertising and Design* sign I'd personally supervised being hung above the door was gone, replaced by a slightly off-kilter neon-orange *G*.

"Did the sign break?" I asked the empty hallway, and then pushed open the door. The loft glittered with shards of light thrown by an actual chandelier. Our cubicles, lugged so carefully across town, had disappeared. Long tables lined the perimeter of the open space, white and glossy against the exposed brick, with sleek oversized computer monitors equally spaced, keyboards hidden beneath. Bright orange plastic exercise balls replaced our practical office chairs, six in total. It looked like a modern art installation, real furniture glossed and shellacked, *Portrait of the Modern Office*. I couldn't spot a single personal item—where was my photo of Trey at eleven, all braces and rounded cheeks? The sand dollar found on a silvery Naples beach on our last trip as a family, a quickie jaunt to Florida? All personal items were gone. Only Jackie, in her sneakers and jean jacket, stood like a startled owl, staring at me with heavily made-up eyes wide and beseeching. "Where is everything? Where is *everyone*?"

Our panic ratcheted up a notch when we heard the clapping.

"Conference room," I said, grasping Jackie's hand as we dashed down the hallway. The door was shut, but I could hear Lukas closing up the meeting.

"Do we go in?" Jackie whispered.

The door opened before I could answer, nearly knocking us on our asses. The staff filed out, each person carrying a box with their name written in bold letters on the front in black marker.

"Oh, dear God, did the company go under?" Jackie said, her voice shaking. "Is everyone fired?"

But they were smiling, talking animatedly to one another. A few gave a general nod in our direction, but whatever they were discussing was too enthralling to make time for pleasantries. Excitement was in their bright, young, cheerful faces. For some reason, that made me more fearful of what was to come.

We stood to the side until everyone passed out of earshot. With one shared look of apprehension, Jackie and I walked in to face Lukas. He sat at the head of the blindingly white conference table, thumbing through a hardcover book. Two boxes formed an odd centerpiece on the table, with *Jackie* scrawled on one and *Paige* on the other. The photo of Trey sat atop my pile.

"You're late," Lukas said, but he kept his tone neutral, more of a general announcement in case we hadn't heard the news.

"It isn't nine yet," I managed.

"Was there an e-mail?" Jackie said hurriedly. "I didn't get the e-mail."

Lukas closed the book he was reading and smiled at us. "By nine o'clock you should be completely present—e-mail checked, coffee drunk, administrative tasks already completed. I called this meeting at eight thirty this morning, and everyone was present but you two."

Jackie grimaced, her face slowly turning a shade more purple than my favorite Pantone color, a deep burgundy. *Don't do it,* I told myself. *Do not show any trace of guilt.* I kept my mouth shut to stop the apology on the tip of my tongue and waited for him to continue.

When he realized we weren't going to fall prostrate at his feet, Lukas pushed the book in my direction. I caught it just before it hit the floor. He reached behind him and passed another book to Jackie. "This is your new bible here at Guh. Don't just read it, commit it to memory. Allow its ideas to marinate in your brain, soak it in, live by it."

I cleared my throat. "So the *g* is pronounced . . . *guh?*"

"It's a simple name change," Lukas said tightly, pointing at the book in my hand. "Rebranding is necessary to escape a rut. Read chapter 7."

I didn't immediately flip open the book, but took in its cover. *The Petra Principles for the New, New Creative Workplace: A Primer for More Than Success* by Petra Polly. The woman on the cover was photographed as she hung upside down, her knees curled around some colorfully painted monkey bars, while artfully dressed children played in the background. Her golden braids hung straight to the pile of woodchips beneath her head. She was cute—round, thickly lashed blue eyes, flushed cheeks, a smile like a baking-show contestant. I think I'd spotted her outfit at Anthropologie. It was a half-knitted, half-silk jumpsuit in a jumble of textures, patterns, and hues, the kind of thing that could only be worn by someone young and thin. The girl was very, very thin and very, very young.

"We're adopting the Petra Principles here at Guh," Lukas said proudly. "Starting with one of her most important dictums, 'Intraoffice competition will only be productive if it is both friendly and fierce.'"

"Competition?" Jackie mouthed the word slowly, as if she'd only learned English five minutes before.

I folded my arms across my chest. "Fierce like Beyoncé, or fierce like Vladimir Putin?"

"Petra doesn't discuss humor until chapter 10, so let's table the wit, okay?"

I nodded and pursed my lips. A reprimand from Lukas felt like a congenial threat. Apparently, "oxymoron" was the go-to word of the day. Friendly and fierce. Congenial and threat.

Lukas offered us a tight smile. "Petra believes that what is good for the human body is good for a company. Very forward thinking, wouldn't you agree?"

Jackie and I nodded dumbly.

"The first chapter discusses cutting the fat. 'An overweight body will harm a person's health, both in the now and down the road,'" Lukas recited. I got the feeling he'd been listening to Petra spout her wisdom on the audiobooks he was constantly listening to while awkwardly sprinting at his treadmill desk. I wondered what she sounded like.

"You want us to drop some weight?" Jackie asked, and I was thrilled to hear a hint of rebellion in her voice. "I'm fifty-one years old. If I want to drop a pound, I have to eat four hundred calories a day. That's only one Lean Cuisine—"

"I'm not requiring *you* to lose the weight," Lukas interjected as his eyes scrolled over Jackie's muffin top. "Our *company* should shed a few. To survive, *and thrive*, we need to be lean."

"We can get rid of the Christmas party," I said, my mind reeling. "And the company picnic this summer. We don't really need kombucha delivered every Friday, do we?"

Lukas shook his head. "Staff. We need to cut two jobs."

Your dad hired these people just over a year ago. I didn't say it out loud. He hadn't said which jobs, but Jackie and I were by far the highest paid, making at least one of us most likely to get the boot. I shuddered at the thought of life on the unemployment line. When your professional life is about to end, it's not your personal history that flashes before your eyes, but your bills—mortgage, car note, tuition, utilities. I had to ask, "Were you thinking of any two people in particular?"

Jackie inhaled sharply.

Lukas tapped the book in my arms. "That's the beauty of Petra's philosophy. It's completely democratic, and so will the process be of who gets let go." He smiled as if to alert me that what he was going to say next was a gift. "Did you notice the new desk configuration?"

Pretty tough to miss, I wanted to say, but instead, I bit the inside of my mouth and simply nodded.

"Petra believes in community," Lukas continued on enthusiastically. "All the computer terminals are now shared property. That way, we can all learn each other's jobs, helping when appropriate, filling in when emergencies arise, sharing the workload. What if you need to take the afternoon off for a doctor's appointment? Rhiannon can finish up your work. Or Seth or Glynnis or Byron. Petra says we shouldn't believe in passwords, we should believe in *passwork.* Imagine it."

I could imagine it all too well. Though a talented designer, Rhiannon snorted Adderall like an '80s coke fiend on her lunch break, and Seth thought the workday should primarily consist of scrolling through inappropriate websites and choosing exactly which porn episode he'd spend quality time with later in the evening. I wondered how he would fare in this new democratic, passwordless office. Byron was all talk and swagger, marginal talent. And quiet, mousy Glynnis? She'd barely made a peep in months. Maybe Jackie and I, stalwart and reliable, had nothing to worry about.

"These principles make sense to me," Lukas said earnestly, breaking into my thoughts. "And I hope they do to you. The next few months will be a time of sweeping change for Guh."

"Why not Gee?" I couldn't help myself.

"What?"

"If I see the letter *g*, my brain reads it as *gee*." Jackie nodded in agreement.

"That's a hard *g*," Lukas explained. "Petra believes names should be both symbolic and easy to remember. Clients should feel working with Guh is completely effortless."

"It's your dad's name," I said, unable to hide my disapproval. "Giacomo."

"Exactly," Lukas said. "My father did an amazing job laying the groundwork, but he left it to me to take it to the next level."

My cliché meter had grown stronger since dealing with people who, after Jesse died, told me everything happens "for a reason." I opened my mouth to call Lukas on his triteness, but then he lifted the box of my personal belongings and dropped it into my hands. It wasn't as heavy as I'd thought. "Read the first chapter of Petra's book," he ordered. "It provides a comprehensive overview of her philosophy."

I hoisted the box to my hip. "And do you have a timetable for letting people go?"

"We will be participating in fierce and friendly competition in the coming months. Terminations won't happen until the end of the summer."

"I've been here twenty-two years," Jackie croaked.

Lukas briefly touched her cheek. "What are you talking about? We've only been here for a few months."

~

"So, we're talking fierce as in Hunger Games."

Jackie and I sat on a bench on the outskirts of the Gossamer Space parking lot. The lot itself was unusable, as the first day of the farmers' market had finally come. We'd talked about it in the office—would there be local honey? Fresh bread? Hemp T-shirts? Moonshine?—but now that the stiff white tents stood tall like meringue, blocking our view and forcing us to park half a mile away, we weren't so enthusiastic.

"Frank would never stand for this," Jackie said as the smoke curled from her lips.

I nearly laughed at the look of repulsion on her face. "I'm pretty sure you're not allowed to smoke in the vicinity of so much fresh produce."

"Frank wouldn't stand for all this vegetable bullshit either," she said bitterly.

Frank isn't able to stand at all anymore, I thought. *Perhaps if he had tolerated the occasional vegetable . . .* I shook off the unkind response and focused on the practicalities. "What we should do is get our résumés in order and start looking for something else."

Jackie nodded, but I knew her thoughts jumped to the same frightening scenarios as mine. The market was terrible. We weren't cheap. We secretly hoped to stay at Giacomo's until retirement.

"Then again, maybe some of our competition will leave," I said. "Lukas said he wasn't going to let anyone go until the end of the summer. Maybe they'll get tired of the stress and quit?"

"Maybe," Jackie said unconvincingly. "I don't know. They seemed invigorated by it." She went quiet for a moment, then said, "I can't lose this job, Paige. I don't have any backup, and who's going to hire me?" The weariness in Jackie's voice, more than the fear, had me scooting closer, my shoulder meeting hers.

"Compared to the rest, we cost a fortune," she went on. "Do you think it'll be you or me who gets fired? He couldn't lose both of us. We know where all the bodies are buried."

A Big Frank line. I didn't mind the cliché.

Lukas couldn't afford to lose both of us, but he could lose one of us. My heart gave a lurch. I needed my job, too. I didn't have any backup either. I glanced at Jackie, who was sucking again on her unfiltered cigarette.

They say a woman clings to the hairstyle she wore when she was happiest. Jackie must have been ecstatic when Jon Bon Jovi and Van Halen rocked the charts, her thin blonde hair parted down the middle and feathered back (calling it layered didn't do it justice) and highlighted and sprayed to the crispy, fragile texture of spun sugar. She wore jeans to work, sometimes with pleats, and topped them with washed-soft Henleys in various shades of pink. The photo atop her box was from the highlight of her life, when she scored VIP tickets to a Def Leppard show and got someone to snap a shot of her with the band. The drummer casually slung his one arm over her shoulder, and Jackie was grinning as though he'd just told her a delicious secret.

With Jackie Everett, all of your assumptions were correct. Frank never tried to push her from the time warp she'd been living in for three decades. Her work was always good, and anyway, he liked her style. It meant she was safe and dependable. Something told me Lukas didn't see her in the same light.

And under which light did he see me? I caught my reflection in the window beside me. Blonde helmet bob, dated power suit, makeup applied to conceal the evidence of interrupted sleep and too much coffee. Neither of us fit into that sleek office with its neon brightness. Only youth could handle its scrutiny.

Jackie yanked a small bag out of her backpack and unwrapped her sandwich. She paused, waiting for me to dig through my purse for my bento box. "Shit," I said. "I ran out of the house so quickly I forgot to bring something."

"You want half of mine?" Jackie winced slightly when she caught the harshness in her tone. We'd shared lunch plenty of times, but suddenly sharing meant something more. I'd always joked that Jackie was my work spouse—were we getting a divorce, too? The thought brought on a wave of sadness. Not the Big Kahuna of grief, but a breaker that drew my energy out to sea.

I stood and smiled at her, trying to counter the uneasiness between us. "Thanks, but I'll just buy something from here," I said, gesturing toward the white tents. "Can't be too bad, right? Fresh, local—"

"Expensive," Jackie finished.

"I'm sure." I dug through my purse and thankfully found my wallet. "Wish me luck," I said, but she just nodded, her mouth full.

The view from inside the market was impressive. Bustling with vitality, healthy-looking, sun-kissed vendors conducted brisk business with the hordes of downtown workers on lunch breaks. Cheese, meats, veggies, honey, flowers, baked goods—my head spun as I tried to take it all in. Everything seemed a little brighter, and gave the impression of people living lives that were better, richer, more wholesome, like the produce they were hawking.

"What are you looking for?" called a woman wearing a brightly colored housedress over a pair of destroyed jeans. She'd piled her bright magenta curls atop her head and secured them with what looked suspiciously like a carrot.

I smiled tightly. "Just browsing."

"You can be browsing with purpose," she said, grinning back. She was missing an eyetooth, and I felt shameful relief at the evidence of poor life choices.

The girl went on in a singsongy voice. "We've got every little thing you need."

Oh, yeah? I wanted to shout. *You've got my husband in your truck? Job security? A teenage son who doesn't seethe with unexpressed anger? You've got all that hanging out with the asparagus and early onions?*

She separated out a bunch of vibrant greens, tied them together with a spindly length of raffia, and tossed them on the table between us. "What about these?"

"What are they?" I snapped.

She smiled again, and I wondered if she was amused or smug. "Dandelion greens."

"People eat those?"

"They do. Cleans the liver. Helps you flush out the bad stuff."

She was smug. Just a little, but it was there. I was sick of people younger than me feeling superior. Sick of hipper than thou looking on me with pity because I was so ignorant. "I have a toilet for that."

She laughed, unperturbed. "Why not give this method a try?"

The greens were a perfect verdant green, maybe too perfect. "No, thanks," I said, and walked straight back up to the office, pausing only to stuff a few crinkly dollars into the vending machine Lukas had threatened to do away with. The machine stuck, and I had to shove my hand up into it, freeing my energy bar from its noose.

CHAPTER 3

The employees of Guh spent the afternoon trying to prove that Petra's common-space concept was a revelation, not the awkward, slightly adversarial game of workplace musical exercise balls it was proving to be. The millennials were nothing if not polite, but after a few hours I'd grown tired of the constant "Is it okay with you if I take a look?" and "Would you mind explaining why you do it that way?" Fidgety, I stood to adjust the blinds and found myself plopping down on Seth's lap when I sat back down. As we fumbled to right ourselves, bouncing halfway across the room, I could see Lukas in his office, arms crossed, watching us.

"I wanted to see what you've done with the salted caramel gelato ad," Seth explained quickly, and I could see a blush rising from the edge of his scruffy beard. "I thought you were getting up. Sorry."

"No need to apologize," I replied, my smile so broad it hurt. I brought up the ad I hadn't yet finished, swallowing down my irritation at showing my work before it met my standards. "The background color isn't right yet, but I'm happy with the dominant image."

"I can do some tweaking," Seth offered, loud enough for Lukas to hear behind his closed office door. "If you're okay with that." He ran his gaze over the ad, frowning. "I can see what you mean about the color.

And are you sure you're happy with the size of the image? I can mess around with it for a while."

I was fairly certain Petra Polly disapproved of intraoffice strangling. "Knock yourself out."

During our exchange, I'd noticed Jackie slipped out for a smoke break. I found her at the bottom of the stairwell, door open to the parking lot. "I don't know if I can do this for three months," I said, leaning against the wall next to her.

Jackie turned to me, tears threatening to make a black, soupy mess out of her mascara. "Why didn't you come back to eat lunch with me? What were you doing? Did you go to talk to Lukas without me?"

I gestured to the still-bustling market. "I felt overwhelmed by all that, so I came upstairs and ate an energy bar. I'm sorry. I should have told you."

Jackie stared at me for what felt like a long time. "I don't want to think that of you, that you'd go behind my back. We've known each other a long time."

"We have," I agreed, wishing for a moment that our friendship wasn't locked into the workday. We didn't do girls' nights out or Saturday trips to the mall. Hell, I hadn't been inside her apartment in years. But we'd grown into the middle years sitting next to each other, and that counted for a lot. I put my arm around her shoulders and resisted the urge to wave the smoke away. "We'll show Lukas that letting either of us go is not in the best interest of . . . Guh."

Jackie shivered. "I can't call it that. It would break Frank's heart."

"We're going to do what it takes," I said. "If that means speaking in phonics and following the lead of some skinny hipster bitch in Heidi braids, so be it."

Jackie flicked her cigarette into the open air, a rare sign of aggression for her. "We're not powerless," she said.

"We're not," I lied. "Not at all."

When five o'clock came, the six of us glanced nervously around the airy loft, not making eye contact, but trying to gauge who would be the first to leave. Did we exit together? In pairs? Would Lukas dismiss us? Glynnis pulled Petra's book from her bag and began flipping through pages in search of the answer.

"Meeting!" Lukas called out from the conference room.

We scurried into the brightly lit room, rushing to take our places around the table. Instead of boxes, the table held six brown paper bags this time, a name scribbled on each.

Lukas took his spot at the head. He steepled his fingers and closed his eyes for a moment before speaking. "Petra Polly believes adaptability is the heart of creativity."

Six heads nodded in unison. Maybe Petra wasn't so bad. There was truth to that assertion. Not a complete truth—creativity was a complicated beast—but close enough.

"And speed is the heart of adaptability," Lukas continued. "The client should not have to wait for your precious inspiration. We're picking up new clients all the time, and they want the work done quickly." He stood and began distributing the brown bags. "I visited the farmers' market earlier and picked up one item for each of you. By tomorrow, I'd like you to create an effective ad for this product, adaptable to all platforms, from a national magazine to an Instagram ad. We'll reconvene to share our work, then I'll rate the ads according to Petra's rubric for effective communication."

Create an ad in a day? Effective ads required a lot of thought, and those thoughts had to *marinate*. Lukas watched too many reality shows.

I wondered if we'd all slink away to study our products in private, but no, for my fellow designers it was Christmas morning. They tore into their bags, pulling bunches of radishes, spinach, and green onions and fresh-baked bread. Triumphant, Rhiannon hugged a bouquet of daylilies to her ample chest. Jackie smiled weakly at her jar of strawberry jam.

My bag sank into my lap, whatever it contained weighing as much as a newborn. With an equally heavy heart, I revealed my product, a flat, gelatinous circle, brown so dark it was almost mahogany, with lighter bits sprinkled throughout. It glistened like an oil slick. "What's this? A cow patty?"

"There's a label," Lukas said, his jaw clenching. "You've got more description than most, Paige."

Vegan chocolate beetroot flourless cake.

Some instinct rose up and told me Dandelion Girl was responsible for this stomach churner. "Would anyone actually eat this?"

Lukas smirked. "It's your job to ensure they do." He directed his attention to the group. "Tomorrow's meeting is at nine a.m. I would say good luck, but you shouldn't need it."

Excited by the prospect of getting to work, the good employees of Guh practically leaped for the exit, pushing past me in a blur. I knew I should rush out with them, putting my enthusiasm on display, but I took my time gathering my things, overwhelmed by all I had to carry—Petra's book, the odd cake, my box of personal belongings. I pushed out of the building awkwardly, the box nearly sliding out of my arms.

"Let me help you with that."

Dandelion Girl. Her dark forearms were smudged with something neon pink, and the carrot had half slid out of her hair.

"I've got it," I said through gritted teeth.

"No, you don't. Stop being ridiculous." She took the box from my hand and shouldered it. "Where to?"

"My car. I had to park a ways away because of the market."

We walked down the main boulevard in silence. I'd never been good with silence. I had to fill it. "Who's watching your tent?"

"No one," she said, grinning. "I have faith in my fellow humans."

Good luck with that, I thought, and refrained from saying anything else until I spotted my car. "That's me," I shouted in a way I hoped meant, *you can go now.*

She didn't take the hint, but waited patiently until I opened the trunk, and carefully tucked the box inside. "You're gonna love that cake."

"Did you make it?"

"I sure did."

"Is it . . . good?"

"I'll let you decide. I will say this, though—some people call me a magician when it comes to cooking what I grow."

Magician. That could be interesting. Inspiration wasn't exactly knocking, but it was definitely lurking. "Are you? How so?"

"I can do anything with vegetables," she said, and somehow it didn't sound like a boast, just a simple, unadorned fact. "I'll serve you something you'll swear is this buttery, flavorful steak, and it turns out to be a slab of butternut squash. I'm this seasoning guru. Like, an alchemist."

The ideas flipped through my head like cards in a Rolodex. Magician, guru, creation . . . "Thanks," I said, opening my car door. "Do you want a ride back?"

"Do I want to ride for three blocks?" She laughed. "No. I'd start worrying about my priorities if I agreed to that."

Before I could come up with a retort, she'd loped down the block, arms swinging, escaped curls bouncing, not a care in the world.

I kind of hated her.

CHAPTER 4

Excerpt from Petra Polly: Chapter 1—Maintain Fighting Weight at All Times

When a company is carrying a spare tire around the middle, it sinks to the bottom of the pool, becomes depressed, earthbound, slow moving. To avoid this, exercise your employees regularly—host competitions and contests, keep their creative muscles taut, promote competition that is friendly and fierce. Burn the fat away with mental interval training—tear those muscles down, and build them back stronger and more resilient!

The vegan flourless cake—dense, chocolaty, delicious—was a marvelous surprise. I didn't care if it was created from tree sludge and sawdust—it tasted amazing. I'd scarfed nearly half of it as I read Petra's book. *Take that, Petra, and your fighting weight,* I thought, bending to search our pantry for a bottle of wine, my knees protesting. I found one slightly covered in dust, by the cans of tuna fish Trey had taken to eating every day after school until someone warned him about the evils of mercury poisoning, and he'd sworn never to touch them again. A stack of them formed a mini skyscraper in my pantry, and behind it, treasure. A nice

Bordeaux given to Jesse by a client. I'd been saving it, but for what? Jesse would never be back to share it with me. I heard his voice so clearly, though, telling me I'd better get drinking before it turned to vinegar. I popped the cork from the bottle and didn't pause to let it breathe. My need to breathe was stronger.

I poured the wine and took a sip. *Heavenly.*

Odd choice of word, I thought. Did I believe Jesse was somewhere in the clouds, looking down at what had become of his wife? I wasn't sure. I kind of hoped not. When Jesse died (I'd stopped using the euphemistic "passed away" after about a year), there were two things people said to me with regularity—*he's always with you* and *he's in a better place.* Try as I might, I couldn't see how both of those could be true at the same time. When I was honest with myself, I hoped neither was accurate. If he were with me, then he could see my tears, my depression, my zombielike inability to engage with the life we'd built together. And how could anyone think there was a better place for Jesse than with his wife and child? That thought, meant to comfort, seemed unnecessarily cruel.

I forced my thoughts to shift—what would Jesse's version of heaven be? Probably a glorified Container Store. Jesse was seriously organized—we both were. Every single thing in our house had a place. We both took great pleasure in our community, a gated, private subdivision on the outskirts of Willow Falls, with its own rules and bylaws. Jesse and I loved rules and bylaws. We loved order. For us, the best day could be described as one that ran "smoothly."

I glanced at the wineglass, and there was only a swallow left, as my grandmother used to say. Jesse and I used to open a bottle every Friday night. We'd each have two glasses, then two glasses on Saturday, with dinner we ordered from our favorite Italian restaurant. I held up the bottle and poured myself another generous drink.

The second glass was going down way too easily when I remembered that Trey was staying at Colin's place, and I hadn't yet spoken to his mother. Jesse and I tried hard to avoid helicoptering Trey, but our rough childhoods made it difficult to avoid making automatic assumptions about others. Trust was not given readily; it was earned only after careful observation and analysis of actions. I'd never met this woman, and Trey would be sleeping under her roof. The prevailing attitude around here seemed to be if you could afford to live in Willow Falls, you at least checked some of the boxes on the list of "good person" attributes. But Jesse and I knew we could never buy into that kind of naïveté. We'd seen too many folks from places like Willow Falls cruising our old neighborhood, looking for drugs and trouble. They usually bought the first and caused a great deal of the latter.

I found my cell phone after much fishing around in my purse and checked to see if Trey texted me her number. He had, and I smiled to myself like I always did when Trey did something he should be doing, like keeping a promise.

Her name was Charlene.

She answered just before it switched over to voice mail with a clipped, "Yes."

I introduced myself and thanked her for hosting Trey.

Silence. I thought my phone had gone out when she said, "Trey says you have no running water in your home."

"We have water!" I said defensively. "Just not hot. I meant to call the guy, but today's been craz—"

"Trey devoured his dinner. He said there's often not any food in your house."

I took a deep breath. Wasn't this the woman who was supposed to be a hands-off, you-guys-are-now-adults kind of mother? What had Trey been telling her?

"I'm doing the best I can since my husband died." I didn't often play the widow card, but if there was a situation that called for it, this was it.

"Trey said that was two years ago." It was a statement, but also an accusation.

She waited for my response—did she want an apology? I thought of something Big Frank said to me after Jesse died: *You're gonna have to deal with people who've never had to grieve before.* "I'm doing the best I can," I said, struggling to keep my voice even.

"I'm sure you are," she responded, her tone softening a smidge. "And I can . . . sympathize. I've been married for twenty years, and I can't imagine."

No, I thought. *You can't.*

"Perhaps you need to be a little more open to help," Charlene said. "Have you tried therapy?"

"Thank you for hosting Trey," I choked out. "I'm going to go now."

Charlene paused, and then said, "He's having a wonderful time. It's our pleasure."

After I hung up with Charlene, I put the rest of the beetroot cake on a plate, refreshed my wineglass, and took both out onto our patio.

The temperature had dropped to somewhere in the low sixties. Shivering, I sat at the edge of the concrete and pulled my cardigan close around my middle. Our backyard, a healthy size for even a suburban plot, stretched out before me, velvety in the darkness.

Charlene's comments weighed heavy, but I tried to shake them off, focusing my attention on an effective ad campaign for beetroot cake. It was fudgy, gooey, and delicious, but it resembled something you'd scoop up after your dog. I thought about what Dandelion Girl said. Alchemy, magic . . . though I could use a little of both in my life, my brain couldn't figure out how to make them work for the slab of gelatinous goo on my lap. I shrugged and shoved a big scoop of it into my mouth. Maybe the skinny hipster know-it-all was right, and I had to train my brain.

I raised my second (third?) glass. "Here's to you, Petra Polly." It went down the way a good Bordeaux should—smooth and easy but grounded enough to bring you back to earth. I cut another slice of the cake, and that went down handily as well.

"You've got dandelions coming up," said a masculine voice.

I started. "What?"

Mr. Eckhardt, my grumpy neighbor, bent over our low fence. Given the hour and our weak porch light, I couldn't see much but his crew cut–topped head and condescending expression. "You haven't had the service come in well over a year, and your son barely does a passable job mowing. If you don't take care of the weeds right away, the problem will continue to worsen. Next year, your backyard will look like a vacant lot in a crack neighborhood."

"Maybe I like dandelions," I said, hearing the slur in my words.

Mr. Eckhardt gave me a surprised look. He'd heard it, too. His mouth flattened into a line of disapproval. "No one likes dandelions. They're a nuisance. A predatory nuisance." He looked at me again, hard. "If you can't pay for it, I will."

"Don't," I said, waving my glass at him to bolster my point. "Dandelions aren't the enemy. We can eat them—did you know that? They clean out your organs. All the toxins come right out."

"I'll call the service tomorrow," Mr. Eckhardt said, pretending I hadn't responded. He pushed himself from the fence, and I could only see the tip of his pointy nose. "At this point in the conversation, I believe you should be thanking me."

"I don't want you touching my lawn."

"I won't be touching anything of yours. The service will spray, and the problem will be eradicated."

"Maybe I don't want my problems . . . eradicated."

"Oh, now I don't think that's the truth, Mrs. Moresco. Though no fault of my own, I've been privy to your problems over the past few years. If you could call a service to spray away your problems, I think you'd do it in a heartbeat. I'm doing you a favor. I'd appreciate if you remember that."

His nose disappeared, and I heard the sharp crack of a door being slammed. I poured myself the last of the bottle and sipped thoughtfully, remembering all the times Jesse and I had giggled at old Mr. Eckhardt while he devoted entire Saturdays to landscaping his yard, even to the point of edging the difficult-to-reach spots with nail scissors. We were neatniks but not entirely rigid. Our neighbor's obsession with perfection meant everyone else fell short in some way, including us. He was obsessive and unfriendly and had disliked us since the day we moved in.

But . . . he was right.

If I could spray Grief-Be-Gone all over my life, I would, toxins be damned.

Disheartened, I kicked off my shoes and dug my toes into the cool grass. Once upon a time, our backyard resembled a stretch at Augusta National Golf Club—smooth and flawless, not a weed to blight its green perfection. Like most artificially beautiful things, our lawn required constant maintenance. I pictured Jesse, T-shirt dotted with sweat, pushing the lawn mower every Saturday, with Trey carefully working the edger around the perimeter. I watched from the kitchen window as I made lunch, bringing lemonade and sandwiches when they took a break. Jesse and Trey didn't talk much while they worked, but they didn't need to—completing a task that had tangible, measurable results appealed to both of their personalities, and bonded them in a way I could understand but couldn't replicate.

I shook off the memory and took a hard look at what had become of our lawn. Mr. Eckhardt wasn't exaggerating—weeds had sprung up all over, dotting the green, pushing up along the fence dividing our property, skirting the edge of the patio I sat on. The old me would have been mortified. The new me? Well . . . I nudged at one healthy dandelion head with my big toe and popped it right off the stem.

The casual destruction felt good. *Really* good.

Grabbing my spoon, I licked off the remaining beetroot cake and dug out the root of the weed. Then I proceeded to toss it over the fence. I did it again, and again, and again, until the small patch of lawn surrounding me was covered in little craters. It looked like the surface of the moon, and I howled. It felt good in a way I hadn't felt in years.

I wanted more.

The earth, still cool and hard, nearly bent the spoon in half. Woozy, I stumbled my way to the garage. We had a garden spade somewhere, or maybe a shovel? I knocked down half of Jesse's tools, but I found a rusty old digger behind a pile of rakes.

My normally boring suburban yard appeared dark and mysterious in the moonlight. I pushed the shovel into the ground, flipping up a chunk of sod, and then another and another, continuing on, stopping only once, to open up another bottle of wine.

CHAPTER 5

The alarm blared, but I awakened slowly, reflexes dulled by the heavy weight of a wine hangover. My pillow felt gritty against my cheek, and when I raised my head, more dried dirt fell from my hair onto the white linen.

Dirt was everywhere. Smeared across my sheets, lodged under my fingernails. Grains of it stuck to the inside of my bra. When I hauled myself up, I could see my feet were filthy, the bottoms blackened as though I'd charred them in the night.

Memories of what I'd done came back, watery, dreamy images. How long had I stayed out in the backyard, stabbing at the ground? Gingerly, I walked over to the window to sneak a peek and found myself staring at a large hole, the approximate length and width of a grave.

"Fuuuuuuck."

I'd have to worry about resodding it later. I'd have to put off evaluating my mental health as well. Lukas had called the meeting for nine in the morning, and here I was, dirty as an unsupervised toddler, with nothing to wear (why hadn't I done laundry yesterday?) and nothing to show Lukas (why hadn't I worked last night?). I would think in the shower. The best thoughts came in the shower.

Except when the shower was so icy the droplets felt like tiny needles pricking the skin (why hadn't I asked Jesse who to call?). I stayed in the shower only long enough to rinse the dirt off, shivered in a towel until I could find the suit I wore yesterday, and attempted to make myself presentable.

When I left for work, Mr. Eckhardt was standing in front of a pile of dandelion carcasses, his long pale index finger shaking with the effort to command my attention.

"Unacceptable," he said before I could apologize. "Completely unacceptable behavior."

"Give them to me," I said, thrusting my hands over the fence.

Without another word, he scooped them up and dumped them into my waiting arms. I tossed them onto my patio.

"You need to—"

I didn't let him finish. I got into my car, dirty hands and all, and sped off to work.

~

The parking lot showed no sign of the farmers' market, and without the stark white tents and colorful people, it looked a little dreary. Still, I could park within a few yards of the door. That was a plus.

9:08 a.m. The conference room door was shut, and I heard the low sound of one voice, female, and knew they'd already begun.

If Big Frank were alive, he'd have shoved a cup of coffee in my hands and made a crack about being glad I'd decided to show up.

If Jesse were alive, I wouldn't have been late.

Since my first day at Giacomo, my work performance would have been rated exemplary, had Big Frank actually believed in annual reviews. Frank understood that I was both responsible and artistic, a combination he felt was rare. He'd tried to balance it out with the other employees (Jackie and Glynnis had practical, grounded souls, and Byron, Seth, and Rhiannon, while not the most reliable people, were idea factories). "But you're the whole enchilada, kiddo," Big Frank frequently told me, and I appreciated his appreciation. It took a great deal of work to give myself the freedom to create while helping Frank maintain an organized, well-run operation. I made every deadline he set for me. Until Jesse died.

I'd fallen apart like a sloppily sewn scarf, a thread here, a thread there, until the unraveling got to be so noticeable that Big Frank picked up a needle and did some repair work. "Pick a few things you don't want to let slide, and let the rest sort itself out," he said gently after one particularly rough day. "When someone leaves this world, everything else gets jostled because of the empty space. You're gonna land in the wrong spot for a while. Sooner or later, you'll find where you fit again."

That kept me going, until it was Big Frank who left a hole, and I found myself surrounded by emptiness.

~

I slipped into the conference room as quietly as possible, but every head swiveled in my direction, disapproval etched on each face. Glynnis, standing in front of her ad, let whatever was tumbling from her mouth trail off into silence. Her cheeks flushed a concerning shade of crimson.

"Lateness isn't merely a sign of disrespect," Lukas began, his gaze never shifting from the front of the room, "it's an affront to the creative process. Any interruption in the flow can have disastrous consequences. Petra addresses this in chapter 6."

I took a seat quickly. "I'm very sorry. I had some plumbing issues at the house."

"Glynnis," he said, ignoring my apology. "Do you feel you can go on?"

The poor girl looked terrified. I felt horrible then, and had to give this one to Petra—it did suck to be interrupted. I smiled broadly at her. "Sorry, Glynnis. I'd really like to hear about your ad. It looks great."

I wasn't entirely sure it did—I'd forgotten my glasses—but the compliment seemed to work. Glynnis nodded and directed everyone's attention back to the whiteboard behind her. She finished up, and after offering her some generic compliments, Lukas called Jackie to the front.

Jackie had dressed up, which for her meant her usual look dialed up a notch. Creased mom jeans. Frosted lipstick. I could see the curling iron marks in her hair. She wore a button-up shirt with a pink tank underneath. She looked fantastic. Like a suburban, middle-aged Lita Ford.

Up went Jackie's ad. She'd used a stock photo, a cute, freckled kid about to stick his fingers into a jar of jam. In bold font at the bottom, it read: *This is only going to get better.*

"Nice job," I mouthed to her.

The others sat silent, turning their heads and attention from the ad to Lukas. "What do we think?" he asked, and I could tell from the tilt of his head that he knew exactly what he thought.

"It's cute," I said loudly. "Appeals to both mothers and kids. I can see bits of fruit in the jam, which makes it seem natural and wholesome."

Jackie flashed me a quick smile.

Rhiannon clucked her tongue, which I was fairly certain was the most annoying sound in the world. "I'm not so sure," she said slowly, pretending to ponder my contribution. "Mothers and kids? Haven't we all agreed using that demographic is dated and pointless? How many mothers still make their kids' lunches? And anyway, they're already buying jam—shouldn't we be targeting the people who would normally pass it by?"

Lukas nodded sagely. "Go on."

Rhiannon unwound her legs from their yogic position and straightened up. "Well, I hate to use the word 'hip' . . ."

Lukas laughed. "We all hate to use that word. You're not alone."

The others nodded so vigorously I worried for their cervical spines.

"I just think the whole point of this assignment was to focus on *fresh*. This doesn't feel fresh. I'm not saying it's bad, Jackie—"

"Oh, no," Jackie said quickly. "Of course not. Because it isn't."

"Jackie," Lukas warned.

Jackie's voice wobbled when she said, "I've been doing this for thirty years."

"That's apparent," Rhiannon said under her breath.

Lukas steepled his fingers, and I readied myself for a lecture. "We know you're experienced, Jackie, but collaboration must be part of our process if we're to succeed. This isn't a critique session—it's, as Petra calls it, a *group exploration into the possible*. Do you understand how that works?"

"Perfectly." Jackie switched off her laptop and took her seat.

"Paige?"

"What?" I'd been so distracted by Jackie's defeat that I hadn't realized Lukas had recalibrated his laser beam stare for me.

"You have the next opportunity."

"Opportunity for what?"

"You're up," he said tersely.

Working in advertising had taught me to think on my feet, but this required more than a quick joke or a tossed-off tagline. Lukas's expression, a slightly predatory look of anticipation, clued me in on how important my success was, and I basically had nothing. An idea had occurred to me as I rushed through the kitchen, but it was so fuzzy and unfinished I knew it would look exactly like what it was—my very last resort.

I pulled the ziplock bag from my purse and walked to the front. Six heads tilted, and fingers began punching at laptops.

"Did you send it to everyone?" Rhiannon asked.

"Er, no. What I have is a visual presentation."

Puzzled, she kept tapping at her keyboard. "What do you mean? Did you post something to YouTube?"

"No, I brought something with me." During the endless walk to the front of the room, my brain was like a contestant on *Supermarket Sweep*, dashing around my skull and grabbing whatever it could. Trembling, I took the cardboard plate from the plastic bag and held it up to the whiteboard. The beetroot cake had left a circular mahogany stain, crumbs stuck to the center. Splashes of red wine dotted the space surrounding it, along with a dark smear of dirt.

I pointed to the one remaining white spot. "Imagine a line printed here that reads, 'When a vegan clears her plate, you know it was good!'"

Seth groaned.

Lukas leaned forward. "Seth, can you verbalize what you feel is the issue with Paige's ad?"

"She's insulted vegans, the main demographic for the product," Seth said disdainfully. "It isn't funny enough to get away with it."

"I thought it was pretty funny," Jackie contributed.

Rhiannon ignored her. "The line sucks, but the image isn't bad. We could work with it."

We. My presentation was shit, but it was mine. "I could rewrite it. The concept isn't—"

"Isn't right," Glynnis quietly offered. "But it could be, Paige, and then the ad would be fine. Good, even."

She meant well. I smiled weakly in her direction.

"Let's help her out," Lukas said, sweeping his arm to encompass everyone but me. "How can we make this ad shine?"

Seth jumped in immediately. "I like the circle. The richness of color, the crumbs sticking to it offer depth and texture. The dark line—what is that?"

"Dirt," I said, unable to think of anything else. "It's dirt. I was eating outside."

Lukas flinched. "Regardless of how unsanitary that sounds, it does add something to the sum total. We'll leave it in."

Glynnis cleared her throat. "It reminds me of a work of modern art, like something you'd see at MoMA. Who is that artist I'm thinking of? With the colors and lines and shapes?"

Every single artist who ever lived? But then I saw what she was getting at. "Rothko," I said. "Glynnis, you are onto something. What if I put a frame around it, and instead of a line at the bottom, it reads something like this—" I picked up a black marker and wrote:

Beetroot Cake
Beetroot, cocoa, and brown sugar
Mom, Family Dinner, 2016

"People won't get it," Rhiannon pronounced.

"Unless you set it on a wall, next to other stained plates made to look like art hanging in a museum," Byron suggested.

"Or in a dining room," Seth added. "That would broaden the appeal."

"I guess I like that idea," Jackie said.

Rhiannon pushed back from the table and crossed her arms. "Though it is sexist. Replace 'Mom' with 'Dad' and I guess I'm in. What do you think, Lukas?"

Lukas stood abruptly, his face resplendent. "I'm thrilled—not so much with the ad, but with your process! This is exactly what Petra is talking about. We've taken a lackluster idea and together turned it into something we wouldn't be embarrassed to present to a client. I gave you a challenging assignment—not impossible, but definitely difficult—and not only did you all bring something to the table, but you offered substantive suggestions in the spirit of collegiality. Impressive." He fell back in his chair, apparently exhausted by such a show of emotion. "But there is always room for improvement. Petra has so much more to say about working collaboratively. I want you all to read chapter 2. I guarantee you will find it absolutely enlightening. We'll discuss the concepts next Monday, and at that point I'll fill you in on the next challenge."

~

The day felt endless, and when I finally pulled into my driveway, I'd almost forgotten about what I'd done to my backyard while drunk and moonstruck, so it was a shock to find Trey sitting at the edge of the patch of dirt, his stuffed backpack propped next to him.

"I didn't do this," he said before I could get a word out.

"I know you didn't, because I did it."

He shot me a dubious glance. "Seriously? Why?"

I removed my heels and dropped onto the grass. "I honestly don't know."

"It looks . . . raw," he said. "Like something we shouldn't see."

"It's just dirt."

"You hate dirt."

I shrugged. "Maybe not so much. But I need to figure out how to fix it, or Mr. Eckhardt is going to have a coronary."

"I'm surprised he hasn't called the police on you."

"I'm sure they have better things to do."

Trey snorted. "Not in Willow Falls. Nothing happens here."

I wanted to tell him he was lucky to live in such a place. I certainly hadn't when I was his age. But he'd never experienced that kind of fear, and I didn't want to put it in his head.

"Were you bored?" Trey asked, because that was something he could understand.

"I guess that's what it was." I nudged his shoulder. "Come on. I need to call a plumber, and then I'll help you unpack. We can order a pizza with extra cheese. I'm too tired to cook." I slowly got to my feet, joints creaking, and held out my hand. "I'll even watch a few episodes of *American Ninja Warrior*. We can make a night of it."

Trey didn't take my hand. Instead, he dug the toe of his sneaker into the dirt. "I just packed that bag. I want to stay at Colin's again, maybe for a couple of days. His dad bought a new sound system, and he wants to teach us how to install it. That's okay, right?"

No. No, it wasn't at all okay. I wanted Trey sleeping in his own bed. But then I thought about how starved he must be for a male influence. "Is his dad a nice person?"

"Yes," he said, rolling his eyes. "Of course he is. He also gives good advice. He wants me to make decisions for myself."

"Is the implication that I don't want you to?"

Trey made a sound of frustration. "Why do you take everything so personally? Colin's place has a great vibe. That's it."

"What does that mean?"

"It's not a big deal."

"Then why can't you explain it?"

"Colin's trying to figure out who he is. He's *exploring*. I can relate."

"You can? What exactly is he exploring? Wait, what are you?"

"I knew you'd take this the wrong way."

Desperate to be right about something, I said, "Does that include learning how to drive? Are you ready for that? We can *explore* that together."

"I don't want to drive."

Trey would be a senior next year, and still he hadn't signed up for a driver's ed class. The school wouldn't let him graduate without it. It was a sore subject between us. He claimed his refusal was political (*They can't force us to consume oil!*), but of course there was more to it, a fear he attempted to hide underneath his anger. The image of Jesse's Volvo, battered and broken, never really left our minds—it sat there like a nightmare that didn't fade once morning came.

"Colin said this was the time for me to really think about who I want to be, creatively. Soon, I'll be so wrapped up in trying to decide which college to attend and what I'm going to do with my life, and there will be no time left for myself, for just being me in the moment. Colin said I need to figure out who I am with minimal interference."

"Apparently Colin talks a lot. But I think I understand."

"Do you? Like I said, it's nothing personal. Colin's going to set up a gallery wall at his place. We've got some friends coming over to help."

Trey's desire to take pictures for a living was one of the many things Jesse and I had been in perfect agreement about—we both felt it was a bad idea. As the son and daughter of working-class people, we had trouble with our child pursuing a creative degree. Not because we were dismissive of art, but because we were distrustful of debt. We knew the true price of owing money, whether it was to the guy on the corner or Uncle Sam. Jesse had been quieter about his disapproval, assuming Trey would come to his senses, but I'd made the mistake of telling him photography would be a really nice hobby.

"So, basically you're saying only rich people's kids should get degrees in creative fields," he'd huffed in response. "That's so elitist. And you're a hypocrite. You use your creativity to make a living."

"I minored in business. My job relies more on those skills than anything. Maybe if you minored in photography and chose a major like accounting? Or, international business?"

"Could you see me in a suit?" he'd countered. "Like, sitting at the head of a table in some boardroom?"

Yes, I'd thought. *I could.* But then I could also see him living like the many photographers I knew through my job, scrambling for the next gig photographing a car dealership, or busy placating bridezillas at weekend weddings. It was a lifestyle that ended up producing more anxiety than artistic satisfaction.

When Jesse and I talked about it, late at night, I'd conceded that Trey had made some good points, but we needed to stick to our guns if we were going to put ourselves in financial peril to send him to the university of his choice. Stability was the name of the game. It was the thing that gave happiness a pedestal to stand on. Jesse agreed. Trey would come to understand this, he'd said.

But now, watching Trey twitch with the need to leave, I realized that maybe I should have been encouraging and optimistic, even if I had to fake it. "Well," I began after quickly gathering my thoughts and strategizing, "if you think you can do some self-reflecting at Colin's, then I'm not going to stand in your way."

"You're not?" He was always skeptical of me, always questioning my sincerity.

"Nope. I'll even drive you. Just give me a minute to change clothes."

"Colin's already on his way," Trey said, smiling as he got to his feet. "I'll text you later, okay?"

"Okay," I said, comforted only that he still needed my consent, even if it was perfunctory.

Later, when I was alone, I sat staring into the patch of dirt in my backyard. After a while, I grabbed the garden spade and did the only thing that made me feel better. I dug.

CHAPTER 6

Excerpt from Petra Polly: Chapter 2—On Collaboration

Not only is there not an I in 'teamwork,' there isn't a U either.
    Expect all of your employees—including yourself—to work together.
Seem obvious? Well, consider the following questions. How often do you
allow office doors to remain shut? Cancel group meetings because of per-
ceived busyness? Allow conversations to be held entirely electronically?
    The company is a singular, multicelled organism that must work in
complete harmony to bring life to your organization. When one cell goes
rogue or isolates or mutates, the organization becomes ill, sometimes peril-
ously so. The prescription is simple. Breathe the same air, ponder the same
ideas, eat together whenever possible, and encourage real-time, in-person
conversations. There is a T in 'teamwork,' and it stands for 'togetherness.'

"If we start going to the bathroom together, that's where I draw the
line." Jackie spoke into my ear so the others wouldn't hear her muti-
nous comment. The employees of Guh sat on the postage-stamp-sized
patch of lawn behind Gossamer Space, discussing Petra's latest words of
wisdom. The farmers' market had returned, so outdoor real estate was

at a premium, but the weather was near perfect, and all of us wanted to get outside. Lukas demanded we all eat lunch together for the foreseeable future; however, he was conspicuously absent, spending his lunch hour at the municipal building, officially putting the name Giacomo Advertising and Design to rest and replacing it with the single-letter designation. I would have paid a fortune to see the look on our village clerk's face. Mrs. Cruikshank was ninety and had known Big Frank since he was born.

Glynnis was the only one smart enough to bring a blanket. It was the serape variety, the kind you get at tourist traps and (once upon a time) Dead shows. We were huddled on it, Glynnis, Rhiannon, Jackie, and me, our lunches held precariously on our laps. Seth and Byron sat with their backs against the building, long legs stretched in front of them, vape pens at their mouths.

"Vaping? You guys are such losers," Rhiannon announced.

"Two of us are going to be losers," Byron said. "By the end of the summer." He had a knowing, sardonic way of speaking, so even the most mundane comment begged a reaction. Glynnis smiled at him. She had a crush.

"What I don't understand," I said, "is how we're supposed to work as one body and still engage in healthy competition."

Rhiannon snorted. "That's the beauty of Petra Polly. She doesn't have to make fuck-all sense."

"It works," Seth countered. "She's number one on the *New York Times* bestseller list."

Rhiannon shook her head, not budging. "That only means she's trending, or has a fantastic publicist. It doesn't mean her stupid rules work."

"You don't seem to have any problem following her stupid rules when Lukas is around," Byron countered.

"I need this job," she retorted. "Do you know how long it took me to find it?"

"We all need the job," Jackie said miserably.

We ate in silence for a while.

"I have an idea," Glynnis said, her voice nearly inaudible. "We still have some time left, and we're supposed to be bonding or something, right?"

"Don't even think of suggesting we do trust falls or play truth or dare," Rhiannon snapped.

Glynnis shifted so she could rise to her knees. "Nothing like that. I think we should go around the circle and say one interesting thing about ourselves. Something memorable. Let's humanize each other."

Seth made a noise of protest. "Are you kidding? Not going to happen."

Glynnis clapped once, sharply, and then offered a timid smile. She must have been a Girl Scout in a prior incarnation, or an eager church group volunteer. "It can happen if we keep it simple," she said. "Answer this question—why did your parents name you what they did?"

Jackie pointed at Rhiannon. "Well, she's got the most obvious story."

"Why?" Seth asked. "I don't get it."

"Fleetwood Mac, you dolt," Rhiannon said, covering her head with her hands. "Why didn't they name me Stevie? I would have liked that better."

"Rhiannon's the white witch," Jackie said. "I think that's pretty cool."

"You would," Byron muttered.

"What about you?" I asked him. Byron was starting to grate on my nerves.

"I thought that was obvious. Lord Byron."

I had to admit that was impressive. "Were your parents academics?"

"They own a dry cleaning business."

"Oh."

"Well, that's interesting," Glynnis remarked. "Did you work there?"

Byron flicked his gaze at her. "Are you kidding?"

Glynnis didn't skip a beat. "What about you, Paige?"

What about me? I hesitated, wondering if I should reveal too much of myself. *What the hell,* I decided. "I was named by a nurse at the hospital. My mother had a drug problem and took off as soon as she was physically able. It took a while for my grandmother to find me."

Glynnis had no idea what to do with that, and neither did the others, their stares vacant, mouths slack. Even Byron dropped his vape pen onto the grass. He leaned over it, assessing me with new eyes. "Are you shitting me?"

I held up three fingers. "Scout's honor."

"I didn't know that," Jackie said. She didn't seem hurt, but perplexed. "Did Big Frank know that?"

He had, but I shrugged it off just as he did, unwilling to go down the path of uncomfortable explanations. "It's not such a big deal."

They longed for detail, begging for more, but I stayed silent. Reluctantly, they turned to Seth.

"I'm named after my uncle," he said apologetically. "Not too exciting."

"That's nice," Glynnis said.

Jackie checked her watch. "We need to get back."

We cleaned up and rose to stretch our legs, moving briefly, as Petra Polly suggested, as one. Then Seth and Byron started goofing around on the grass while Rhiannon reapplied hot-pink lip gloss and Jackie fluffed up her hair.

"We're forgetting something," Seth said. "But I don't know what it is."

"Then it doesn't matter," Rhiannon snapped. "Let's get back inside, do what we need to do, and get the hell out before Lukas announces that Petra thinks we should work weekends."

I fell in step with Glynnis.

"I was named for a valley in Ireland," she said, slowing her pace.

"We forgot your turn! I'm so sorry." Impulsively, I reached out and tucked a stray lock of her strawberry-blonde hair behind her ear. "Your name is lovely."

"But your story is better," she said. We watched Byron and Seth jokingly fight over who held the door for Rhiannon. "I'm going to be one of the losers, aren't I?" she continued.

"It's impossible to say. It could be any of us."

She shook her head. "Some things you just know."

~

Saturday morning, I awoke to the sound of male voices arguing. For a moment it was comforting—my house had been quiet for days—and I eased back into lounge mode, but then I heard my name rip through the relaxation. The voice was unmistakable.

Jesse.

Frantic, I leaped out of bed and scrambled for a bra. I ran a comb through my hair and managed to brush my teeth. The capri sweats that seemed so comfortable the night before made me look like a Walmart meme, and there was a large oily stain on the hem of my T-shirt, but they were gray, and he liked me in gray. My head was still fuzzy with sleep.

Paige!

I ran full tilt down the hallway, and then stopped at the edge of the stairs. I'd been with Jesse long enough to know the edge to his voice meant he was annoyed, but that wasn't why I hesitated.

I wanted to hear it again.

Paige!

There. How many times does a married couple call out to each other during the course of twenty years? Thousands? I'd lived without it for two years now. Part of me knew it was fantasy, but I shoved that part off to the sidelines. I was like Trey—he'd give up sugar for weeks, but sometimes, sometimes you longed for a taste, even though you knew it wasn't good for you. I'd find him in his room, surrounded by candy wrappers.

"Mom?" Trey sounded unsure.

"I'm coming!"

They were outside, standing at the ragged patch of dirt I'd dug up. It was no longer the size of a grave, but round and approximately the size of an aboveground pool. I'd left the garden spade on the patio. Trails of dirt marked the concrete. The dandelions, dead and wilted, still lay in a pile. Trey took a seat next to the weeds, his eyes watchful.

"Paige!"

The voice I'd heard was not Jesse's but Mr. Eckhardt's. I shook the remaining cloudiness from my brain and tried to focus, but grief pulsed in my throat so violently it brought tears to my eyes. Death was final, but grief wasn't; it was a dirty street fighter who rose again and again even when I thought I had successfully knocked it to the ground. King of the sucker punches. Swallowing my emotions, I turned to Mr. Eckhardt. "What do you want?"

Mr. Eckhardt, his white crew cut standing with the same straight, unflinching posture as his spine, said, "Your son doesn't believe you did this on purpose."

Ignoring him, Trey took my appearance in for one agonizing moment, and then, puzzled, said, "Is everything okay?"

"Peachy," I responded.

Trey studied the dirt pond, brain obviously scrambling for an acceptable explanation and coming up with nothing.

"You'll need to get this resodded," Mr. Eckhardt insisted.

"I'm not getting it resodded," I said evenly. "I like it."

Trey nodded, his reaction automatic. "Okay, Mom. Whatever. But what is it?"

"It's . . ."

"Lunacy," Mr. Eckhardt finished. "Utter lunacy."

47

"It's mine," I said, curling my toes at the edge of the pit. "All mine."

"Your mother isn't thinking correctly," Mr. Eckhardt said to Trey. "Now, you're old enough to talk some sense into her. I won't have this. She's breaking the law."

"Which law?" I interjected, forcing him to address me. "Is there a law about digging in your backyard?"

"Community standards," Mr. Eckhardt retorted. "You're violating them. We live in a gated subdivision. Buying property here means you agree to certain terms, one of which is not destroying the character of your portion of the land. Are you having trouble understanding what that means?"

Trey walked over to the older man, his movements uncertain. Jesse and I had impressed upon him the importance of being respectful to adults, and I could see him struggling with honoring those lessons. His fists clenched and unclenched, but before I could intervene, he said, "Thanks for your input, sir. My mom and I are going to have a private talk about it, inside. It'll be taken care of, no doubt."

"I don't doubt it," Mr. Eckhardt said. "Because if you don't take care of it, I will."

~

"So what's going on, Mom?" Trey said while putting the teakettle on. "Are you digging your way to China?"

"No, just digging," I said with a shrug. "It felt good to do it the other night. So I did it."

"It's . . . a weird thing to do. You know that, right?" Trey made himself busy around the kitchen, the constant movement a shield against any talk of Jesse. Trey only wanted to talk about his father when he could control all the possible routes the conversation might take. Any possibly dangerous emotional paths were to be avoided.

I shot him my best sane, motherly smile. "I don't think it's weird. It's just . . . something different."

"It's irrational," he said, sounding so much like Jesse the tears almost returned. "And that's not like you. It's a little crazy." He moved to the far cabinet to grab the tea and stopped short. I'd left the two empty wine bottles in the corner because the recycling bin was full and I hadn't had the time to empty it.

"Did you drink those?" The shock in his voice was almost heart-warming. His mother didn't drink. His mother did not ever lose control.

"I did." For some reason, inappropriate as it was, it felt good to admit it. I'd managed to hide the ravages of my grief from Trey. They leaked out at work, mostly, and in the privacy of my bedroom, where some nights I could wring out my pillow and fill a swimming pool.

Trey broke into a broad grin. "Oh, you were drunk!" The explanation pleased him—crazy was difficult and scary; drunk he could handle. "Why didn't you say so?"

"I wasn't drunk." Drinking was one thing; admitting intoxication gave him an excuse to write off what I'd done. "I was drinking, but not drunk. There's a difference. I was fully aware of what I was doing."

"And what is that, exactly?" Trey shot me a skeptical look.

I didn't have an answer I could articulate. "I'm . . . I'm not sure."

Trey poured me tea and popped open a can of sparkling water for himself. After I thanked him, he shook his head and said, "Just resod it like Mr. Eckhardt said. He's an ass, but he's kind of right."

"But what if I want to keep digging?"

"Why? I think you're going to need a good reason to keep Mr. Eckhardt from getting in your face all the time. You don't even have a reason at all."

"I don't have to justify my actions to him."

Trey shrugged, and then gulped down his sparkling water. He needed time to make sense of things, and so did I. Where was this impulse coming from, this need to keep digging up the grass in my backyard until I completely destroyed it? Was this grief in action, or the opposite of that—healing? I needed to figure that out. Until I did, I'd keep digging.

"Let him think I'm going to resod the backyard," I said to Trey, giving authority to my words. "I need some time. Okay?"

"I guess," Trey said. "But time for what?"

"To make sense of things."

"Good luck with that."

CHAPTER 7

That night and all the next day, I dug. The weather turned, sun shining with vigor, and my skin turned pink and then mottled red. I didn't care. I kept at it, even when Mr. Eckhardt threatened to call the police (he didn't), and Mrs. O'Shaunessy from down the block warned me to call the utility company before I dug farther, or I might hit a gas line (fingers crossed!). The dirt patch grew, amoebalike, its perimeter uneven but spreading. When Monday morning arrived, I was sore and sunburned, dirt in every crevice of my body. Trey asked me if I was having some kind of a breakdown, and if he could film it if I was. I told him I didn't know, and I'd think about it.

I was so exhausted I sat in front of my computer screen, staring at the Seth-manipulated image of caramel gelato. Something wasn't right about it, but my brain, muddled and dirt clogged, couldn't figure out what it was.

Midmorning, Lukas tapped me on the shoulder, just as the sunshine of an idea began to burn through my brain fog.

"May I have a word?" he asked, overly polite, and I felt like the headmaster had called me into the hallway. I followed him to his minimalist, Instagram-ready, feng shui–approved office, where he sat, spine straight as my garden hoe, in a swivel chair seemingly constructed from wrought iron, duct tape, and the tears of young art and design students.

"We scored a meet and greet at Landon Cosmetics later today," Lukas announced.

I flopped down on the overstuffed white couch in front of his desk. "That's fantastic!" Landon Cosmetics was a retro-inspired line of lipsticks, glosses, and cheek tints, the packaging all done up in old-school movie posters from the '40s and '50s. Headquartered in downtown Chicago and helmed by Trinka, a gorgeous woman who could double for Dita Von Teese, Landon would be a major client for a suburban agency.

"I feel really good about this," I added, taking in Lukas's youth, his glossy looks, his carefully chosen attire, the rightness of him. It filled me with equal parts pride and shame. His father sweated through every dress shirt he owned, and had tufts of hair growing out of his ears, but I loved every messy part of Big Frank. Could I grow to love Lukas's perfection if it worked for the company? Big Frank wouldn't have gotten one foot in the door at Landon Cosmetics. I had to admit that Lukas seemed to know what he was doing.

"I could join you," I offered, trying to keep my tone casual.

Lukas smiled tightly. "That's what I wanted to discuss with you. I am going to take some creatives with me, but I've chosen Seth, Rhiannon, and Byron."

"But I'm more experienced," I said, fully aware of how defensive I sounded. "I know this business, and I know how to talk to people like your dad did. I can draw them in."

"Look at your hands," Lukas said, his voice clipped.

My gaze dropped to my filthy, ragged fingernails. I quickly flipped my hands over and saw dirt embedded in the whorls of my fingerprints.

Lukas clucked his tongue. "And your suit."

Crumpled, stained, smelling faintly of BO.

My face burned. I'd never been such a wreck at work. *How did I get to this point?* "I can run home for a few minutes to freshen up."

He shook his head. "We're leaving in a few minutes."

"I'm sorry," I said, suddenly feeling as though I had failed him. And Guh. And myself.

Lukas's expression softened. "I don't want to pry into your personal life, Paige, but Petra Polly has a wonderful chapter on underperforming employees—"

Wait a minute. "I'd hardly say I'm underperforming."

Lukas paused, one eyebrow creeping up to meet his receding hairline. "Really? Because what I see is someone who is letting her personal issues affect her day-to-day performance. I can't take you with me because one look at you and Miss Trinka will think we aren't up to the task. Rhiannon is quirkier than Zooey Deschanel with a side of ModCloth. Seth and Byron look like matching hipster salt and pepper shakers—one light, one dark, one bearded, one not, both flannel. She's going to love them."

"So, she doesn't love older people? It's a retro company—she adores the past."

"Vintage, yes. Spent and exhausted, no."

I crossed my arms over my middle, hiding my hands. "This conversation sounds vaguely discriminatory."

Lukas sighed. "Oh, Paige. It's not that they're young, it's that they *care*. I'm wondering how much you do."

"More than you know," I said with what I hoped was conviction. I'd been devoted to Giacomo for seventeen years.

Lukas stood and shrugged into his too-tight leather jacket. "I'm glad," he said while he mussed up his hair. "I don't want you to be one who goes. Sincerely. My father really liked you, and I do, too. That gelato ad is . . . coming along nicely."

"Thanks." Was he being sarcastic? Sincere? I wasn't sure.

Lukas patted my arm, choosing sincerity. "How about you run the office for the rest of the day? We won't be back until after closing hours. Miss Trinka likes to hold forth. She likes a *salon*." He opened the door, and I saw Rhiannon, Seth, and Byron waiting outside like eager little puppies. Before they took off for greener, more glamorous pastures, Lukas turned and said to me, in a low voice but audible enough, "Read Petra's book, chapter 8. I think you'll find it enlightening."

"Thank you," I murmured, wondering exactly what I was being grateful for.

"No, thank *you*, Paige," Lukas said. "I see your value, but I'm wondering if you do. 'A good employee is a confident employee,'" he recited.

"Petra, huh?"

"Not Petra," Lukas said, a wistfulness in his tone. "Big Frank."

∼

"Lukas left me in charge, and I say it's okay."

It was four o'clock. Lukas and his *creatives* were gone, and I was trying to get Jackie and Glynnis to leave early so we could go to the farmers' market.

"I don't want to go there," Jackie whined. "It makes me feel bad about my life choices."

"We're supposed to stay until five," Glynnis said, eyeing the wall clock. "What if Lukas comes back? Won't we get into trouble?"

The old Paige would have reacted the same way. The new Paige grabbed a hand from each of them and pulled them to standing. "It's a field trip. We need ideas, don't we? Let's go bombard our minds with possibilities!"

Glynnis frowned, but Jackie quirked a smile. "I think Petra covers that in chapter 9," she said, her smile turning into a grin. "Okay. Let's go."

Dandelion Girl, perched on a stool behind her table, noticed us immediately and started waving.

"That woman has a carrot in her hair," Jackie whispered.

"I kind of like it," Glynnis said.

Just another week into the season, the market was already more bountiful. Endless rows of boxed strawberries stretched out before us, their aroma sweetening the air. Green onions, new potatoes, asparagus, and rhubarb—the beauty of the produce had me wondering, what could I grow? I had plenty of dirt. The only area I was lacking in was experience, but how hard could it be if a woman who used a carrot as a scrunchie could do it? Eccentricity aside, she seemed like the type of person who'd be willing to help even someone like me.

Dandelion Girl hopped off her stool and began to pack up. At this hour, the greens had begun to wilt, and a handwritten sign was hastily posted beneath them, *Cheap! Cheap! Two-for-One Deal!*

"What's the deal?" Jackie asked her.

Dandelion Girl smiled. "However much you're willing to pay. I don't want to pack those up again. In another five minutes, they'll be free."

"I can wait that long," Jackie said. "I'm gonna go for a smoke. When I get back, I want some of those."

"People still smoke?" Dandelion Girl teased.

Jackie pulled a cig from her pack and stuck it behind her ear. "That they do," she said, and went off to find the small patch of cement dedicated to those who did.

Glynnis walked off to marvel at the flower displays. Dandelion Girl continued to load her truck, watchful for anyone who came by but completely focused on her task. I stood there, toying with a strawberry, awkward as a middle schooler at her first dance.

"Are you gearing up to ask me out?"

I was so spaced out I was completely unaware she'd come up next to me. "What?"

"You look like you want to ask me something important." Dandelion Girl's tone was light, her sense of humor still present, but there was an underlying seriousness to what she was saying. She put her basket of strawberries down and crossed her arms over her chest. "Well?"

My earlier confidence shriveled up like her lettuce. I felt foolish, and old . . . very old. But it felt good to dig in the backyard, and I didn't want to stop. "I'm trying to plant a garden in my backyard," I explained, still wondering if that was what I really wanted to do. "I don't really know what I'm doing. I kind of . . . just started digging and kept going. I've got a large plot now."

Dandelion Girl snapped into professional mode. "What's the square footage?"

"I don't know. It's . . . big."

"How big?"

"Approximately the entire length of the house, and then going back a ways. I could measure it, if you need specifics."

She smiled. "You just dug up your backyard out of the blue? I like that."

I took that as encouraging. "What if I brought a photo with me on Thursday, and you can see what I'm dealing with?"

She fished around in the pocket of her housedress and found a chewed-up pencil and a slip of paper that looked like a receipt. "Tell you what," she said, handing them to me. "You write down your address, and I'll stop by on my way home. It's better if I see your mess in person."

I bent to write my details, but then I hesitated. Was I about to give my address to a stranger wearing a carrot as a hair ornament?

"My name is Mykia," she said, amused. "And I don't need to come over if you're uncomfortable."

"I just wasn't sure what I was doing after work," I said, lamely trying to cover my suspicions. I scribbled my address and handed it to her. "I'm sure you're a very nice person," I blurted, my face warming.

Mykia slid the paper into her pocket. "Oh, I wouldn't be too sure about that."

She was kidding, right?

"Why don't you invite your work buddies, too?" she said. So Mykia was not only an alchemist, she was a mind reader. "Those two can help us measure."

"I've never had a plant that didn't die," I admitted.

"I kind of figured that. Whatever. Doesn't matter. Everything can be learned, you know? Some people learn sooner, others later. Not a big deal if the outcome is the same."

CHAPTER 8

I wasn't prepared for company, but my guests didn't seem to mind, especially my new friend Mykia. She'd taken one look at my backyard, and then announced she needed to eat before she could think about where to start with my small ecological disaster. After a quick trip to her truck to grab some produce, Mykia began to familiarize herself with my kitchen.

"Are these spices from this century?" she asked, holding up some jars I barely recognized. "I think they've permanently adhered to the side of the jar."

I squinted at the labels. "Coriander and marjoram? When were those ever a thing?"

"They're always a thing. You can't mix up herbes de Provence without marjoram, so how would you make herbed pork loin or roasted goose? And could you imagine making Moroccan tagine without coriander?"

I couldn't imagine cooking any of those things because I never had. But I didn't admit that to Mykia. "I thought you were a vegetarian," I said, changing the subject.

"What gave you that idea? I like everything. I eat everything." She surveyed the pantry, stopping at the tower of tuna. "Are you a pescatarian?"

"Those are my son's."

"You have a son? Where is he?"

Mykia was probably just curious, but her question gave me pause. She was a stranger. I had a stranger inside my house, going through my things, talking about my son.

I crossed my arms over my chest, sending what I hoped was a clear message. "He's out with my husband," I lied. The lie felt strangely comforting.

"Cool," was all she said, and she got to work setting pans on the stove. She washed the veggies and then began to slice them, a peaceful, satisfied look on her face. She hadn't asked us what we wanted for dinner. She hadn't asked for help. I felt petty and mean, my judgment getting the best of me.

"So," I began, telling myself I was initiating small talk, "do you have any ownership stake in the farm you work for?"

She smiled faintly. "Why does it matter?"

"It doesn't." But it did, though I couldn't put a finger on why. Did I need to feel superior? Did some better part of me want her to have something of her own?

She gestured outdoors, toward Glynnis and Jackie, who sat companionably on the patio. "Do those gals have a stake in the company you work for? Have you ever questioned it, or is it just who I am that's bothering you? You're skittish as a cat having me in your house—"

"That's not fair. I know them. I'm happy to have you over, but I don't know you."

"No," she said, after an uncomfortable beat. "You don't. I'm sorry. I've got a small chip on my shoulder. It wasn't placed there by me, but for some reason I can't get rid of it. It's probably implanted itself by now."

"I've got one, too," I admitted. "I'm not from around here originally. I guess that feeling never quite goes away." I knew for sure that feeling never moved on. Jesse always felt the past was something we had to outsmart—if it got the best of us, we'd find ourselves struggling to survive in the world of poverty, drug addiction, and violence that beset both of our families. He succeeded in this by playing by the rules of suburbia, a society that made sense to him. We had good jobs and a nice home, we paid our bills on time, and we gave back to the community in small but significant ways. The one time Jesse let something lapse, it ended in catastrophe—when he died we were in the process of changing insurance companies, and we'd decided to hold off on life insurance policies because I felt we could shop around for a better deal. Taking such a risk truly bothered him, but I'd said it was only a matter of a few weeks. What could happen? So much could happen. Death could happen. I'd apologized to him a thousand times in my head. For Jesse, security was the best thing he could give us, and I'd taken that away from him.

"Your mind is a million miles away," Mykia said, her voice full of wry humor. Something in her eyes told me she knew what I was thinking about wasn't all that funny. She began to chop an onion, methodically, precisely. "So, my father is from Jamaica. My mother was German. I'm a halfsie."

"Was?"

"She's passed on," she explained, "but my father is still around. He wants me to go back to dental school. On his dime."

"You were in dental school?"

"I'm going to ignore how surprised you sound."

"Sorry," I said, my face growing hot with embarrassment. "I'm terribly judgmental. Can't help it."

She smiled. "There are worse things."

I thought about all the part-time jobs Jesse and I worked when we were young. How exhausted we were, and how fearful. "Why would you say no to someone footing the bill for college?"

"Because I'm saying yes to this," she said, gesturing toward the vegetables brightening my countertop.

"It's tough to get into dental school. You just walked away one day?"

"I did."

"Why?"

"Because I know what's what."

What? I wanted to shout. *What* is *what?* I felt like I had no idea what she was talking about, and I desperately wanted to know but didn't know how to ask without sounding foolish. Instead, I asked, "Did you leave before they could fix your tooth?"

Mykia laughed. "I pulled my own tooth, because it would probably need it eventually, and I wanted to see what it felt like. I haven't gotten around to doing something with it."

I just nodded. Usually, when someone said something that highlighted how starkly different we were, it made me take a step back. With Mykia, I wanted to get closer, to keep peeling back the layers of her personality. She was bold enough to yank out a tooth. She was confident enough to call me on my bullshit. I thought she was exactly the right person to help me with the backyard of destruction.

I watched as she worked her magic, taking a box of pasta, some cream I hoped hadn't gone sour in my fridge, an egg, and a random mix of spring vegetables, and turned it into savory Italian goodness.

She twirled the pasta around a fork and held it out to me. "Try it."

Wow. Just like Mykia, the dish was a multilayered miracle of taste. "That's pretty incredible."

She smiled, self-satisfied. "Uh-huh."

I helped myself to another bite. "You're going to help me, aren't you? With this garden."

"I don't exactly know why, but I'm going to try," she said through a mouthful. "It's not looking too good."

Someone rapped on the French patio doors. Jackie stood there, frowning, her French-manicured index finger tapping at the glass. When I opened the door, she said, "There's some people here to see you. And they don't look happy."

~

Mr. Eckhardt led the charge, followed by a ruddy-complexioned, barrel-chested Willow Falls police officer and two women of about retirement age, one dressed head to toe in symbols—Tory Burch, Chanel, Michael Kors—and one wearing sensible sandals and khakis. Both frowned at me, lips curled in disgust as though I were the dog who pooped on their expensive carpet. Mr. Eckhardt shook with barely controlled fury—it would have struck me as funny had I not been the focus of his outrage.

"Unacceptable," he spat, gesturing at the dirt pit. "Completely unacceptable."

Jackie moved next to me, and Mykia was on the other side, so it was a fair fight.

"This is private property," I said. "My property. If I want to dig, I can dig."

"You just need to watch out for the gas lines," said the police officer. He looked faintly amused. "Call Nicor, and they'll send someone out."

"It's not that simple," the label lover said. Her voice, smooth and confident, had the assurance of someone who didn't question herself and expected others to follow suit. She placed one hand on Mr. Eckhardt's forearm, much to the alarm of the khaki-clad woman. "We are long-time members of Willow Falls. This community has standards that were established long before you bought this house. You must abide by those standards."

Miss Khaki, red faced but determined, stepped to Mr. Eckhardt's other side, and placed *her* liver-spotted hand on his forearm. "There are rules," she said. "And there are consequences for not following them."

"What kinds of consequences?" Mykia said. Her voice matched her opponent's—cool and unperturbed.

"Do you live here?" the khaki-clad woman asked.

"Does it matter?" Mykia countered. "I'm just talking sense."

Label Lover addressed me. "You have a corner house. Anyone walking by can see this eyesore. It's not good for the community, and we take the well-being of the community very seriously." She reluctantly removed her manicured hand from Mr. Eckhardt and placed it on my shoulder. "I take our citizens' well-being seriously as well. Bill has filled us in on your tragic situation. If you need financial help—or if you need to speak to someone—my husband, bless his departed heart, was a renowned therapist. I'm well versed in grief." She glanced at an uncomfortable Mr. Eckhardt and added, "Though the past is past and I do feel moving forward is important, in every way."

Her concern oozed over me like a BPA-filled plastic film. I couldn't stand her false pity, so I looked down, my feet at the edge of the dirt pit. I leaned slightly forward and let my shoes sink into it.

"Well?" she said. "Are you ready to talk solutions? Are you ready to let us help you?"

"Help me?" My brain suddenly felt fuzzy, my thoughts muddy as my shoes. "How would this help me?"

The silent pause that followed was brimming with awkwardness. The two women pretended I hadn't said anything and looked at me with feigned compassion. Mr. Eckhardt seethed. Jackie went off to have a smoke. Glynnis began to fold into herself for protection from their scrutiny.

"Can I ask you to step over to my vehicle?" The cop's voice was raspy, but still it sounded too loud.

"What?" Was I being arrested? Should I ask someone to grab a phone and start recording? I scanned his chest for a body cam.

"She doesn't have to do that," Mykia said. There was steel in her voice. The cop smiled, revealing crooked teeth. His eyes twinkled. With his red hair and bristly red beard, he resembled an overgrown, slightly chubby leprechaun.

"I'm not hauling her into the station . . . yet. I just think a private conversation at this point would be most productive," he said, and gestured for me to follow him to his copmobile, parked in front of my house.

"I'm recording you," Mykia said, holding up her phone. "It's not illegal to do so."

"Go right ahead, ma'am," he said.

"I'd prefer all conversations to be had in front of everyone," Mr. Eckhardt said, using his voice of authority.

"Sir, I think it would be more productive for me to speak with Miss . . . uh . . ."

"*Mrs.* Moresco," I said. "And if you give me your word you aren't going to try to bully me, I'll talk to you."

He placed three fingers over his heart, like a Boy Scout. "You've got my word."

"Every move you make," Mykia called out as we walked toward the squad car. "Every single move you make. I'm recording everything!"

Once out of earshot, Officer Leprechaun started laughing, a great big guffaw. "Lady, what the fuck are you doing?"

My mouth dropped open. "Did you just swear at me?"

"I did. Your friend's phone won't pick that up, so you'll have trouble proving it in a court of law," he said, still laughing.

"I'm having trouble figuring out the source of your humor."

"It's just I haven't seen that trio so worked up since that homeopathic doctor opened her doors downtown."

"Oh. So, I'm off the hook?"

His expression turned more serious. "They weren't blowing smoke when they said there are ordinances. I'm not well versed in the bylaws of this particular subdivision, but I do know people who stop mowing their lawn or put a car up on blocks are soon convinced to change their habits ASAP. I don't even think they allow garage sales."

"Who stops them? You?"

"Not me." He glanced over at Mr. Eckhardt, who was sandwiched tightly between the two elderly women. "However, I do need to come when they call the police, or else I'll hear about it from my sergeant. And I wasn't kidding around when I said you need to call the gas company. You start digging seriously and that could go wrong pretty quickly."

"A garden," I said quietly. Suddenly my plans felt foolish. "I want to plant a garden."

He whistled. It was an old-fashioned sound, and I smiled despite myself. "Have you ever heard of starting small?"

"I've always started small," I said. "I figured it was time to go big."

"That's a good attitude, but fair warning—you're going to have a battle with them. They don't give up easily, and they're always convinced they're right."

I smiled up at him. "I'm learning to deal with people like that."

He smiled back. "And how's that going?"

"Not good," I said. "But I'm optimistic."

❧

"I swear that tasted just like a bowl full of heaven." I sprawled over the lawn, full of food and satisfied, and stared up at the darkening late-spring sky. We were all stretched out over some old blankets I'd found in the linen closet. Somewhere in the pantry Mykia found a tray Jesse's aunt Tess had given us, and it made a nice centerpiece, citronella candle burning away in the middle. Still, we alternately swatted at the early mosquitoes sucking our blood, enriched as it was with the sweetness of the strawberries Glynnis had bought at the market.

"I told you," Mykia said. "When it comes to food, I'm a genius."

"Alchemist," I said as I poured us all some more wine. "That's what you called yourself. I like that better, turning something boring into something spectacular."

"I'm not sure what that means exactly," Jackie said, "but that was amazing, and I don't even like vegetables."

"Anyone can do it," Mykia said, her voice growing soft. "Like anything else, it just takes a little effort."

"I don't know," I mused. "You planted those vegetables. Cared for them. Plucked them at the right time and made something incredible from them for us to enjoy. Circle of life right there."

Mykia turned on her stomach. She toyed with one blade of grass, not snapping it, but not letting it go, working it between her fingers. "You'll do the same, in time. That's the goal, isn't it? Some kind of subsistence garden?"

"I don't know. I started digging because I was feeling shitty and it felt good. Then I kept digging because I liked the feeling. The idea of actually planting something came later. I didn't seriously start thinking about it until I saw your stuff at the market today."

Mykia nudged me with her foot. "I always tell my father that gardening gives me endorphins. You know, like a runner's high."

"I believe it."

We grew silent for a moment, taking in the great gaping hole of dirt, which suddenly seemed to beckon with possibility.

"Well, you have to do something with this," Jackie said. "It seems a shame to sod it over, and I don't even know why. This is a fancy suburb. It does look awful. That snobby lady was right about that."

It didn't look awful to me. The dirt was dark and rich and teeming with worms. That should have grossed me out, but it didn't. "I'm not going to cover it up. I'm going to keep digging."

"It's not too late to plant this season," Glynnis quietly contributed. "My mom always put in tomatoes late, and peppers, eggplant, zucchini. It usually worked out."

"That's not the way to do this," Mykia said, shaking her head. "You should do raised beds, maybe build a small greenhouse on one side of the yard. This requires planning. You can't just dig up your yard and drop in a few plants."

"How much would the raised beds cost?" I had no idea.

She thought for a moment. "You could fit about six here, maybe eight. Fifteen hundred dollars? And that's conservative."

"I don't have the money for that right now."

Mykia took her time before she spoke again. "Well, I guess dirt's dirt. If you're not going to resod that hole, then you might as well do something with it. We've got some guys who work at our farm. I can send them out with a rototiller if you're serious. I've got some scrap wood, and they can squeeze a few raised beds out of my stash. It's not going to be pretty, though."

"And how much will that cost?" I asked, expecting the worst.

"About a hundred bucks."

Jackie's head whipped up. She raised an eyebrow at me. Mykia was obviously giving me a deal. I wasn't above taking it.

"Okay. If I toss in another fifty, can they help me get more of this lawn up?"

"Done." Mykia grinned. "This subdivision is full of perfect lawns and Stepford wives. Your neighbors aren't going to be happy."

"Nope."

"See if your association will give you a permit," she added, her smile widening. Mykia was getting a kick out of this. I had the feeling that thumbing her nose at authority revved her up.

"You sure about this, Paige?" asked Jackie. The voice of reason. But I wasn't feeling particularly reasonable.

"No," I answered. "I'm not. But I'm doing it anyway."

CHAPTER 9

Excerpt from Petra Polly: Chapter 8—The Underperforming Employee

Imagine you are dealing with a small child who insists on heedlessly running into traffic. At first, you admonish her and attempt to explain the danger. Next, you threaten punishment. Finally, you purchase a leash or quit walking altogether. Neither of these solutions is particularly desirable. They both teach the child nothing.

For management, dealing with an employee who has lost her way offers similar choices. Multiple warnings or write-ups, the threat of dismissal, forcing more restrictive rules, outright firing—these tactics are only rarely necessary and ignore the real issue at hand.

Your employee feels unchallenged and seeks attention.

So you must give it to her. Hang a brass ring. Draw a finish line. Engrave a trophy.

Set the standard necessary for achievement. Sit back and watch her run.

I thought about Petra's words on my way into work later in the week, turning her ideas over and over. The meeting with Landon Cosmetics had gone well, and Lukas had set a meeting for later in the day to discuss the next step forward. Rhiannon, Byron, and Seth had stayed pretty tight-lipped all week, and Jackie and I tossed around ideas about what it meant. Was Landon giving us a chance? What would have seemed unlikely a few years ago was now a definite possibility, and I had to admit it felt pretty good.

And, if Landon were ours, would Lukas give me a chance to shine? If he still followed the gospel of St. Petra, then yes, it seemed he would hang that brass ring for me. Landon Cosmetics was big-time. Was I?

It was market day, which meant I parked a few blocks from Gossamer Space. The white-peaked tents kept me from seeing inside, but I imagined Mykia, charming customers, doing brisk business. I hoped so, because the sky, heavy and gray, promised a downpour before the afternoon was out.

I stopped in my tracks. Rain. The possibility hadn't occurred to me. Mykia's men had showed up a few days before, machines in tow. My backyard had gotten a Brazilian—only a single strip of grass grew along Mr. Eckhardt's fence line, hugging his property. The friendly, efficient men had tilled the soil, disturbing it, then turned it over again, leaving a dark, blank canvas for me to begin to fill. I'd meant to get over to the nursery to pick up some plants and paving stones but hadn't been able to find the time. Would a storm wash all the topsoil away? Was I going home to a mudslide?

I wanted to jog back to my car and dash home. I could buy a tarp on the way. I could call the lawn service and pay a fortune for a sod emergency.

But I couldn't miss the Landon meeting. Leaving early meant leaving myself professionally vulnerable. What was the worst that could happen? A little runoff onto the sidewalk? Mykia had promised the men would dump some mulch on the corner of my property. Maybe the weather would hold out, and I could buy the plants on the way home and get them in before it rained.

With renewed confidence, I walked into the offices of Guh, head held high, heels clacking on the shiny hardwood floor.

"What's gotten into you?" Jackie said. She sat at her workstation dipping jicama into a tub of what looked like a strawberry smoothie. I'd never seen her venture into anything even remotely exotic. Then it hit me; she'd been shopping at the farmers' market on her own.

"Did Mykia sell you that?"

Underneath her caked-on foundation, Jackie blushed. "Maybe. I guess. It's really good." She handed a stick to me. "Go ahead. Try it."

The sharpness of the jicama was tamed by the strawberry sauce. I tasted honey and something else, something vinegary. "This really wakes up the palate."

Jackie shrugged. "I'm not one for fancy foods, but I know what's good. This is even better than good."

"What do you think?" I asked as I settled in front of a computer station. "Of Mykia, I mean."

Jackie chewed thoughtfully for a moment. "She's like some of the young people who work here. I can't deny that they do good work, but I can't shake the feeling that part of them is already on to the next thing. They aren't in it all the way. Mykia seems committed to what she's doing because she's got nothing to lose. In our case, we're committed because we've got everything to lose. Does that make us better at what we do? Hell if I know."

Jackie rarely uttered more than a sentence or two, and she slumped a little, her hand reflexively reaching for her purse. "I need a smoke," she said. "Or maybe three."

~

"It's like dropping pearls before swine," Rhiannon muttered.

The spring line of Landon Cosmetics lay scattered over the white conference table. Byron and Seth poked at the merchandise with clinical detachment.

"What's this again?" Seth asked as he gingerly held a sleek chrome tube between his index finger and thumb.

"Mascara," Lukas said. "Landon is expanding into eye makeup. Weren't you paying attention when Trinka was speaking?"

"Of course," Seth said too quickly. "I'd just forgotten."

Byron and Rhiannon shared a look. Rumor had it Seth was quite taken with Miss Trinka, CEO of Landon, and had paid little attention to anything but her ample cleavage.

Lukas directed our attention to the makeup with one expansive swoop of his hand. "Familiarize yourselves with the product line. Think outside the box—forget the box even exists. Petra discusses awakening your creative juices in chapter 5. I'd suggest you read it again."

"Or for the first time," Jackie mumbled, but she was taken with the cosmetics, just as I was. Since its inception, Landon Cosmetics meant old-school glamour—Trinka's bestselling lipstick, an indelible true red, evoked Marilyn at her finest, yet looked good on every woman who tried it, regardless of skin tone. High-end department stores couldn't keep it on the shelves, and her online business boomed. She'd recently offered corals and pinks, the color palette of midcentury-modern craze, and she'd done well.

But now she'd moved into the space age. Frosted lipsticks; thick, natural-looking false lashes; fast-drying liquid liner—she was reinventing herself.

"Landon is ours?" I said, too shocked to keep the disbelief from my voice. "Really ours?"

Lukas took a moment to answer. "Not yet," he said evenly, "but there is no reason why it can't be."

"What does that mean?" Jackie said bluntly.

"Miss Trinka is interviewing candidates. She wants a full presentation of ideas for this new line. In two weeks." Lukas smiled, letting his eyes roam to make contact with each of ours. "We are more than up for the task."

I picked up a rocket-shaped tube of lipstick. A bold shade of pink called "One Large Step for Womankind." Miss Trinka knew what she was doing. I hoped Lukas did.

"Who'll be the lead?" I asked. Lukas couldn't pull his democratic office bullshit when a client such as this was at stake. We needed to focus, bring our A game, as Big Frank would say.

"There should be a lead," Jackie said, nodding in my direction. "Frank would have chosen one." As the words left her mouth, she realized she'd overstepped. "It just seems like a good idea," she muttered.

"Let's sit down," Lukas said, and my stomach sank to my knees. Lukas had a *plan*. The set of his brow, the way his lip curled in when he was deep in thought, the slow push of his forefinger against the glossiness of the conference table, leaving a mark—he was about to get into why we were really in this room.

"Quite simply, the work we present to Landon needs to be exemplary in every way. There needs to be no question that not only are we the best, we offer something so new, so fresh, the other agencies seem stodgy and dated in comparison."

His tone implied that we were somehow lacking. I felt like one of us should say something to defend ourselves. "We can do it," I said, and Glynnis nodded. "Whatever it takes."

"Ah, but we've never been challenged like this," Lukas said, offering a smile I took as condescending. "When I left Miss Trinka's office, I told myself we'd need to approach this in an unusual way. She's absolutely unique and deserves a campaign worthy of her originality."

We were all nodding now, though by habit. What was he getting at?

Lukas stood, placed his hands on the table, and leaned in. "By the time you leave this room, the outer office will be reconfigured."

"Again?" Jackie said.

"Temporarily," Lukas responded. "The computers will be set in pairs, and so will you. Each duo will have two weeks to design a campaign for Landon. At the close of the competition, Miss Trinka and I will judge the winner. It's a bit unorthodox, but I've discussed it with her, and she's thrilled."

"Doesn't it make us look indecisive?" Rhiannon blurted.

"Not in the new, new creative workplace," Lukas intoned, quoting the ever-present Petra. "To Miss Trinka, it appears that we've devoted our entire staff to her company. She'll have one stellar campaign to run with and a backup if she changes her mind."

"But there's a third," Byron said. "If we're going to be divided in twos."

"Which also works for us. The third-place duo will be terminated." Lukas had the decency to look faintly apologetic. "As you recall, competition should be—"

"Friendly and fierce," Glynnis said miserably.

"Exactly," Lukas said.

"You said we had until the end of the summer," I said, trying to keep my voice steady. "I don't think that's fair."

"I'm taking advantage of an opportunity," Lukas responded. "I think this is a very fair way to handle the dismissals. It's merit based. I don't think you can argue with that."

I could, but I wouldn't. I stayed silent.

Lukas shifted his attention to Byron. "Rhiannon and Byron, you'll be working as a team."

The undercurrent to his words was, *you're the A team.* Byron winked at Rhiannon. Seth, Jackie, Glynnis, and I all shifted in our seats, wondering where we should place our allegiance.

"Seth and Jackie, you'll be working together," Lukas continued. "And, Glynnis, you'll be with Paige."

Seth stared blankly at Jackie, who'd unconsciously gathered the cosmetics to her chest during Lukas's speech. "Oh," she said, looking down and pushing them away. "Sorry."

Glynnis moved her chair closer to mine. "We're being set up," she whispered, so faintly I almost didn't hear her. "We're the most likely candidates for termination."

I swallowed, acknowledging silently that she was right. Still, it wasn't going to stop me from fighting. "Doesn't mean we can't win." I tossed the lipstick into the air, launching the rocket. Lukas had hung the brass ring. I'd need both hands to grasp it.

~

Lukas demanded that we spend our lunch hour aligning forces with the other half of our duo. None of us could focus. We stayed inside, and I squirmed as grayish clouds hung heavier and heavier, the promise of rain was one that would be kept. We barely ate, and talked in low, protective voices. Glynnis was carefully mapping out a division of duties in her notebook, and I glanced around the room. There should have been a villain, someone to secretly hope would get the boot, but my mind wouldn't easily go there. Byron could be smug, Rhiannon obnoxious, Seth pervy, Glynnis too wallflowery, Jackie too behind the times. And me? I was distracted and not working to full capacity. But we were all decent people. And I knew without a doubt that, for various reasons, we all needed this job. Was one person's reason better than another's? Probably. But in the end, what mattered was what we would create. Surprisingly, the plan of action suddenly made sense to me. Lukas *was* creating a merit-based office world. I couldn't fault him for it. Heck, I thought Frank might be frowning at the methodology but approving of the outcome. Instead of being coddled, we were being pushed to be our best. Lukas was right—it *was* hard to argue with that.

"How do we decide which concept to use, mine or yours?" Glynnis's voice brought me back from my musings.

"We can't let our egos get in the way. You come up with something, and I'll do the same."

"But who *decides*?"

The idea that there wasn't some arbiter, some authoritative decision maker, pained Glynnis. I realized that it would have bothered me a few years ago, too, so I tried not to give her a hard time. "We decide," I said. "Together."

She nodded, though I sensed she didn't believe it would work.

"Can we work at your house?" she asked. "I still live with my parents, and they'll want to involve themselves somehow."

I thought about how I worried about helicoptering Trey and smiled. "That's fine."

"And maybe I could help with the garden?" she asked, the question lined with hope and vulnerability.

"Of course. I need all the help I can get."

"No, you don't," she said. "But it's nice of you to say."

I grabbed her hand. "Hey. Listen to me. When someone wants your input, they aren't being nice, they're hoping to gain something from it. You understand that, right?"

Glynnis sighed. "I guess."

"No guessing. It's true."

"Whatever," she said. "Can we get started? So should we each try to come up with something or try to do this together?"

"If we each present something, then we have two ideas to work from."

"You can go first," Glynnis said quickly. "I'm okay with being second. Really, I am."

I started to tell her that wasn't an asset, but then I shut my mouth. Some things needed to be experienced to be learned. "Thank you," was the only response I could come up with.

CHAPTER 10

The rain began after lunch, in the steady, cooling drizzle of late spring. I fidgeted through the afternoon, futzing around with the gelato ad, avoiding Glynnis's plaintive stares, and meeting Jackie outside to complain about everything. "We're fucked," she kept saying, blanching slightly at the curse word. "Byron and Rhiannon actually met Miss Trinka. That equals a head start."

"Seth met her, too. Maybe he can offer you insight."

Jackie rolled her heavily made-up eyes. "I don't think Seth even looked her in the eye. That boy has his mind set on one thing, and makeup ain't it."

I couldn't counter that one with positivity. She was right. "There's time," I went with. "You and I both know how well we work when we've got the time to think."

The rain tapered off as Jackie finished her cigarette, the clouds lumbering out of the sun's way. The warmth it brought rejuvenated my spirit. "What are you doing later?" I asked Jackie.

"Nothing," she said. "A whole lot of nothing."

"Want to go to the nursery with me? I need to buy some plants."

"You're gonna need a lot. You know that, don't you?" Jackie said, but I could tell by the humor in her voice that she would join me. She shrugged. "All right. Got nothing better to do."

"Glad for the company."

"Don't expect me to plant anything, though," she added as we walked back inside Guh. "I just had my nails done."

~

"Those were some slim pickings."

Jackie sat in the passenger seat of my car, a sad-looking tomato plant propped between her knees. The plants stuffed into the back seat and trunk were an equally sorry lot. Yellowed, withering leaves, teetering stems, dry soil—even the nursery employees had given up on them. "After Memorial Day, they just don't care," she said, shaking her head. "Shame."

"They'll be fine," I assured her. "After we get them in the ground, they'll perk up."

"Uh-huh."

"Tell you what. You help me unload them, and I'll make you dinner."

Jackie mused about the offer for a moment before answering. "Okay."

The rain returned as we cruised the streets of Willow Falls, a steady pummeling. "Do you think it's a bad sign Lukas didn't put us together for the Landon assignment?" Jackie asked, her smoker's voice barely audible as we turned the corner onto my street.

Yes, instinct told me. *It means he's definitely going to get rid of one of us.* Jackie sounded so dejected I didn't have the heart to tell her the truth, but I didn't have the heart to lie either.

I didn't have to choose. When we pulled up to my property, the sight that met me stole my ability to speak.

~

When we were thirteen, Jesse and I practically lived at the library. By that age, we'd run through most of the paltry fiction section, so we'd set our sights on nonfiction. He would head straight for the hard-science books while I meandered through the history section. I once pulled a book about Woodstock from the shelf, a book consisting mostly of photographs I found shocking but enthralling all the same. Hippies danced in the rain, mud covering their half-naked bodies, ancient creatures rising from the earth, at one with the natural world. I envied them, the joy they took from not caring, not giving even the tiniest bit of a shit. It looked exhilarating, their freedom, and I knew if I could somehow find the right door to open that I could be that free. At thirteen, I'd thought I would love the sight of all that mud, that I would roll in it and roll in it and maybe never come up for air.

At forty-three, getting dirty had lost its luster. If freedom really was another word for nothing left to lose, I didn't want it. I *had* things to lose—a home, a son, and, hopefully, a garden. If that meant I wasn't free, then I didn't want to be free.

I pulled the car over with a jerk of the wheel. Jackie gasped as we exited the car. "Oh, Paige. What's going on here?"

The soft earth was no match for the rain. Dark pools of water pockmarked the yard. Mud ran onto the sidewalk in wide streaks.

"AAAAYYYEEEEIIIIAAA!"

Jackie and I watched, wide-eyed, as a vaguely human-type form dashed from my back patio, making squelching sounds as it ran through the muck, leaping through the air, only to land on what looked like a tarmac made of garbage bags and duct tape.

"Trey?" I screeched.

He came around the back patio, plastered head to toe in mud. When he saw it was me, he did an about-face, took a running start, and skidded over the homemade slip-and-slide, spraying mud onto Mr. Eckhardt's pristine white fence.

Another kid followed his lead. And then another, until my back-yard resembled that Woodstock photo from so many years ago. It was impossible to tell how many kids slithered around in the mud, their limbs intertwined, their laughter sounding light and musical as the rain, Trey's ringing out over the rest. I hadn't seen him this happy in a long time. He looked alive.

He didn't look like Jesse. He didn't look like me.

He looked free. Really, truly free.

Maybe freedom had nothing to do with loss. Maybe it had every-thing to do with joy.

Jackie bent over and removed her shoes and tucked her socks inside. She tossed them into the car and then carefully rolled up her jeans.

"What are you doing?"

"I dunno," she said while she waded into the muck. Weighed down by water, her blonde hair hung heavily down her back. She wobbled a little until she found her footing. "Can I try?" she called out to the group of kids but didn't get an answer.

Jackie didn't wait for one. She awkwardly slogged over to the patio. Without waiting for an opening, she half ran, half stumbled onto the slide, falling on her ass when she got to the end. She sat there for a moment, unmoving. "Paige?" she finally said. "I think I might have hurt something."

❧

Jesse didn't like to get dirty. I didn't either, but for him, staying clean was a near obsession. It didn't take a psychiatrist to figure out why Jesse had such an abhorrence of dirt; it merely took a glance at a few old photographs of the apartment he grew up in. The hodgepodge of relatives crammed into it had little time for keeping tidy. Jesse's tiny room—narrow twin bed made with military precision, scratched dresser without a speck of dust, books shelved in alphabetical order—was an oasis of calm in a sea of chaos. Neatness and order became talismans for him, things to keep him steady when the twin tornadoes of poverty and crime swept through the world around him. He kept his habits into adulthood, and I was happy to join in. I liked the feeling of satisfaction brought on by cleaning my house. Feeling satisfied was right next door to feeling safe. And that was close enough for us.

Until death filled me in on a little secret—there was no such thing as a safe life. As much as I hated to admit it, that sense of satisfaction, that feeling of accomplishment when everything was in its rightful place, was gone. Jesse wasn't in *his* rightful place, so what did it matter?

Jesse avoided dirt while he lived, but in death he was surrounded by it.

Now I was.

And I didn't have a talisman to keep the tornadoes away.

~

"That was awesome," Trey exclaimed, studiously avoiding eye contact with me. I'd hosed down all of Trey's friends, sent them home with one old towel each, and put a pot of coffee on for Jackie. She'd twisted her ankle on her way to her ass, and now her foot perched atop a stool in my kitchen.

"That was so far from awesome," I said. The rain had stopped temporarily, but I worried about what would happen if it started pouring again. Would all of my topsoil run off into the gutters? I wished I could ask Mykia to come over, but she was fifty miles away at her farm. She would know what to do. Her men had the foresight to throw a tarp over the pile of mulch—too bad they didn't have a supersized one to cover the whole backyard. Maybe I'd text her later, but maybe I wouldn't. I needed to start learning things for myself if I was going to get serious about this garden. I had a date with Google later.

"You're going to help me put the plants on the porch and at the side of the garage," I told Trey. "Tomorrow, if the backyard dries out enough, you're going to help me plant the tomatoes. Those we can put in rows."

Trey made a face. "I'm going over to Colin's tomorrow."

"No, you're not."

He went silent for a moment and then said, "Fine. I'll help you. But afterward, I'm going to Colin's. His dad's painted the gallery wall, and I want to hang some of my stuff."

"What kind of stuff?" Jackie asked innocently, though I thought she'd caught the look that said, *sensitive topic!*

"I'm kind of into photography," Trey answered, suddenly shy. "Wait, *I am a photographer.* Well, sort of. Colin's dad said I shouldn't belittle myself just because I'm young and lack experience. He says talented people are born that way, so technically I have a lot of experience, even though I'm not an adult."

What a bunch of horseshit, I thought, but knew enough to keep it inside.

"He's right about that," Jackie said.

Trey and I responded at the same time. "He is?"

"Big Frank used to say something similar—'fake it till you make it.'" Jackie gestured to me. "You can only fake it well if you know what you want to be." She flashed her nicotine-stained teeth at Trey. "You just gave us a good reminder. Your mom and I are fighting for our jobs because we forgot how to fake it until we could figure out what to do."

Trey turned to me, his face pale. "You might lose your job? Why didn't you tell me?"

"It's not likely," I assured him, shooting Jackie a surreptitious dirty look.

"Forget I said anything," she muttered. "But I'm right about the faking it part."

She was. Jackie and I needed to up our confidence game. Here I was worried about Glynnis's self-esteem, when I could use some lessons myself. "We don't need to fake it," I said, still thinking the opposite. "You and I could write a hundred campaigns for Landon Cosmetics, and they'd all be fantastic."

"Landon Cosmetics?" Trey wrinkled his nose. "What's that?"

"Makeup. They do retro products. Red lipstick, cream blush." I fished around in my bag for the sample lipstick I swiped before walking out of the meeting. "Here, check this out. They're getting into sixties stuff, and we might work on their campaign."

Trey accepted the lipstick case as though it might double as a hand grenade and studied it closely. "It looks kind of like a rocket."

"I call that one," Jackie said quickly.

I took the lipstick back from Trey. "You can have that idea. I think we need to move beyond the obvious."

We. But we weren't "we." Jackie and I weren't on the same team. That was vaguely unfair and depressing, but it was the reality of it. "We've both got to work our hardest on this, and I don't think we should help each other until we've got a solid idea down on paper."

"I don't think we should help each other at all," Jackie said, frowning. "One of us is going to be disappointed, and I couldn't stand the burden of feeling that I hadn't helped enough."

"What are you two talking about?" Trey said, his gaze wandering back and forth between the two of us.

Briefly, I explained Lukas's obsession with Petra and the competition he'd set up, carefully editing out the part about two of us losing our jobs. But Trey was sharp, and he'd picked up not only on the tension but also the true effect the competition could have on our lives.

"One of you needs to come in first, and the other second," he said, working through it aloud. "That's doable, isn't it? What does this Byron guy have over you? Or Rhiannon? That's a stupid name."

I smiled to myself. It'd been a long time since Trey was on my side about anything.

"They're younger," Jackie said miserably. "Hipper. And Rhiannon is a beautiful name."

"Well, 'hip' is definitely a stupid word," Trey interjected. "Why does Lukas have you following a book? Is it any good?"

I pulled Petra's book from my work tote and handed it to Trey. He stared at the cover for a long time, and then paged through it while Jackie hobbled outside for a smoke. (I told her to exhale in Mr. Eckhardt's direction.)

When Jackie returned, Trey pushed the open book to the middle of the breakfast nook. "She's hot. And British. Did you notice?"

I slid the book toward me and flipped open the back cover. "She is? I hadn't noticed."

"Why should we listen to someone who isn't even American?" Jackie added. "That's weird."

"I'm guessing the principles of business don't vary much, Western nation to Western nation," I said.

"Frank would use her book as a coaster," Jackie said grimly. "Or he'd leave it in the john for bathroom reading."

Trey's addition to the conversation was, "She's seriously hot."

A smaller photo of Petra Polly stared back at me. I read the short biography aloud, "'Petra Polly lives in the London area with her three kittens, two dogs, and pet cockatoo. She is currently developing a line of business products based on her popular philosophy.'"

Jackie rolled her eyes. "Of course she is."

Trey paged through the book while Jackie and I drank another cup of coffee.

"Check out what she has to say about the creative process," he said after a while. "This Petra is pretty slick."

Chapter 5. I hadn't read it, and from the look of mild interest on Jackie's face, I could tell she hadn't either. I began reading aloud:

Petra's Rules for Creative Engagement, Part 1

1. *An idea has both a body and a soul, just like a human. The soul is the initial spark. The body is what you share to your group—the practicalities, the plans, the blueprint. The key to success is retaining the energy of that spark through the life span of your project. After a while it will become greater than you, and only then will you achieve success.*

"Does she think she's the freaking Dalai Lama?" Jackie grumbled. "Come on. That doesn't make any sense."

"I think it's kind of interesting," Trey said. "Keep reading, Mom."

Trying to please both of them, I rolled my eyes in solidarity with Jackie, but cleared my throat and read on:

2. *How does one enrich the soul? Reveling in nature. Falling in love. Eating a delicious meal. This is how you prepare your idea to live in the world. Expose it to the elements. Share it with others so that they may become entranced. Feed it with the contributions of your peers.*

"I'm not feeding my idea with anything Seth wants to cook," Jackie said. "This is stupid. Petra is stupid."

I closed the book. "I don't know. Maybe she's got a point. When you came up with that great ad for Castorelli's Deli, didn't you fall head over heels in love with it?"

"Was that the dancing pickle?" Trey asked, laughing. "I loved that pickle."

"It was a good idea," Jackie said slowly. "And I came up with it on my own and designed the whole thing myself. I don't think these tips, or whatever they are, are practical. Or fair. I've been doing this longer than anyone at . . . the company. I know what I'm talking about."

"You do," I said. "But maybe what we're talking about and what they're talking about are two different things."

"It's all advertising," Jackie scoffed.

"I don't know," Trey said. "I kind of dig this Petra chick."

Jackie made a face and went outside for another smoke.

"You live for your work," Trey said quietly. "What are you doing when you're there, Mom? You've never worried about losing your job before. You're freaking obsessed with it. Is this guy picking on you?"

"No," I said. "Not really."

"Then what are you doing?"

I heard the fear in his voice. Trey knew more than I wanted to tell him about our financial situation. Children shouldn't need to know about lapsed life insurance policies and low-return 401(k)s and college savings accounts that would only cover one year's tuition. Jesse and I had been diligent about our money, but that didn't seem to have the results we'd anticipated. Even careful people couldn't save enough to cover retirement, college tuition, and the constantly rising costs of everyday living. Trey had a right to be worried. I had a responsibility to hide that I was terrified.

"Don't worry about it. I've been a star at Giacomo for seventeen years. That means something." The lie left a sour taste in my mouth. I filled a glass with water and squeezed some lemon into it. Trey stared out at the backyard.

"I can't believe I'm actually saying this to you," he said, "but you need to focus."

I thought about the hundreds, perhaps thousands, of times I'd said those same words to him.

"I'm always focused."

"You're giving too much attention to weird stuff, like this garden idea. You've never done anything like this before. You would have grounded me until the next decade if I did something like it."

"Maybe I'm exploring, like you are."

He smiled faintly, and then shook his head. "You aren't allowed to do that."

"And you are?"

"Yeah. I'm not a parent."

"I'm not being irresponsible, Trey."

He pointed at my shoes, encrusted with dirt, that I'd forgotten to take off when I came inside. "You sure about that?"

CHAPTER 11

"Is he going to watch us the entire time?" Trey asked, shooting a nervous glance in Mr. Eckhardt's direction. "He's really creeping me out."

We were on our knees digging shallow holes for the tomato plants. I'd actually had the foresight to buy stakes and some wooden lattices, and it seemed I could at least prop up the wilted vegetables until they grew heartier. The back portion of the yard I'd devote to herbs. The pickings were slim at the nursery, and I knew I was planting the lesser-used varieties—sage instead of basil, marjoram instead of oregano, borage instead of parsley, lemon balm instead of mint. Behind the garage, I'd found some large, flat paving stones left over from the previous owner that we'd never gotten around to throwing away. I could use them as dividers.

Neither of us wore gloves, and the earth was still damp, sticking to our skin and wedging under our nails. We'd stopped wiping smudges of dirt off our faces about five minutes in, and we resembled matching coal miners, streaked with black.

"He's still watching," Trey whispered.

I winked at him and rose to standing. "Mr. Eckhardt!" I called over the fence. "Would you like to help us with the planting?"

He stood in one swift motion, and I heard not a single joint crack. "You've gone crazy," he said. "This is an ecological disaster."

"Isn't that overstating it a bit?"

"The first thing I'm doing when I go inside is calling the village police department." He leaned over the fence. "Do you understand me, Paige? This has gone too far. If you're having a breakdown, do it privately, instead of tearing apart your lawn for attention."

"She's not having a breakdown," Trey said.

"Your *family* had a breakdown," Mr. Eckhardt said. "I'm sorry for your loss, but you are letting it destroy your sensibilities."

I took a step closer to him. "That was uncalled for."

Mr. Eckhardt crossed his arms over his chest. He had to have served in the military. I thought of Hollywood movies with the drill sergeants yelling at privates until they broke down or cried. I would do neither of those things. "What are you waiting for? Go inside. Call the police." I thought of Officer Leprechaun's twinkling eyes. "Go right ahead and call them. You can use my cell."

He stared at me a moment with cold, empty eyes. "Don't think I won't," he said, then turned on his heel and disappeared into his dark kitchen, one I curiously had never seen. I had lived next to the man for over a decade and never once saw past his foyer.

"Do you think he'll call the police?" Trey was trying to come across as nonchalant, but I could tell he'd been rattled.

"I don't know, but at least I got rid of him. That man is a menace to society. He just wants his way or no way. It's not a wonder he never married."

Trey didn't seem to want to converse, so we worked in tandem for a while longer, silently, but a conversation was gurgling underneath the placidity of our quiet. It was dangerous, a possible volcano of emotion, so I started moving more quickly, hoping to avoid it.

"You know, there is some truth to what he said." Trey fingered a tomato plant leaf instead of meeting my eye.

"What's true?" Though I knew what he meant.

"Our family did break down. Without Dad . . . it's not the same. It's broken."

I tossed the trowel I was holding. My hands had begun to shake. Trey rarely spoke of Jesse—was this why? Because he thought we were irreparably damaged? "Is that what you think, sweet boy?"

Trey found the courage to look up at me. When he did, I could see he wore an expression I was not accustomed to—a very adult, almost clinical look of analysis. "Dad held everything together. When he died, it was like"—he struggled for the word—"the *mechanism* had broken down."

At least he hadn't said "the center" was gone. I'd spent two years trying my damnedest to be a strong center, to hold everything together, but it was like being the center of a tornado. Eventually, I'd have to deal with the swirling emotional forces threatening to level us.

"I can be a mechanism, too," I said, trying to reassure myself as much as him. "Or I can at least try."

"Yeah, you can," Trey said, but he sounded unconvinced. He finished packing the dirt around a sad-looking tomato plant and said, "I'll text you from Colin's when I get there. I'm taking my bike."

"I could drive you."

"And ruin the show for Mr. Eckhardt?"

"*You* could drive you, if you had a license," I said, trying desperately to keep my tone light. "I'd let you use my car, honey. Anytime."

Trey ran his hand over his face, smearing the dirt farther, up to his hairline. He sighed deeply, a sound that was so like his father's that I felt Jesse's presence. "This is what I'm talking about, Mom. You stay so focused on the surface things, the meaningless things. The wrong things."

That insight, even if it was faulty, found its mark. I bristled. "What's that supposed to mean?"

"I'm searching for . . . stuff. Myself, I guess. I thought about what we said last night, and figured maybe I was being unfair. Maybe you do have a right to explore things. I thought you tearing up our backyard meant that was what you were doing, but I think you just want to piss off Mr. Eckhardt."

I studied my nails, broken, dirty. A year ago I would have run to the manicurist at the first sign of a chip, but now? "That's not true."

"Sure about that?"

Was I still thinking in superficialities? I had started digging in the adrenaline rush of anger, fueled further by booze. I kept on digging because . . . I'd have to think about that one.

"These plants will probably die," Trey said. "What are you going to do then?"

"I won't let them die."

"You can't control everything," Trey said as he kissed my cheek goodbye. "Why is that so hard for you to accept?"

I wanted to lash out, to tell him *he* was the one having control issues, but thanks to some newfound wisdom I'd mysteriously acquired, I stayed silent and let him think he had the last word.

~

After Trey left, I decided to plant the two blackberry bushes I'd bought. He was right in a way—I couldn't control the weather, pests, or the bunnies and squirrels that frequently thought they owned our backyard, but that didn't mean I shouldn't try. The man at the nursery said the berry plants had a 50/50 shot of taking root, but I bought them anyway, even though I would have much preferred blueberries. Like the other plants I'd purchased, the humble blackberry was second best. It wouldn't even start producing for a year, at the least, but I didn't care. It was the thought of them that gave me the energy to start digging up a spot.

The only place it made sense to plant them was at the corner of our property, up against the fence we shared with Mr. Eckhardt. I liked the thought of plump, juicy berries falling on his side of the fence, staining dots of deep purplish blue on the painted wood.

The backyard was perfectly quiet, the afternoon shifting into evening gear. Mr. Eckhardt's house was still and dark—he obviously hadn't called the police. It didn't mean he wouldn't ever call them—but for some reason, tonight he'd decided to back off. And anyway, Officer Leprechaun would probably write me a warning, at worst. At best, he'd probably help me plant the young blackberry bushes.

I got a shovel from the garage—berry bushes needed a much deeper hole than our delicate tomato plants. The sun began to dip. I couldn't remember what Google had told me—was I supposed to plant things in the evening? It didn't matter—I had to get them in the ground. And regardless of what Trey or Mr. Eckhardt thought, I had a feeling those bundles of roots were hearty and waiting for the opportunity to burrow in.

I put myself fully into the task, using my foot to wedge the shovel deeper in the soil, getting perilously close to Mr. Eckhardt's property line. I glanced again at his house, but it was still dark. I needed to dig out a section just under the fence between us. Technically, it was right on the dividing line, but getting to it required standing on his side to make it even.

Casually, I walked around the fence, moving as swiftly as I could, my hand drifting over the fence posts. When I reached the corner, I was reasonably sure the angle would make it difficult for Mr. Eckhardt to see what I was doing. Then again, he probably had supersonic bat ears and could hear even the subtlest shift of the dirt.

I slowly worked the shovel into the soil, brought up a wedge, and gingerly dropped it onto my side of the fence. It still hit the ground with a thunk, and I impulsively shushed it.

I repeated the process a few times, getting the shovel in pretty deep. When it was ready, I decided to dig out just a little bit more, figuring if it was too deep I could fill it in a little, but if I'd misestimated, I didn't want to have to return to the Eckhardt side of the fence.

When I pushed the shovel in one more time, I stopped short, nearly clipping my chin on the handle. I tried again, but from the scraping sound, something solid blocked my shovel from digging in. Had I hit a stone?

Oh my God. Had I hit a gas line? Was my whole property about to blow?

Carefully, I twisted the shovel and realized it was scraping against metal. Ditching the shovel, I bent over, thrusting my hands into the hole I'd made, and my fingers felt something smooth and flat and undeniably metal. It was too broad for a gas line, and buried in between the two properties, right under the fence. I skulked back over to my side, hoping to free it without disturbing Mr. Eckhardt's grass. With a shiver of excitement, I dug, lying on my stomach, pawing at the ground like a puppy. I used the shovel to loosen the edges of the hole and dug some more, eventually clearing enough dirt to pull what I now realized was a metal box, sort of like the ones military guys used. It was heavy but had handles at the sides, and, squatting, I hoisted with all of my might, falling backward when it came free. Then I tucked it under my arm and ran inside like a quarterback.

~

"What do you think is inside?"

Jackie eyed the dirty, rusted box on my kitchen table with wary skepticism. "Could it be from the fifties, like when everyone had a bomb shelter? Maybe there's Yoo-hoos and Twinkies inside."

"It could be a bomb," Glynnis said in a whisper. Jackie and I gave her a look, and she flushed. "Well, you never know."

Deciding I wanted coconspirators to deal with possible unearthed treasure, I'd texted Jackie and Glynnis, and both had accepted my invitation in seconds, which I wasn't going to overanalyze. They'd come immediately, and brought snacks and wine. As far as I was concerned, this was a party. It was Saturday night, and I hadn't actually cared about a Saturday night in years.

When I could see the box more clearly, I could tell it was old, but not that old, and not military. There were no identifying numbers. There was, however, a rusty lock keeping us out. Jesse'd once bought bolt cutters when he had a brief flirtation with handyman status, and I stood holding them, wondering if my natural curiosity would win out over my suspicion that I was getting myself into something I would have a hard time extracting myself from.

"Open it," Jackie said, a mischievous glint in her eye. "What if it's full of money?"

I eyed her wineglass. How much had she drunk?

"Nooooo," Glynnis said, shaking her pale red curls adamantly. "What if it's a time capsule? You'd ruin it."

That gave me pause. I was violating someone's privacy. But . . . technically it was half on my property, and I was curious as hell. I slipped the nose of the cutters underneath the lock. With some effort, I cut through the metal. "Are you ready?"

"Yes," said Jackie.

"No!" said Glynnis.

I opened the box. It creaked, and some dirt crumbled onto the table.

Glynnis gasped. "What is that? Oh, we shouldn't have done this."

Neatly placed inside, wrapped in watermarked silk fabric, was a gauzy dress, a simple ivory shift, the kind sold in tourist traps all over Mexico. Age had stiffened and yellowed the fabric, but it was cut simply, in a style that never seemed dated. A beautiful red patterned scarf was wrapped around the waist.

"There's something else in there," Jackie said, pointing to a small, flat box.

I was pretty sure it was a jewelry box. Opening that seemed more personal, but I did it anyway.

"Oh, those are so pretty," Glynnis said.

I held the finely etched silver hoop earrings in my open palm. Though tarnished, they looked handmade by someone who'd lovingly crafted them.

While Glynnis found the courage to run her hand over our trea-sure, Jackie narrowed her eyes. "Where did you find this?"

"Sort of under the fence, on the line between my property and Mr. Eckhardt's."

"How long has he lived here?"

The question chilled me when I realized the implications. "Forever. Like, I think he's been here since the houses were built."

We stared at each other, wide-eyed.

"What if he's a serial killer?" Glynnis said, terror clearly etched on her face. She snatched her hand back from the box and cradled it to her chest. "What if that's a souvenir of his victim?"

"What if there are boxes buried all over the yard?" Jackie added, running with it.

I took a gulp of wine, and the alcohol loosened my imagination. I pictured dozens of metal boxes, buried under Mr. Eckhardt's property, full of dresses and jewelry and the sad belongings of the women he'd strangled.

"What does the inside of his house look like?" Glynnis asked.

I took another sip of wine and said, "I've never been inside."

An ominous pause. What if he had a skin suit in his living room, à la *Silence of the Lambs*?

Glynnis placed her hand protectively over the dress. "Should we call the cops?"

I thought of Officer Leprechaun laughing at me through his reddish whiskers. With a start, my common sense returned. If Mr. Eckhardt was a mad murderer, why hadn't he done away with me and put my yoga pants and Pandora bracelet into a box and buried it? "Maybe it belongs to the woman who used to live here."

"Who was she?"

"I don't know," I said. "Jesse and I saw the house unoccupied, and I believe it was sold from an estate, but I don't remember. I guess I could look at our original closing papers."

Jesse had always been in charge of storing all the old file boxes, and I had no idea where to begin looking. Searching through all those memories seemed like opening a can of worms. I needed my worms for my garden. "But isn't that information a matter of public record? I could look it up at the village hall."

Jackie raised an eyebrow. She could tell I was practicing avoidance. Glynnis was too young and inexperienced. "I'll go with you," she said eagerly, forgetting for a moment that she'd concluded we had a serial killer right next door. "If you don't mind me going."

"I'd love to have you along. We'll sneak out at lunch sometime this week."

"Petra wouldn't approve," Jackie said, her words dripping with sarcasm.

"Oh, but I think she would. I'd be going for the brass ring and all that."

"I hate the brass ring," Glynnis said. "But I do like a good mystery."

~

Later that night, I wiped the dirt from the box and carried it up to my bedroom. With the blinds firmly shut, I turned on the soft light next to my bed, took off everything but my underwear, and tried the dress on. It fit, but it probably would have fit someone twenty pounds heavier than me or twenty pounds lighter—it was one of those dresses. I tied the scarf around my waist to make it suit me, and then I walked up to the full-length mirror and held the earrings up to my ears. Who did they belong to, and why would someone bury something so pretty?

I could always ask Mr. Eckhardt, but then he'd probably call the police for real and have me arrested for trespassing.

They did, in all likelihood, belong to the woman who lived here before us. Who was she? Did she mean for someone, someday, to unearth her secrets?

Because I was sure the story attached to this box was juicy. Scandalous, even. The thought appealed to my imagination.

But as I was carefully refolding the dress, my Pandora bracelet caught on the hem and snapped one of the fine threads. Was it symbolic? Was I unleashing something I couldn't contain?

CHAPTER 12

Excerpt from Petra Polly: Chapter 5—Petra's Rules for Creative Engagement, Part 2

1. *Now that you've enriched your idea's soul, you must cultivate it. Let it breathe. Socialize. Work its muscles. Turn its face to the sun. But be patient. Ideas are like houses—they need to settle, but then they need to expand and grow.*
2. *When your idea is at peace with itself, then its soul is ready for the next world. Will it go viral? Will it become part of our cultural lexicon? Your ownership of it will cease to matter. It will become known, and, in the process, so will you.*

"This is such a stinking pile of horseshit," Byron announced when he was certain Lukas was out of earshot.

We had decided the patch of land was simply too crowded on market day, and had given up and decided to walk around the stalls, hitting all the sample stations. We huddled around the cheese man, who was scooping burrata into small cups. Our group had been by twice already, and he kindly pretended not to notice. Lukas had drifted away from everyone almost as soon as we entered the market. I spotted him, of all places, at Mykia's stall, sifting through a tub of zucchini. He'd pick up a vegetable, hold it up to the sun, and reject it, one after another. I hoped Mykia's patience wasn't being tested. The look on her face said that it was. Lukas said something to her, and Mykia bared her teeth in a smile that looked almost feral.

Byron continued to complain, and I knew what he was really doing, which was throwing all of his energy into whining. It was what we "creatives" did when we were stuck. And we were all stuck. Cranky, distracted, and impatient, the six of us had spent the morning bouncing around on our exercise balls like a bunch of toddlers, rudely bumping into each other, as if we could smash a good idea out of ourselves. We'd even settle for a halfway decent idea. Lukas knew what was going on and wisely left us alone. If he breathed down our necks at all, we'd all probably have simultaneous nervous breakdowns.

"This cheese is amazing," Rhiannon announced, bending over to throw out the biodegradable sample cup. Once the bearded, suspendered cheese man got a good look at her cleavage, she slowly rolled up and winked at him.

"A vile display," Byron seethed. "But . . ." Byron's eyes glazed over, and he got *the look*, the one that said that an idea had finally burst into the right side of his brain. He grabbed Rhiannon's hand. "Let's go back to the office."

"What?" She yanked her hand back. "Don't touch me."

"Sorry," Byron said, sheepish for once. "But I've thought of something."

Rhiannon's whole demeanor changed. "You did?" With a final wink at the confused cheese man, she pushed Byron in the direction of Guh. "Run. Now. Get it down on paper."

After they left, a restlessness hit us, and we went our separate ways, searching for our lightning bolt idea, hoping a little bit of Byron's magic had leaped to us. My mind moved in endless circles, and I wandered through the stalls, not really seeing anything.

"Your boss has got some issues," a voice said, and it took me a moment to realize it was Mykia. I'd been drawn to her stall, again and again, but I was simultaneously avoiding Lukas.

"Did you give him some dandelion greens to help him out?"

She laughed. "I think he needs some stronger stuff."

"He's a stress case," I agreed.

"I think there's more to it than that." She shrugged. "But what do I know? Let's talk about you. How's the garden?"

I described the raised beds her men had constructed, the rows of tomatoes, the blackberry bushes. When I got to them, I told her about the metal box and the treasures we found inside.

"Glynnis and Jackie think my neighbor might be a serial killer." I should have included myself in that theory, but I sensed the story was less tabloid sensational and more plain old human sadness.

"Did you ask him?"

"No! That would be . . . awkward. And anyway, he's furious I started the garden in the first place."

"I say ask him. What do you have to lose?"

A secret, I thought. Finders keepers. It felt good to hold something inside that didn't have anything to do with grief.

Mykia tossed a bundle of peppermint at me. "Make some tea with this. But don't plant any in your garden."

"Why?"

"It's invasive, and you're not experienced."

"But I like mint." I smiled at her. "What would a mojito be without it?"

She shot me a measured look. "You want something else in control of your garden, or do you want to be in charge?"

"Well, when you put it that way." I found my reusable produce bag and started to fill it with Mykia's produce. I chose randomly, focused on a variety of colors instead of using my supermarket strategy of planning meals in my head. My sense of smell helped—the sharp tang of onions, the earthiness of asparagus, the childhood-memory-inducing sweetness of ripe strawberries. My grandmother always made shortcake. It was Jesse's favorite.

"What are you making tonight?" Mykia asked.

"I hadn't thought of it. Maybe I'll just mix all this stuff up and call it dinner."

Mykia paused before saying, "I can come over and help you out. You'll have to pay attention, though."

That was usually a problem. Jesse's death diminished my attention span to zilch. Mykia would get frustrated with me. Why bother?

But then I thought I should try.

Jesse and I were never a social couple. We'd had to lean on each other for so long that we'd gotten used to being a duo. Our uniquely shared history made it difficult to get to know another couple in a meaningful way, and our innate distrust of strangers made it hard to get to know us very well. Sure, we went to school fund raisers, and when Trey was younger, I met up with some of the neighborhood moms for coffee or drinks. Jesse coached Trey's T-ball team, but Trey's athletic career was short-lived, and Jesse missed out on most of the bonding rituals of the local dads. He didn't stop off for a few with the guys after work, and I usually worked late, even on Fridays. When I got into my car after such a long day, it never even occurred to me to head anywhere but home.

Typically, Jesse and I loved being homebodies. We ordered in and rented a movie on most weekend nights, especially after Trey discovered a social life of his own. Once in a while we'd splurge and go into the city in search of some new hot spot Jesse had read about in *Chicago* magazine. Some might have seen our life together as boring, but we knew how valuable boring was. Like order, boring was safe. We could rely on it.

We were happy together. We lived in a bubble.

But that bubble had burst. I needed to build a new life, and widening my social circle was one way to do it.

I smiled at Mykia. "I get off at five thirty. Do you need help packing up?"

~

When Trey arrived, trailed by the slim-hipped, bespectacled Colin, we'd already sat down to dinner. Jackie and Glynnis had pitched in, and we had chopped some early potatoes with some green onions and Swiss chard, topped them with some cheddar, and stuck them in the oven. Then we'd fried some bacon I'd found in the freezer and a half dozen eggs Glynnis had bought from the market and whipped some fresh cream to accompany the strawberries, which Mykia had said were on borrowed time.

The boys grabbed plates, their movements awkward, almost shy. For all Trey's talk of Colin's rebelliousness, in a room full of women they both returned to boyhood, all jerky limbs and mumbling. Glynnis stood to make room for them at the table, and both boys blushed furiously as they found their places. We ate silently until I couldn't stand it anymore.

"What do you think of the garden, Colin?" I said in his general direction.

Colin finished chewing, a long, laborious process, before he spoke. "Are you having a midlife crisis?" he said, blue eyes boring into me.

"That's what I asked her," Trey mumbled.

Colin's expression was one of anticipation. This one liked to stir the pot.

I thought for a moment. *Crisis.* What did that really mean? I was in crisis when Jesse died. That was pure existential terror. How did my feelings of meaninglessness and isolation compare to run-of-the-mill, pass-me-a-glass-of-Chardonnay-I'm-in-my-forties anxiety?

I fought my irritation whenever I heard women complain about their fine lines and premenopausal weight gain, about their husbands always traveling for business, and, in this neighborhood, about the high cost of maintaining a summer home while saving for retirement. But they complained without true fear. The aging process didn't seem nearly as daunting when you had someone to age with. I would never have that. Did that meet the definition of crisis? It was more than that. Like watching your future undergo a full nuclear meltdown, Fukushima-style. The effects threatened to last long after damage control was complete.

"I wouldn't call it a crisis; it's more like exploration," I said to Colin, borrowing a word from his father. "Sometimes people change slowly, because life moves slowly." I leaned forward, warming to my topic, though there was a definite possibility I was talking out of my ass. "For example, my grandmother's sight diminished over years and years. First, she squinted at traffic when crossing the street. Then, she got glasses when she could afford them. Then, the doctor upped her prescription every year. Finally, she couldn't see a thing unless she was wearing her glasses. She adapted to it over time. She kept her glasses on her night-stand, and during the day she wore them on a string tied around her neck. She adapted. She changed. But it was over many years."

"Seems like an easier way to do it," Mykia said as she helped herself to more eggs.

"But wasn't that a necessary kind of change?" Glynnis asked. "Your grandmother had no choice but to adapt. What about change that you choose for yourself?"

I smiled at her earnest desire to understand. "I would argue that all change is necessary."

"What about Dad?" Trey said, his tone bitter. "Was that a necessary change?"

"We can't control life and death," I said. "But we can control how we react to them."

"Is that what you're doing by digging up the backyard? Reacting? Dad would never have done that to the backyard."

"No, he wouldn't have," I said after a moment. "And I wouldn't have when he was still alive."

"So you're saying you're a different person now," Colin said, satisfied with his deduction.

"I think the fundamentals stay the same, but parts of me are different."

Trey snorted. "Which part of you dug up the backyard?"

"The part that wants to build something meaningful."

"That's the heart," Mykia said. "You had a heartshift."

"I had a heartbreak," I admitted.

The table went silent.

"I want to know . . . ," Glynnis said quietly.

I smiled at her, encouraging. "What?"

"I want to know what the other kind of change is. The kind that isn't slow."

Tears burned at my eyes, hot and quick. "It's the kind that pulls you by the hair. The unexpected jolt. It's merciless, and it doesn't allow you to change cell by cell, cushioning the blow with time. It smacks you into a new reality. It forces you to examine things you'd rather leave under a rock."

I paused, embarrassed. Why had I said that? I was happy with my life, but the life I had before required Jesse to make things work. We were just fine living in the small world we'd created for ourselves. It worked for us. But what happened when "us" became "me"? Isolation. Loneliness. Fear.

The tears began to flow. Trey's eyes filled, too.

"That kind of change is the kind that's fucking unfair," he said. "It's the sucker punch."

"And the only thing you can do when that happens," I added, reaching out to touch his arm, "is to breathe your way through the pain."

"But it's hard to breathe sometimes," Glynnis said. "It's so hard to breathe."

Mykia set her fork down. "Do you ever see, when people are hyperventilating on TV, someone hands them a paper bag to breathe into?"

Glynnis nodded.

"You have to find your paper bag when you feel like you can't get the air in," Mykia said. She had an air of authority that had both boys hanging on her every word.

"Is that what my mom's doing?" Trey asked. "Is the garden her paper bag?"

"Well," Mykia said, resuming her dinner, "you *are* smarter than you look."

CHAPTER 13

The following week, three days after it was official on the calendar, summer danced its way across the farmers' market. The sun shone brighter, high up in the sky, hot enough to warm my skin through the thin cotton of my blouse.

"I've got little green ones," I said to Mykia.

"What?" She tilted her head back to take in the sun, and a carrot fell out of her hair.

"My tomato plants have green fruit popping up all over." I couldn't keep the joy from my voice. I'd gotten up early to water the garden, and to my surprise, the tomato plants were bearing gifts seemingly overnight.

"You've got to watch out for pests," Mykia warned. "Keep a close eye." She squinted up at the sun. "You're going to be inundated with tomatoes. What are you going to do with all of them when they ripen?"

"Could I sell them here?" I said, a bit sheepishly.

Mykia squeezed my arm. "Sorry, but no. I'll be dealing with an onslaught of my own. I end up canning enough to last through the zombie apocalypse."

A memory, Technicolor sharp, ran across my consciousness. Jesse's mother teaching me to make her secret salsa recipe, one of the few treasures his family owned. She taught me when she knew I would soon be a member of the Moresco family, tattered and spare as it was. She passed away a few years later, and it was our only real lasting legacy.

"I'll make salsa. I have an incredible recipe."

"I don't have a decent salsa recipe," Mykia said, a smile forming. "That's not something I do. But if it's something you end up doing, and doing it right, test run some jars in my booth."

It was work to keep from tearing up. "I'll learn how to can properly," I said, struggling to stay practical when all I wanted to do was hug her tightly. "I promise I won't give anyone botulism."

"The lawsuit will be yours if you do," she said. "But if it's a hit? I'll take you on at ten percent."

Anything would have been a deal in my eyes. "Done," I said. We shook on it.

As we shared a pint of strawberries, I watched Glynnis wind herself through the market, reaching out to touch plants and produce and never quite making contact. "If things keep going the way they're going at work," I told Mykia, "salsa making will be my only source of income."

"That bad, huh?"

"That bad. We're supposed to have a presentation next week for Landon Cosmetics." Glynnis and I had not a single idea. Not one. Not even a file full of bad, in-case-of-emergency-only ideas. Jackie and Seth had found some common ground. I had seen them locked in intense conversation, nodding at each other like bobbleheads. Byron and Rhiannon swaggered through the office like they'd seen the future and knew they had the competition in the bag. We wanted to pelt them with copies of Petra's book until they screamed for mercy.

"What do you do when you feel all tapped out?" Mykia asked. "I work on the farm. Hard labor. It gets the juices flowing again."

"Whenever I was stuck, I'd talk to my husband, and he'd ask the right questions to loosen the spigot." Had it been that long since I'd felt supported while I was being challenged? Over two years?

Mykia frowned. "Husband, past tense. You had me thinking he was still around. I had to figure out that he wasn't from what your son was saying. How long were you married?"

"I'm sorry. I have trust issues. And . . . twenty-one years married, longer than that together."

Mykia whistled. "That's pretty monumental. No wonder you're digging up your backyard. Why didn't you want me to know?"

I shrugged. Sometimes the explanation required more energy than I was willing to give. But then sometimes the simplest explanation was the one that could be best understood. "Sometimes I feel vulnerable without my husband around. You were a stranger then, for the most part."

"I hear you. No offense taken."

"Good."

She whistled. "I haven't got any advice for dealing with that kind of grief. My longest relationship lasted a year, and he was in Doctors Without Borders. We Skyped more than anything."

"That's not unusual when you're young," I said, sensing she saw this as a fault.

"I've got nothing for you as far as ideas go. If you want to know the best ways to cook carrots to get maximum flavor, I'm your girl. But advertising tips? Sorry."

"I don't think there's any work advice that could help me at this point, unless you have a solid, kick-ass idea for selling retro frosted lipstick and false eyelashes."

Mykia laughed. "Not in my wheelhouse."

"Clearly not in mine any longer."

"That could be," Mykia said, growing serious. "I was thinking about what you said about change. I thought about when I left dental school, and at first I felt I'd experienced the quick change you spoke of. But that wasn't right. I'd been slowly moving in this direction since I was a teenager. I just didn't notice. Isn't it possible that you didn't change overnight either? That your garden is something you've been moving toward for a long time?"

I wasn't sure how that made me feel. Had I been unhappy and not realized it? Acknowledging any unhappiness while Jesse was still alive felt like a betrayal. Recognizing it when he was no longer around to defend himself felt grossly unfair. But still, I had to ask myself—was I unfulfilled and didn't know it? "I don't know," I said. "And I don't know how valuable it is to dig that deep."

A slow smile spread over Mykia's pretty face. "Worst pun ever."

I laughed, and it felt like a release, an exhale. "Yeah. I guess so."

She handed me a bunch of dandelion greens. "On the house. Keep getting those toxins out."

Without thinking, I grabbed her shoulders and gave her an awkward hug. "Thanks," I said, emotion muddying my voice.

Mykia pushed me away gently. "Go back to the office and figure out how to sell your shit. My grandmother used to love her false eyelashes. She looked like Diana Ross, but with better hair."

And then there it was. The lightning bolt. I waved the dandelion greens at Mykia and dashed for Glynnis.

~

I handed Glynnis my phone with the video I'd found on YouTube.

"They're gorgeous," she said after watching, "and they sound great. I'm pretty sure I've heard that song before."

It was "Stop! In the Name of Love" by the Supremes. Pretty sure? It was my mother's generation's music, but still. Sometimes Glynnis had the ability, with just a single phrase, to make me feel like one of the ancients.

"How are we going to use it?" she said, brow furrowing. "It's the era Landon is trying to evoke, but the ad can't be stuck in the past. Trinka's targeting a younger demographic. Does that make sense?"

I brought up a photo of Diana Ross backstage before a show, sitting in front of her makeup mirror, carefully applying liquid eyeliner. Then I brought up one of Tina Matthews, a pop star I'd seen on the cover of *Teen Vogue*. It was an arty photo of her pressing a lip gloss wand to her pouty lips. It had a retro feel.

"We can't use these," Glynnis said. "They're proprietary."

"But we can use the general impression. We'll tell a story of how these women use makeup to build themselves up for a concert, but it's their confidence that really shines through. One from the past, one from the present, connected. Get it? Not ancestors, glamcestors! The performers from today got their cues from the ones of the past, the ones who set the mold. Landon becomes both a homage to those women and a modern link to them."

"Isn't it a little too obvious?" Glynnis said, drawing out every syllable of the last word as if to annoy me thoroughly and completely. "But I guess we don't have much else."

"We don't," I said tersely. "You can handle the modern image, and I'll do the retro one. We'll find common ground and put them together when we're done."

Glynnis shrugged. "I guess it's not too bad. But I don't know."

I bit my tongue so hard I was surprised it didn't fall out on the desk between us. So much about my life confused the hell out of me, but professionally, I thought I knew what I was doing. Was I wrong? Maybe Glynnis didn't like the idea because it was me suggesting it. Or maybe the idea sucked. When had I lost my confidence? I gathered the tattered shreds from some corner of my brain.

"What's your idea? Let's hear it."

Glynnis flushed. "You know I don't have one."

"Exactly," I said.

We sat there for a moment, in the silence of a passive-aggressive tug-of-war.

"If this isn't good enough," Glynnis said softly, "we'll lose our jobs. I need to be sure."

I put my hand on her arm. "I know. But we don't have time to be sure. It's better to have something than nothing."

"I'm always trying to have something," she said miserably, "but I always end up with nothing."

"Not this time," I assured her, though I wondered if it was a false assurance. "Not this time."

CHAPTER 14

When I got home that night, the house was quiet in a way that made me feel a deep loneliness, but the garden's silence had a velvety softness that had me sitting on my small patio, breathing deeply and wondering if I could just stay there forever.

Some of the tomato plants had already yellowed at the bottom, and the blackberry bushes looked a bit peaked, but, overall, the plants took every opportunity to burrow in and make my yard their home. My garden had a chance.

I was briefly entertaining the fantasy of success at the farmers' market, my salsa a big hit, when I heard the siren. Since Jesse's death, the sound of wailing sirens picked and prodded at my imagination like a dentist poking at a bad tooth. I wasn't there when Jesse was taken, his breathing ragged and labored, to the hospital where he would pass before I arrived. I imagined being there, holding his hand, telling him to stay with me—the Hollywood version of a death scene, but I didn't know any other. The only thing I was fairly sure of was that I could have said something to him, something meaningful, something other than *Remember to pick up the dry cleaning*, which were the last words I said to my husband of twenty-one years. It could have been worse—he could have stormed out after an argument, or we could have not said anything to each other at all—but it also could have been better. So much better.

The siren blared. It was getting closer. Some instinct, the sixth sense of one who has experienced tragedy, sent me walking to the front of the house just as a cop car cruised slowly down our block past the neighbors and, as my stomach sank to my knees, stopped directly in front of my driveway.

The siren cut off abruptly. Officer Leprechaun exited the vehicle with a nod to me and opened the back door. I recognized the boots that hit the pavement, the tattered jeans, the holey concert T-shirt.

Trey.

"What happened?" I didn't know whom I was asking, but Trey didn't answer, and focused his attention on the ground.

"I want to know what's going on," I said to Officer Leprechaun, but I moved toward Trey, protectively. "Was that siren really necessary?"

"I wanted to impress upon Trey the seriousness of his actions," he said, and I wanted to extinguish the twinkle in his eyes with the hose I used for my garden.

"And those actions were . . . ?"

Officer Leprechaun glanced at Trey. "Shoplifting."

"What?" It was my turn to bore a hole into Trey's skull with my eyes. "Is this true, Trey?"

"Not guilty," Trey said, but he wouldn't look at me and instead stared at the house.

"The owner of Pizza City said he wouldn't press charges if I spoke to you," Officer Leprechaun said, with a note of something meaningful in his voice. What was it? Apology? Pity? Embarrassment?

Anger took over. I grabbed Trey's chin and forced him to look at me. "What is he talking about? You stole some pizza?"

Trey didn't respond. I thought about when he was a toddler and stuck a small rubber ball in his mouth. He had clenched his lips together and wouldn't give it up until I'd pinched his nose and he had to open up to gasp for air. The ball had bounced on the floor in front of him and then into the toilet. The look on his face—horror, anger, astonishment—had surprised me. There was no fear. But now, now I saw the swirling mix of emotions in his deep brown eyes, and fear, well, that was front and center.

"What *happened*?" I asked again, but this time I tried to imply comfort with the words.

"I took the ketchup and mustard dispensers," he said, voice monotone. "Someone saw me and called the cops."

"That would be me," Officer Leprechaun said. "I happened to be down the block at the coffee shop."

Daisy's Coffee Express was notoriously popular for its donuts. I swallowed my inappropriate laugh.

"I was going to bring them back," Trey said. "I wanted to use them for an art installation."

"We have ketchup and mustard in the fridge. Why would you need to take them from a restaurant?" I tugged on Trey's sleeve, motioning toward the house. "Thank you, Officer. I can handle this now."

"I'm sure you could," the officer said, "but I told Richie down at Pizza City that I would have a talk with you, and I intend to keep that promise. Richie could have pressed charges, and that would have made a lot more work for me and a lot more stress for you, financial and otherwise."

I noticed Mr. Eckhardt standing on his front steps, a look of disapproval directed toward us. I gave it right back, arching an eyebrow. I wondered what Officer Leprechaun would think of the clothes buried in the backyard.

"Let's go inside," I said tersely.

They followed me into the kitchen, none of us uttering a word. I put a kettle on and directed Trey to sit at one end of the kitchen table and Officer Leprechaun on the other side. I took the middle.

"You're not a child," the officer said to Trey. "Can you explain why you'd take something like that? Was it a prank?"

"Technically, I am a child in the eyes of the law," Trey said under his breath.

I warned him with a kick under the table. "Then I'm going to treat you like one," I said. "You're grounded. You will also write a note of apology to Richie at Pizza City."

Trey shrugged. "I did a stupid thing. People do that, you know."

"Mistakes are different from conscious decisions to break the law." Even Officer Leprechaun had to know that one wasn't going to hit its mark. Sure enough, Trey snorted.

"Except for school, you are not to go out this week," I said. "You'll help me around the house and in the garden."

"How's that coming along?" said the officer, likely already bored by the domesticity of punishing a teen.

"It's ridiculous," Trey said. "She doesn't know what she's doing."

The officer straightened in his chair. "If I still had a mother, I'd show her some respect."

The teakettle went off, and Trey almost did as well. His jaw clenched, and tension rolled off him and gave the room a feeling of oppression.

"Go upstairs," I said. "We'll talk more later."

The chair scraped against the floor with the force of him rising. Without sparing either of us a glance, Trey bolted from the room. I listened to him bound up the stairs. When he slammed the door, I felt the sound in my teeth.

"Teenagers," I said, hoping that would shut down the conversation.

Officer Leprechaun studied me for a moment. "That doesn't explain much."

"Don't you remember being that age?"

"I didn't go around stealing condiments." He softened his comment with a smile. "Richie wasn't going to press charges for something so trivial, but he's known Trey awhile. He's worried."

I am, too, I wanted to say, but I didn't know this man very well, and our family's grief was private. It was *ours.* "I know you hear this from every mother, but my son is a good kid."

"I didn't think otherwise, but even good kids act out when life isn't going their way." He took a sip of tea, winced at the heat, and then blew over the top of the mug. He wasn't going anywhere. He was also waiting for me to say something.

"My husband died two years ago," I blurted. "I thought we were doing okay, but maybe we're not."

I waited for the usual questions: How did he die? How old was he? Are you doing okay? But Officer Leprechaun simply nodded. I waited another moment, but he didn't respond, didn't encourage. He was probably really good in interrogations. His patience made me want to explain, to tell him that what he was seeing wasn't really us, but a temporary us, brought on by stress and missing the person who made the family work. But then I thought death was permanent, so I couldn't say that honestly. The stress would always be there. The missing, too.

"Can I take a look at how the garden is doing?" he said after the interminable silence.

"What?"

"I'd like to see what you've done out there since the village threatened to shut you down." The twinkle was back in his eye, and this time I didn't want to put out that light.

When we walked onto the patio, I tried to see the garden through the eyes of someone who hadn't seen it struggle to survive every day. It had a haphazard look, like thirty gardeners had come in and done their own thing. The overall effect was messy and disorganized, but I could see some improvement, some growth.

"It's getting there," he said kindly. "Don't know if those tomatoes will make it."

"They will," I said.

"Confidence is a good fertilizer."

"Are you trying to say I'm full of shit?"

He laughed. "Nothing of the kind."

We walked around, my pride growing as I realized how hard the plants were working to take root. They wanted to flourish. They *wanted* to live. "It's a lot of work, but I like it."

"My grandmother had a kitchen garden, but not as big as this one. Still, she always had a lot of produce left over to share with the neighbors. What do you intend to do with all your bounty come August?"

Suddenly shy, my deal with Mykia seemed like a pipe dream. I didn't want to tell him about my salsa enterprise, but then I didn't want to seem unfocused either. I cleared my throat. "I'm going to make salsa and sell it at the farmers' market. Hopefully. I just need to learn how to can without giving someone botulism."

He knelt down, knees and cop gear groaning, and studied the tomato plants up close. "Gonna still be a while until these are ready," he said, pointing to the now plump green tomatoes.

"So I have time to learn," I said.

He peered up at me, squinting into the sun. "What are you doing on Sunday?"

"What?" I choked on the word.

He stood. "I have the day off. My grandma taught me how to can. It's easy, and I could teach you in an afternoon."

It was like a wintry wind swept through the backyard. My hands went cold, and my heart . . . was he asking me out? I'd be lying if I said I hadn't thought about dating. Actually going through with it was another matter entirely. The feelings it brought up—guilt, worry, guilt, sadness, guilt, fear, guilt, and a heart-stopping, gut-clenching excitement—were uncomfortably strong. It felt like cheating. It felt undeniably wrong.

"Paige?"

But this man, this ruddy-faced bear of a man, seemed sweet. Maybe it wasn't a date? Maybe he pitied me and wanted to help out the poor widow?

"Don't overthink this." He smiled, the mind reader.

I looked away. "I'm just mentally checking my schedule. I think it'll work."

"Good. Just keep in mind . . . the process is messy."

"Noted." The thought of another man in my kitchen made my stomach lurch.

He walked me back to the patio. "I don't have any children myself," he said before leaving. "But I've seen plenty of teenage boys in my time on the force. He's a good kid, but sometimes circumstances make sure that doesn't matter. I know you'll keep an eye on him."

"Always," I said as Officer Leprechaun got back into his cop car. He made a U-turn, flicking the siren on momentarily as a goodbye. Breathing deeply to quell the little earthquakes erupting inside me, I went in to see to my son.

~

Later that night, I shut off all the lights in the house, checked the locks, and watched the green lights blip on the fire alarms. Safety was never guaranteed, but there were a few things I could control. Then I checked on Trey. His door was shut, but a thin strip of light underneath it told me he was still up.

"Yeah?" he said when I knocked.

"Can I come in?"

"No."

Just as I had when he was younger, I weighed the cost and benefit of accepting his rejection or pushing past it. My anger at his immaturity paled in comparison to my worry for his state of mind. *Do I leave him to his own thoughts or try to add my own to his musings?* Grief made regular, run-of-the-mill worry completely irrational. The mind skipped to worst-case scenarios because of the realization that the worst could actually happen. Was Trey depressed? Would he harm himself? I flung open the door.

He sat on his beanbag chair, his copy of *The Lord of the Rings* open and facedown on his lap. Some kids used food for comfort, or drugs—Trey used Tolkien. Tears streamed down his face.

"Oh, honey . . ."

"I told you to go away! Don't you respect anything?"

"I'm sorry. I—" As with so much lately, I had no idea what to do.

"You're right. I shouldn't have taken those things," he said, voice listless, as his attention turned to the window. "And I'll stay in all week. I'll help you around the house, but I will not help you with that garden. It's just as stupid as me stealing the ketchup bottle from Richie. Those plants are going to die, and we'll be left with a big mess. It just doesn't make any sense. I'm admitting I did a stupid thing. Can you?"

CHAPTER 15

Excerpt from Petra Polly: Chapter 9—Dealing with Failure by Forgetting about Success

So your idea fails. What now? Some will worry, some will give up, and some will keep pushing the dying idea until it is a lifeless, floppy mess. None of these will help. What will help is forgetting. Forget the concept of success, at least temporarily. Forget the failure. Forget the stress and the disappointment. Don't analyze what went wrong. Don't flog a dead horse. Forget it all so you can be reborn. A clean slate. No ideas ever existed before this very moment. Free yourself from the pressure of success, and you'll free yourself of the oppressiveness of failure.

"What happened to reaching the brass ring?" I asked Jackie while she blew smoke in the other direction. The Landon presentations were scheduled for the evening, and the atmosphere at Guh was nearly intolerable. Each duo guarded their project with police-dog ferocity—even Jackie hadn't told me what she and Seth had come up with. She stalked across the office, looking miserable when she asked me to join her for a break, so I assumed things weren't going well. I thought Glynnis and

I did a decent job—not spectacular, but not merely passable. We had a chance.

Jackie made a disapproving sound. "Petra Polly was drunk when she wrote this. Like Rhiannon said, she makes fuck-all sense."

"If we see her in a bar, we're beating her silly."

"I want to yank those golden braids. Hard."

"She's probably the type who'd like it."

We laughed, but there was no joy in it. Because it came from fear.

"We're not ready," Jackie said after a fierce inhale. "Seth thinks we are, but we're not. I don't think he understands what's on the line here."

"I think he does," I assured her. "But even if he doesn't, you know what you're doing. You've got this."

Jackie shrugged. "I didn't tell you, but I sent out some résumés about ten days ago. I haven't heard a word. Not a word. I can't lose this job, Paige."

"You won't. It's not going to be us that get the boot. It can't be."

"I don't see Rhiannon and Byron failing." Jackie quietly finished her cigarette. We gazed out at the empty parking lot.

"I miss the market when it's not here," Jackie said. "Hard as it is to admit."

"We need to have another dinner at my house." I checked my phone. It was five o'clock. "It's time to get back upstairs. Lukas is going to be prompt."

Jackie put a hand tentatively on my arm. "Paige, if it is me, will you still keep up our . . . friendship?"

There was so much insecurity in her eyes. There shouldn't have been. We'd known each other for nearly two decades. It shamed me to think I hadn't strengthened our connection over the years enough that she wouldn't be so afraid it would snap easily.

"Of course we'll still be friends." I drew her into a quick hug. Her sprayed hair tickled my nose, and she smelled like Poison. "Our friendship goes beyond this office. You know that."

"Does it?"

"Now it does. I know it wasn't always like that."

"I like how it is now," Jackie said, starting to cry. "I'm sorry I wasn't there for you more when Jesse died."

"Oh, but you were." Honestly, I couldn't remember. The months after Jesse died were a blur of people offering gifts I could never repay—food, gift cards, checks for Trey's college fund. I didn't remember even writing thank-you notes, but I was grateful for everything. Had Jackie sent flowers? Brought over a casserole? Hell if I knew. It was easier to assume she had. And knowing her, she'd done something. And I was indeed grateful.

"Thanks for being a good friend," I whispered in her ear.

"But I'm not," she sobbed. "I'm not."

"Why would you say that?"

She pulled away. We were close enough for me to see that Jackie's mascara-stained eyes were full of shame. "There's something I haven't told you."

No one liked to hear those words, as so rarely did they end with an explanation that brought anything but sorrow or disappointment.

I steeled myself. "What is it?"

"I loved him. With my whole heart. I loved every part of him."

My mind reeled. "Who?"

She swallowed. "Big Frank."

I had to let that register for a moment. Jackie and Big Frank? KiKi, aka Mrs. Big Frank, had died only a few years before he did. Had he and Jackie been carrying on an affair? I suddenly felt sick.

"What? How?"

She lowered her eyes. "I never told him. Never acted on it. I obsessed about it, and tried to manipulate situations so he and I would be together at the office. I bought him presents for his birthday and Christmas. I have photos of him in my apartment. That sounds so weird, right? I made a fool out of myself at the Christmas party, trying to get him on the dance floor."

I didn't remember that. I was so lost to my own grief at the office party, and even more so when Big Frank was found.

"I regret that I acted like a love-struck teenager. It wasn't right, even after KiKi died."

"I don't know if you can assign right and wrong to that situation. You couldn't help the way you felt. Do you think he knew?"

She paused before answering. "Yes. Once, a few years ago, he walked by my desk and said, 'Kid, you're one in a million. And I'm not gonna be the only one who thinks it, because it's pretty damn obvious to those who get to know ya. Capiche?'"

Classic Big Frank. So he knew. That was his way, the way of kindness. Of course she loved him. Who wouldn't?

"You think badly of me now," she said.

"Why would I? I think nothing of the sort, though this does change things."

"I know," she said, defeated.

"The way I see it, you're a widow, too. All the more reason for us to stick together. No matter what happens in that conference room, I've got your back, and you sure as hell better have mine. Capiche?"

She put her head on my shoulder. "Capiche."

~

We sat around the conference table, pairs huddled together, waiting for Lukas. No one spoke. Our laptops, open in front of us, didn't provide enough of a shield, and we each glanced around the room, avoiding eye contact. Two of us weren't going to make it through the evening. Hunger Games, indeed.

Lukas walked in smiling, which seemed exceptionally cruel.

"Paige and Glynnis, you're up first," he said brightly.

Glynnis squeezed my hand under the table. Her pallor shifted from pale to snow white, and I squeezed hers back.

"I've just sent you all the file," I said, voice shaking. The others dove into their mailboxes. Were they simply curious or rabid to see us fail? I looked up, and Jackie gave me a subtle thumbs-up. It was enough to give me a little courage.

"Start the video now," Glynnis squeaked.

The short video that Trey and Colin had begrudgingly helped us with looked polished. The music, '60s Motown, began, and the image of Diana Ross sitting at her makeup chair, gorgeous and confident, appeared. The music shifted seamlessly into something more modern, and the image morphed into Tina Matthews, pop princess, in a similar position, her eyes showing that whatever the joke was, she was in on it. Then the ad popped up, the makeup in the foreground, the background split between the past and present. We'd re-created both backstage spaces perfectly. The words were displayed in frosty pink letters: *The Past Makes a Beautiful Present*. Glynnis had added a pink bow around the lipstick at the last minute, and the color contrasted beautifully with the black-and-white photographs.

"I really like it," Jackie said immediately. She looked up at me, and I could see the pride in her eyes. I was so grateful for it.

"Thank you," I said.

"The pink is a little too girly," Rhiannon started, and I wished the earth would open up and swallow her whole. "Overall, I think it's effective. I like the message."

Shocked, I could merely nod in her direction.

"You can't use those images without paying a fortune," Byron noted.

My smile was brittle. "We'd substitute something similar."

He flicked a key on his laptop. "Then the effect is completely gone."

I glanced around the table. All eyes were on me—should I defend myself? I didn't know. "I disagree," was all I said.

Lukas put his elbows on the table and peered at me over the top of his glasses. "Byron has a point. You couldn't go to a client with material that would add substantially to the cost of the project. I like the concept, Paige and Glynnis, really, I do, but I'm not sure of its . . . sustainability."

"It's not a rain forest," I mumbled under my breath, and Glynnis kicked me. The others stared at us in relief. We hadn't hit this one out of the park. We'd made it to first base, but that barely counted, even in make-out sessions.

"Byron, why don't you show us what you and Rhiannon have come up with," Lukas said, turning his attention to the A team. But had they brought their A game?

Rhiannon and Byron shared a smile, and then fiddled on their laptops for a minute. "It's yours now," Rhiannon said. "Take a look."

It was a psychedelic Peter Max–style extravaganza—the colors of Landon's line swirling together in a '60s-inspired wonderland. The two hipstery girls superimposed over this masterpiece were laughing, passing the lipstick between each other. There was no tagline, simply the Landon logo scrolling across the bottom in hot pink.

Pink!

"I guess pink's not all bad," I said to Rhiannon.

"It's a certain shade," she retorted. "I'd almost argue it's got burgundy undertones."

"It's arresting," Lukas said, obviously pleased. "Nice marriage of the past and present."

Glynnis made a choking sound.

"It feels fresh," Lukas continued. "Well done."

"We were going for hipster meets hippie," Byron said, unable to graciously accept his victory. "I'm glad we succeeded."

The table fell silent again, but this time the smugness seeping off Byron and Rhiannon gave it an uncomfortable hum.

"Jackie? Seth? You're up," Lukas said.

I realized then that Seth had been silent up until that point. I also noticed that his color seemed off, his normally flesh-toned Pantone 62-7 color fading into something with a greenish tint. Was he sick?

"It's there," Jackie said flatly.

I found myself looking at an image of a lipstick-shaped rocket hurtling toward a star-laced sky. It was retro, trite, and . . . phallic. Jackie and I had both dismissed that idea as tired when we were sitting around my kitchen table. I caught her eye, and she gave a quick nod and pursed her lips. I noticed how much distance there was between her and Seth. They'd had trouble from the start and obviously hadn't found a way to overcome it. I wished she'd asked for my help, but then would I have been able to offer any?

"Well," Lukas said. "Well."

"The image is well defined," Rhiannon said in a rare show of grace. "The rocket is . . . dominant . . . and . . . shiny?"

Byron groaned. "Did you intend for it to look like a dildo?"

"Enough," Lukas interjected. "It's a traditional take. The space-age theme is a bit obvious, but sometimes that's what's needed." He gathered himself and stood. "Petra Polly does not believe in embarrassing employees, and neither do I. I will share your proposals with Miss Trinka tonight. Tomorrow morning you'll find an envelope at each of your workstations. Inside will be a card that says 'stay' or 'leave.' If you are in the position of leaving, take it merely as a sign that there are opportunities for you elsewhere and that you now have the freedom to pursue them. I do ask, however, that if you are asked to leave that you do so immediately, and through the back entrance. Whoever it is, be aware that we all wish you the best of luck. There is no reason for any long, drawn-out goodbyes."

As we shuffled out of the conference room, bent and defeated, I wondered if Lukas's method of kicking two of us to the curb was Petra's method or his own.

It definitely wasn't Big Frank's.

~

Jackie and I decided to meet at the farmers' market for coffee before one of us possibly lost her livelihood. We grabbed two cups of the best coffee we'd ever tasted and waved at Mykia as she attended to some early customers.

"Seth and I simply could not work together," Jackie explained as she sipped her coffee. "All of his ideas centered around sex. Or something sexist. Or both."

"Well, two of us are going to get the boot. I'm worried for Glynnis. And for myself."

"I'd like to say I'm worried for all of us, but I'm not," Jackie admitted. "I don't want to go, and I don't want you to go either."

"Lukas was toughest on mine. It'll be me and Glynnis." I pushed the unkind thoughts from my mind. The ones that said I wished it would be Rhiannon and Byron, because they were young and would bounce back a lot quicker than I would. I tried to bury my fear down even deeper—what would I do? How would I continue paying the mortgage? How could I help Trey pay for college? But it kept bobbing to the surface, leaving an oil-spill residue of anxiety.

Nervous, Jackie and I both checked the time on our phones. "Let's get it over with," she said.

We climbed the stairs to Guh, our footsteps heavy with foreboding. I'd worked for Giacomo for seventeen years. Nearly Trey's entire life. Would getting the boot ruin me? I thought of the garden, of Lukas's insincere promise that opportunities would abound. Maybe I'd make my own opportunities. Maybe . . .

When we stepped in the office, Byron, Rhiannon, and Glynnis were already at their workstations, saucer eyed. They pointed to the chair where Seth usually sat. An opened envelope, torn in half, rested on the keyboard.

"He's gone," Glynnis said, pink cheeked, likely embarrassed by the relief in her voice. "But he didn't go out the back door."

"Good for him," I said, but then my comment trailed off as I saw the pristine white envelope wedged into Jackie's keyboard. With Seth gone, it didn't take much to imagine what hers said. My mouth opened. "Oh, honey . . ."

She ran to her desk and snatched the envelope, clutching it to her heart instead of opening it. "No," she said. "No way. I'm not leaving."

"I'm sorry, Jackie," Rhiannon said. She stood up and awkwardly attempted to offer a hug. "I really, really am."

Jackie shook her off. She pushed her shoulders back and lifted her chin. "I said no. I don't accept this."

"I don't know if you have a choice," Glynnis said. "I'm so sorry."

Jackie glanced at Lukas's closed office door. "Hell if I don't have a choice."

She marched over to his office, and in a rare show of office solidarity, we all followed her. Jackie didn't hesitate before knocking.

"I'm busy at the moment," Lukas called out. Was that a Madonna-esque fake British accent I'd heard?

Jackie busted into his office anyway. We were at her heels. Adrenaline pulsed through my body with such force I felt light-headed. Jackie, red faced and determined, was nearly vibrating with energy. *You can move mountains,* I thought. *Start pushing.*

Jackie tossed the envelope on Lukas's desk. "Big Frank would never have done this. Never."

I winced. *Don't lead with that!*

Lukas stood. "In case you haven't noticed, I'm not Big Frank. We all agreed to this, Jackie."

"I didn't agree to anything."

Lukas slowly picked up the envelope and held it out to Jackie. "If you'd opened this," he said, "you'd have found a very generous severance check. I didn't have to do that, but I'm thankful for the years of service to Guh—"

"Giacomo!" Jackie screeched. "It's Giacomo. Always has been. It's your name and birthright, but I've given my adult life to this company. I believe in it, I believed in your dad, and I even believed in you! Don't do this." She paused to collect herself. "Please, Lukas."

Indecision flickered over his Big Frank–like features. Lukas took us in, standing behind Jackie. I had put one hand on her shoulder, and Rhiannon had done the same on the other. We were a force to be reckoned with. A beleaguered but energized foe.

Lukas took a deep breath. "I don't believe Petra would approve."

"Petra says we should embrace failure," Byron piped in. "Wouldn't keeping Jackie on best illustrate that principle?"

Byron's smooth baritone delivery made Lukas take notice. Glynnis practically swooned. "He's right," she said in a whisper.

Lukas pondered this for one excruciating moment. "I suppose re-adding Jackie to the mix would make the next contest all the more of a challenge. Petra does discuss the nature of competition more comprehensively in chapter 5." He held up the white envelope. "Upping competition should add an element of risk. You are welcomed warmly back to Guh, Jackie. However, if you lose the next contest, there will be no severance. Do you accept that term?"

I could feel Jackie trembling beneath my hand. I wanted to squeeze her shoulder, but would she take that as encouragement to accept Lukas's offer? I wasn't sure what she should do. How much risk was too much?

"I accept," she said.

Lukas nodded. "That goes for everyone. There will be no severance for whoever loses the next challenge. I'll have our lawyer draw up a legal document. I'll expect you all to sign it."

That was our cue to leave. We filed out, subdued with worry.

"Paige," Jackie murmured in my ear. "Will you go with me to the bathroom? I think I might be sick."

CHAPTER 16

"You've got aphids," Mykia said while peering at one of my tomato plants. "No biggie."

I breathed an enormous sigh of relief. "So they're not doomed?"

"Nope. I've got a spray. Made from chrysanthemum flowers. It'll do the trick. Let me go dig around in the truck. It might be buried, but it'll be there." Mykia had parked on my driveway, prompting a Mr. Eckhardt sighting. He watched us with an eagle's pointed glare, but we ignored him.

Before Mykia arrived, I'd spent the morning fretting about the health of my tomatoes. Trey had slept over at Colin's, so as soon as the sun rose I'd brought my superstrength coffee outside and lay on the ground, watching the families of puffy green bugs congregate on the stems of my beloved plants. I had briefly flirted with the idea of tossing the hot coffee on them, then decided I was not only stupid but also possibly sociopathic, and texted Mykia instead.

The garden was again morphing into something different. The flimsy young plants had taken root for the most part, and they were careening through adolescence like teens on a bender, their leaves seeking independence by growing into places I hadn't predicted. Plants did not merely grow tall; they grew wide, curious about their surroundings, eager to seek nourishment from anywhere they could get it. Sometimes it worked, and sometimes I had to prune them back or watch a branch snap and wilt. My garden was a patchwork of failures and successes. I loved it.

But when it was threatened?

Anger. The fury I felt at Jesse's death, Lukas's antics, and the mere fact that my well-planned-for future could no longer happen heightened my need to protect the few things I did care about. I wanted to scream and rage and storm. I wanted to squish those bugs into oblivion.

"Those aren't going to make it," Mr. Eckhardt said over the fence, startling me. "The fruit will start turning black before turning red."

"How do you know that?" I knelt next to the plants as if to shield them from Mr. Eckhardt's insults.

He gestured toward his backyard. "Have you taken a look at my lawn? I'm an expert."

"An expert on growing grass is hardly an expert in growing vegetables," I said haughtily, wondering if that was actually true.

Instead of getting angry, Mr. Eckhardt looked thoughtful. "I used to grow vegetables, years ago," he said.

"Why don't you now? You've got plenty of space."

He went silent for a moment, and before he could respond, Mykia returned.

"What's going on here?" she asked warily.

Mr. Eckhardt's look of chronic disdain returned. "I was just telling Paige that those plants are going to die."

Mykia began to spray the plants, from the ground up. "Why would you say that? Do you like being mean?"

"Pointing out reality is hardly mean-spirited," he said. "It's necessary at times. Do you prefer to live in a fantasy world?"

"I prefer to live in a hopeful world," she responded. It was a nice sentiment, but her words were tinged with a fierce anger that seemed almost an overreaction.

Mr. Eckhardt's eyes narrowed. "That's simply naïveté." He focused his attention on me. "If those tomatoes start rotting on the vine, you will need to remove the entire plant from the ground."

"Not gonna happen," Mykia said.

He turned to me. "Foolish behavior is not going to bring him back."

"I'm trying to bring *me* back," I said, realizing at that moment that it was true.

Mr. Eckhardt shook his head sadly. "That person you were? She's dead, too. The quicker you realize that, the better off you'll be. I'm just trying to help."

That person—that loving, devoted, oblivious person—was someone I definitely wanted back. She was caught in a quicksand of grief, and I had to figure out how to help her escape. "Your help was not requested," I said, and Mr. Eckhardt's eyes widened with surprise at my vehemence. "I don't need it."

∼

"You're going to be sore tomorrow," Mykia said as we stretched out on my living room sofas. Jesse and I could never agree on which kind to get—he liked leather; I preferred fabric—so we got both and shoved them against each other, armrest to armrest. When Trey was smaller, he liked to run back and forth between us until we all erupted in fits of giggles. It was one of those family things, not quite a joke but funny nonetheless, and one that didn't make sense to others, so I didn't mention it to Mykia. She was lost in a postdinner haze, stirring her rapidly cooling coffee with her index finger. We'd weeded the garden, mowed and edged the front lawn, hauled mulch, and baked in the sun all afternoon. The hot day had turned into a gorgeously mild summer evening, the cicadas softly humming, fireflies popping intermittently into the view afforded by my front bay window, and I tried to remember the last time Jesse and I had enjoyed a night like this. Unfortunately, memories tended to blur when they were no longer shared.

"Your neighbor has a fence post stuck up his ass," Mykia said, drawing me back to the conversation.

"You can't let him get to you," I responded after a beat. "He's a miserable old man. I'm not sure what happened to him, but something must have turned him into something so sour."

"Do you really think that's what happens? You didn't go sour." She paused a moment. "I didn't."

I didn't want to be impolite and ask what she was referring to. Then I gave it a second thought. How did people become friends? They shared parts of their pasts, bit by bit, until the other person had something solid to hold on to. "What are you referring to?"

She poked at her coffee and stared into its depths for a moment before saying, "When my mom died, I was only nineteen. I got a little crazy."

"Crazy?"

She shrugged. "You know."

"I don't. I wish I did sometimes, but I don't." I smiled at her to show her I wasn't judging. "Jesse and I were so focused on not becoming our parents that we followed every rule. We even made up some rules so we could follow them." And I'd been trying so hard to continue living by them, but why? It wouldn't bring him back.

She laughed, but it was hollow. "Following the rules was probably the better choice. I hung out with some unsavory people. I made mistakes. I slept with a lot of guys—"

"There is nothing wrong with that," I stated with fervor. I meant it. I did not abide by slut-shaming.

"I know," she said. "What was wrong was my reasons for it. I had no self-esteem. I wasn't taking my own pleasure, I was giving it to other people so they might like me. When the universe took my mom, I thought it was telling me I wasn't worthy of being loved."

"But you had your dad," I said quickly, thinking of Trey. The thought of one parent not being enough kept me up at night.

"He checked out of this world for a while when she passed." Her voice had grown soft. I knew what that was, when grief memories threatened to take over. It was work to stay calm, but fulfilling work, to learn to accept without letting them destroy you.

"I understand what you did," I said.

"Maybe you do," she said. "But you didn't use circumstance as an excuse to self-destruct."

"Don't you think you're being hard on yourself?"

She smiled wryly. "Do you know anyone worth her salt who isn't hard on herself?"

"Good question." I thought about the women in my life—Jackie, Glynnis, Rhiannon, Mykia. They could all give themselves a good pounding. The question was did it help or hurt? And how was it shaping my son's perspective? "Your dad," I said. "When did you reconnect with him?"

"This is going to sound like psychobabble, but I found my dad when I reconnected with myself. I put my mind into my schoolwork and found I had a love for science. Once my dad realized this, once he recognized I'd discovered a passion for something that wasn't tearing me up inside, he came back to me."

"You brought him back," I said. "That was you, not him."

She went quiet for a moment, and then said, "Maybe. And maybe Mr. Eckhardt had no one to bring him back."

A certain sadness fell over me. Sadness for Mr. Eckhardt, but also sadness for myself. Who would bring me back? Trey? No, I couldn't put that on him—he had to work on finding himself. On exploring what he had to offer. Maybe Colin had a point.

"That garden is doing it for you," Mykia said as if reading my mind. "Even if Mr. Eckhardt is right and every one of those plants dies on the vine, you tried it. You had to find the energy to give it a go. And the passion."

I thought about the garden and what it had come to mean to me. "They won't all die," I promised her. "I won't let them."

"Then maybe it's already brought you back," Mykia said. "Sometimes the brain takes a while to catch up with the heart."

CHAPTER 17

"I didn't do anything," Trey said to the open door. My heart gave a thump when I realized it was Officer Leprechaun.

"He's come to see me," I said before realizing how that sounded. And that my voice had grown embarrassingly husky. What was wrong with me?

Willow Falls' finest walked in, wearing tattered cargo shorts and an ancient Pink Floyd T-shirt. A few inches taller than me, he had a little middle-years paunch developing, but the surety of his steps told me he could move very quickly if need be.

"Oh, you're gonna have to change," he said when he took in my capris and sleeveless blouse. "Find your scuzziest clothes."

Trey gave me a weird look and disappeared. I dashed upstairs to search for something else to wear. Before Jesse passed away, I would have had a difficult time finding something appropriate. But now, half of my wardrobe could be described as "skuzzy." I shrugged on an old tank top and some shorts I'd been gardening in. I'd made them by hacking off the legs from a pair of khaki pants.

"Better," he said when I entered the kitchen. He'd already begun setting up. I spotted a box full of mason jars on the kitchen table and three bags overflowing with tomatoes on the counter. A large steel pot sat tall on the stove, and he rinsed another at the sink.

"Do you wanna help or watch?" he said, laughing.

The simple components suddenly seemed overwhelming. "Where do I start?"

"Load up the dishwasher with mason jars. We need to sterilize them."

"That makes it sound like we're operating on something."

He laughed again, and I realized how booming it was, how infectious. "We kind of are." He hoisted the canner onto the stove. "This is the old-fashioned kind. I don't have a pressure canner. This is yours now, though, old as it is."

"Oh, I can't take that."

"Why?"

"What if you need to use it?"

He shrugged. "Then I'll knock on your door and ask to borrow it."

He was an easygoing man, Officer Leprechaun. It had been a while since anything felt easy. Still, having any man besides Jesse in the house felt vaguely like cheating, and I had to push away the urge to tell him to leave. I used the act of loading the dishwasher to distract me, but the good officer must have sensed my hesitancy because he said, "This isn't a big deal. It's actually not even a deal. I have no expectations."

I wasn't sure how I felt about that. It had been so long since I had allowed myself to expect anything. The garden was the first thing since Jesse passed that I'd allowed myself to invest a little hope in.

I stood a little straighter. "My only expectation for today is that I learn how to can properly. That's a reasonable one, right?"

He moved to touch my arm, thought better of it, and picked up a tomato instead. "We need to start by skinning these babies. You up for that?"

"Bring it on."

~

"It looks like a murder scene in here." Officer Leprechaun stood in the middle of my previously white kitchen. Tomato juice covered every surface, dripped down to the floor in bloodred stripes, and was even splattered on the ceiling.

"Have you actually seen one of those?" I asked. "Willow Falls isn't exactly a hotbed of crime."

He glanced down at his stained T-shirt. "I used to work in the city, so yeah. It's boring out here, but sometimes boring is good."

"I used to think I was boring," I admitted.

"But not anymore?"

"I don't know. Can someone who dug up her entire backyard still be boring? Crazy, yes. Boring? Not so much."

Officer Leprechaun moved closer to me. He stopped before invading my personal space, but still, it felt like an advance. He reached around me and turned the sink on, and I breathed a sigh of . . . relief? Disappointment?

"It doesn't look crazy out there," he said while attacking the mess of utensils. "It looks like life. You'll have something to can come end of summer. If you want, I'll help you. But you don't need my help."

"I think I'll need all the help I can get."

"We could all use help, but need? That's a different thing entirely." He dried his hands on the one clean spot on a tomato-juice-covered towel. The air in the kitchen, already as humid as a Florida swamp, turned heavier. It'd been a long time since a man had looked at me the way Officer Leprechaun was eyeing me up, and I didn't know what to do. I didn't know what I *wanted* to do.

He slowly folded a paper towel, held it under the faucet for a moment, and pressed the excess water into the sink. "Come over here a minute."

He wasn't really asking or ordering; it was more like an offering. Officer Leprechaun had soft blue eyes, the kind that gave the appearance of thoughtfulness. I stared into them for a long moment, and then took one step forward, then another. When I'd moved close enough for him to reach me, he smiled.

"You're a mess," he said, and reached over to dab my forehead. I was still far enough away to lend the action some awkwardness, so I moved a little closer. He continued to gently rub the dried tomato juice from my cheek, my hairline, the side of my neck. I could hardly move, much less breathe, but I could feel his breath against my skin, and the soft weight of his fingertips as they pressed lightly on my cheek. I closed my eyes, no expectations but sensation, and when his lips touched mine, I gasped at the contact. He froze for a moment.

"Is this okay?"

Okay? I didn't know what that meant anymore. Tears sprang to my eyes, grief, the ever-present emotion, waiting to take over from the amateurs—lust, shock, longing.

"I—I don't know."

He leaned back, face flushed with concern and hopefully not embarrassment. "I'm sorry," he said.

"So am I."

We cleaned the kitchen together, making small talk, pretending the moment hadn't happened. Afterward, I walked him outside. Day had turned to night, but the warmth had held on. I bit my tongue to prevent myself from saying something clichéd about the heat. "Thank you," I said instead. "I learned a lot."

"Well, that could be taken in a number of ways," he said, and I was glad to hear some laughter in his voice. "But I'll keep my mind out of the gutter and assume you meant the canning process."

He opened the door but seemed to forget what he was meant to do afterward. "Would you consider seeing me again? I promise to dress nicer and stay relatively clean."

"I'm not sure."

He nodded. "I understand. You're not ready."

"Not exactly." I smiled at him, sheepish. "I don't know your first name. I've been calling you Officer Leprechaun in my head."

He didn't say anything at all for a moment, and I wondered if I'd insulted him. Then a baritone of a laugh rumbled from his chest. "We've spent half the day together, and you don't know my first name?"

"You never said it. And then it had gone on for too long."

He slid into the driver's seat. "It's Sean. Sean Doherty. And now that we're more familiar, can I get another date?"

"This was a date?"

Laughing, he drove away, slowly and carefully, like a good cop should.

"Are you kidding me?"

Trey sat on the front steps. I hadn't seen him, but I was fairly certain he'd seen us.

"He's a nice man," I said by way of explanation. What was there to explain?

"You don't know what you're doing. First, this stupid garden, and now flirting with the cop? The cop who arrested me?"

"He didn't arrest you."

Trey grabbed on to the front railing and pulled himself to standing. Every so often, I was struck by the size of him—in my mind, he was still a toddler hanging on to my pant leg. "Up to you if you want to make a fool of yourself, but don't expect me to stick around to watch it."

"That's not what I'm doing." The tears made a reappearance. "Let's talk about this."

"Nothing to talk about. You want to bone the cop. End of story."

"Trey," I said sharply. I glanced at the garden, away from him, and took a deep breath. He missed Jesse, too. I had to remember that. "I loved your dad, and I would have stayed with him forever. That's not how it worked out. I'm trying to . . . I'm trying."

"Trying to do what? Forget him?"

"You know I would never do that."

"Yeah," he said. "Whatever. I'm going over to Colin's."

CHAPTER 18

"An In-Depth Conversation with Petra Polly," from Adweek *(as read to the employees of Guh by Lukas Giacomo)*

Where do you get your ideas?
I spend a great deal of time thinking about how creativity develops. Some might say I live in my head, but I disagree—I live in a cavernous creative space that happens to be inside me! Ideas come from everywhere, but mostly my sub-subconscious.

Sub-subconscious?
I've decided there's a part of the brain devoted to truly subversive thought. It lies two levels below the problem-solving and logic sectors, and one level below creativity and inspiration.

"It's a good thing Petra Polly isn't a brain surgeon," Jackie whispered, and I stifled a laugh. Still, Lukas caught the spirit of our misbehavior and glared our way before reading on.

How did you learn to apply your ideas to the business world?
The entire world is run by corporations. They've become our sustenance. The idea of treating a creative workplace as a living thing seemed logical—we've become the embodiment of the corporations that dictate every part of our lives.

"If I'm a corporation," Byron interrupted, "I'm Apple."
"And I'm Google," added Rhiannon.
Lukas clenched his jaw. "Please stay focused, people." He read on.

Do you think noncreative workplaces could benefit from your ideology?
I don't believe a "noncreative" workplace exists. When people come together, there is a certain dynamism that results in the energy to spark ideas. Creativity takes many forms. Every company has the potential to be a creative powerhouse. Every single one.

"She obviously never worked at Stanley's Auto Parts," Glynnis whispered.
Lukas paused dramatically before diving in again.

Do you have any future projects in the works?

Another Lukas pause. Irritated, I glanced up only to see him looking so shiny and proud, like a clever little boy who thought he had figured out the meaning of life. "Wait until you hear this," he announced. "What you're about to hear . . . is the future of Guh."
Well, then. We all leaned forward, waiting.
Lukas continued reading from his iPad:

The future is a very exciting place, and I can't wait to visit. The second book in my creative workplace series, The Petra Polly Workbook for the

New, New Creative Workplace, *will release next month. I'm going out on a limb and publishing it myself. I've also created some products to enhance the workplace environment—mugs, inspirational posters, and even laptop sleeves that say "Passwork, Not Password." That's copyrighted, by the way. The goal is a whole line of books and helpful materials to guarantee success. And I mean what I say. I GUARANTEE success.*

"She guarantees success," Lukas repeated with a sigh. "That takes guts. And true belief in oneself." Lukas was positively beaming, as if Petra herself had deemed him her personal press secretary.

Byron said what we were all likely thinking. "Is it a good idea to guarantee success for everyone?"

"That's the beauty of her philosophy," Lukas insisted. "It suits every worker, in every situation."

"That might be true," Rhiannon said, obviously struggling to keep her tone benign. "But is there a reason for reading that interview aloud? I understand studying Petra's book, but that article doesn't exactly help us gain insight, you know?"

Rhiannon is the one with guts, I thought. She wasn't afraid to be confrontational. Lukas, smiling indulgently at her, didn't seem to mind. Was it her relative youth that gave her such confidence, or was it her security in her position? She brazenly challenged Lukas. If Jackie or I had done it, would the effect have been the same? I didn't think so, and I stayed quiet, though I, too, questioned the need to listen to Petra's substance-free interview.

"Petra is touring to promote her new book," Lukas began excitedly, brimming with the need to explain. "When I learned she was expanding her brand, I sent a message to her Facebook page—" Here he paused to generate a little drama. When none came, he went on, though he seemed slightly irritated. "I asked if she needed help with advertising her new products."

I nearly choked on my extrastrong coffee. "You what?"

"I sent her a lengthy message detailing our company's talent and success," Lukas said, unable to keep the smugness from his voice. "Including catching the eye of our most recent client, Landon Cosmetics."

Our recent success with Landon Cosmetics was impressive, and I was proud of my company, but scoring Petra Polly seemed slightly unreal, like being allowed to join Oz behind the curtain. Lukas had written to her like a lovesick fanboy? The other employees of Guh obviously felt the same—everyone shifted in their seats and appeared mildly uncomfortable. Had our leader embarrassed himself?

Lukas's face lit up. "Fate has given us a chance. Petra is making a stop in Willow Falls during her book tour, giving us the perfect opportunity to present our ideas in person."

Byron dropped his pen. "Seriously? Why would she come here?"

"Tomson's Bookshop is one of the top independent bookstores in the nation," Lukas said, grinning.

We all loved Tomson's, but that was pushing it a little.

"So she responded to you?" Rhiannon asked, as puzzled as the rest of us. "Will she come by the office, or do we have to go to her?"

Lukas's glow dimmed ever so slightly. "She did not respond. Sometimes, when you shoot for the brass ring, it requires unconventional methodology. Our solution is to use guerrilla tactics. Given her incredible popularity, Petra Polly will likely have a long signing line, which means she'll be stuck in one place for at least an hour, possibly two."

"So she has no idea we're coming," Byron said, his eyes dancing with amusement. "I'm in."

The rest of us weren't so sure. What if she called the cops? Screamed? Getting kicked out of Tomson's Bookshop in downtown Willow Falls wasn't exactly good advertising for Guh.

Lukas leaned forward and placed his palms on the table. "If we don't take risks, then what are we?"

"Safe," Glynnis said. "We're—"

"Unchallenged," Lukas interrupted. "And being unchallenged, as Petra says, leads to underperformance. Does anyone here want to be accused of underperforming?"

Nope. We all leaned in. If making fools of ourselves at a book signing was what it cost to keep our jobs, so be it.

"Okay," Lukas said, accepting our acquiescence. "Okay, then. We are more than up to the task. All hands on deck for this one."

"No pairs?" Jackie said.

"No," Lukas said. "We're in this together. All of us."

Jackie and I shared a relieved glance. Did that mean he wasn't going to fire anyone?

"Are you still kicking someone to the curb?" Rhiannon asked what we were all thinking.

Lukas steepled his fingers, a gesture that I now found almost unbearably irritating. "I'll be closely monitoring everyone's work, and after we speak with Petra, one person will be free to seek other opportunities."

"That's a yes," Rhiannon said.

"But we've got new business," Jackie said. "Landon will bring in a lot of money."

"I'm looking at long-term financial viability. That's always a concern," Lukas intoned. He wore an expression of such seriousness I wondered if he practiced it in the mirror. He shook his head, as if shaking off the unpleasantness of thinking about something as crass as money. "Strategy sessions start next week. Plan on getting here early and staying late."

"It's summer," Glynnis whispered, and then I immediately saw the regret on her face.

Lukas stood and adopted a stance that was vaguely presidential. "It's game time," he said with a straight face. "Bring me your best."

~

"Petra Polly probably thinks he's psychopathic," I said to Glynnis and Jackie as we strolled through the farmers' market.

Jackie laughed. "I wouldn't be surprised if she filed a restraining order. Do you really think she wants people like us to do her ad work?"

"I doubt she'll even pay us any attention," Glynnis said. "But I guess it doesn't matter. One of us is still getting fired."

I heard my name being called and turned to see Mykia hanging from the back of her truck, beckoning us over. I hadn't seen her since she'd checked out my tomato plants, and I smiled broadly—her joy was that infectious.

"How're my ad girls?"

We filled Mykia in on the latest Lukas drama.

"That guy needs to chill," she said after I was done.

"He should hang out here more often," I said. I had come to see the farmers' market as a calm presence, an escape from the high-stress world of Guh.

Mykia grabbed a bunch of kale and handed it to me. "How's your garden doing?" she said to me when I was done. "Is it still bringing you back?"

It was. Success was spotty—I'd planted some herbs too close together, and the more dominant ones were choking the others out; I'd watered too heavily at times and at others not enough; and weeds were encroaching when I didn't have the time to pull them, but some of it was flourishing, particularly the tomato plants, whose leaves were deep green and velvety, with plump green tomatoes on the verge of turning color. I took deep satisfaction in the process, from the initial planting, to watching the roots dig in, to the plants figuring out a way to flourish.

"I love it," I said, prompting a grin from Mykia. "I really do."

"You should celebrate what it's doing for you," she said. "Have a garden party."

"But there's no room for people. It's a mess."

"I'll help you with it," Glynnis offered.

145

I hadn't hosted a party since . . . since I couldn't remember. Jesse and I had been so wrapped up in making enough money to stay afloat we hadn't had much time for anyone but Trey. At least that was what we told ourselves. The few dinner parties we'd had were overshadowed by our own insecurities and desire for perfection. It was less stressful to go out to eat together, less potential for error. But since Jesse died, I'd been making mistakes with embarrassing regularity, and I was still standing.

"So," I said, "who would I invite besides you two and Jackie?"

"I'm sure you could scrounge up some people," Mykia said with an eye roll. "Invite those uptight people from your village hall. Show them how you've got everything under control."

"I don't have anything under control," I said. And it was true. Not my job, not my kid, not my home.

She laughed. "Of course you don't. But they don't need to know that."

Why not invite Miss Khaki and Label Lover? Maybe they'd decide I didn't need psychiatric help, only help getting my hands dirty. There were also a few women in my neighborhood who offered tips or gave quiet words of encouragement as they walked their dogs past my property. I could invite them. My coworkers, Lukas included, could bulk up the list. I might even extend the olive branch and invite Mr. Eckhardt.

"I'm warming up to the idea," I said. "A garden party. Never thought I was the type, but I'm learning I'm all kinds of types."

"That's a good thing," Mykia said. "But now you've got to focus on practicalities. Where are you going to put the bar?"

CHAPTER 19

"Where are you going?"

I'd picked up Trey from Colin's and impulsively taken an alternate route on the outskirts of town, down a two-lane highway that led to a succession of new but only partially occupied corporate parks.

"I need to see about something," I said vaguely as Trey returned to texting. *Good,* I thought. *There's nothing like the element of surprise.*

I pulled into a large parking lot in front of a deserted loading dock. The lot was rectangular and dotted with concrete-bottomed security lights. *Perfect.* I rolled to a stop.

"What do you think you're doing?" Trey asked, finally looking up from his phone.

I unlatched his seat belt. "We're switching places."

"I don't want to do this."

I kept my tone brisk, no-nonsense. "It's not about want. It's about need."

"I don't *need* to do this."

"You will not be allowed to graduate until you take the driver's education class. There's no special dispensation for people who don't feel like it," I said, reminding myself that sometimes the strongest love was the tough kind. "You've got to face your fear."

"I'm not afraid. Telling me I am is bullying."

"I'm afraid, too, Trey. All the time. It doesn't mean I don't still take action."

"Are we living in the same world? You never take action unless you're forced to. Are you forcing me? I said no. And 'no,' as everyone feels the constant need to remind me, should always mean no. You should respect that."

"Look," I said, feeling my small reserve of patience shrink to nothing, "this is not an argument or a negotiation, and it has nothing to do with respect. Get in the damn driver's seat. You don't even need to put your foot on the gas pedal. Put it in drive, and the car will move slowly on its own. All you need to be concerned with is steering."

After one long, tense moment, Trey slid his phone into his backpack, taking his time, letting me know that though I'd won, he didn't have to like it. Raising a teenager was one long battle for power—the parent was losing it but fiercely trying to hold on, and the teen was taking advantage every time a weak spot was revealed, fighting to gain more ground.

We settled into each other's places. Trey stared blankly out the windshield.

"Adjust the mirrors," I said gently.

"I know," he snapped.

Trey took approximately four years to adjust the mirrors to his liking. I turned off the radio; he turned it on and messed with the stations until something appealed. Then he put his hand on the gearshift and . . . did nothing.

"Put your foot on the brake," I said. "Slide the car into drive."

Trey flexed his right foot. He grasped the gearshift tightly and tugged it into place.

"Perfect," I whispered. "Now ease your foot off the brake."

In the tiniest of increments, he did. The car moved forward with a slight jerk. Trey clutched the wheel with both hands, knuckles going pale.

"What do I do?" he said, panic turning his voice into a screech. "What if I hit something? Or someone?"

"We're going less than five miles an hour. There's no one around, and if you hit some concrete, it'll leave a mark, but I don't care."

"Yes, you do." He jerked the wheel to the side to avoid one of the pylons and slammed on the brake. Both of us shot forward.

Trey smashed his hand against the dash, hard. "I can't do this!"

"Yes," I said. "Yes, you can. You're thinking too much, and it's getting in your way."

"Why aren't you thinking about it at all?"

I knew what he was talking about, but I wasn't sure it was the right time to address it. I stayed silent.

"You're trying to forget what happened," he continued. "I can't. I spend every minute thinking about it. I wonder if it hurt, and if he knew what was coming. I think about him crashing into that concrete while you're worrying about work or digging around in that stupid garden!"

"Trey—"

He pushed the door open with his foot and bolted from the car.

"Trey! Trey!" He sprinted across the parking lot, jumped a divider, and headed toward the highway.

"Shit, shit, shit!" Awkwardly, I crawled across the gearshift and dropped behind the steering wheel. In the seconds it took me to resituate myself, Trey disappeared. Frantic, I spun a U-turn and sped toward the highway. It was two lanes, with a shoulder barely wide enough for a teenage boy. The worst-case-scenario greatest hits reel played through my imagination as I merged onto the road and watched as cars nearly clipped Trey, who walked swiftly, head down and hands stuffed into his cargo shorts pockets.

"Stop!" I yelled as my car approached. I slowed at a dangerous pace, reached over, and opened the passenger door. "Get in!"

He ignored me.

"I'm not going to make you drive again," I promised. "Get back in the car!"

He kept walking, and I kept following, cars honking behind me. We'd gone a few more yards when I heard the siren, and a recognizable voice telling me to pull over. *Where?* I thought, eyeing the narrow shoulder. I maneuvered the car as best I could. The cop car pulled up behind me. Trey kept walking.

A sharp rap on my window made me jump. Officer Leprechaun—er, Sean—stared at me, eyebrow lifted. "Well?" he said. "Do you think you could keep up with the pace of traffic?"

I lowered the window. "Trey's up there." My voice felt clogged, like tears were bubbling up in my throat.

Sean squinted down the road. "I see him. He'll be okay. We, on the other hand, need to get out of the flow of traffic. Meet me at the base of this ramp. Take a right, and we can cut him off at the pass."

I nodded, unable to trust my voice. Sean pulled ahead of me, leading the way. It embarrassed me to think I needed to follow him. Grief had struck again, the argument with Trey pushing it to the forefront of my mind. Sometimes I was struck by the permanence of the whole thing. Other times, the unfairness. But at times like this one, I couldn't help but feel furious with a universe that would take a father away from his son.

Sean blocked Trey with his squad car, and I joined him seconds later, jumping from my car as soon as I shifted into park. "Trey."

"I don't want to talk to you," he said. "You're psychotic."

Sean looked at me with a raised eyebrow again. "Trey, why don't you get into the car with your mother? She's worried for you. It's a long walk back to your house."

I stepped forward, bristling a little at Sean's takeover of the situation. "Let's just go home."

"I'm going to walk home," Trey said, with a certain Jesse-like strength to his voice. "It's not illegal, so Officer Too Friendly here can't stop me. I'm capable of walking a couple of miles."

"It's lonely," I said. "Walking by yourself."

"It's peaceful," Trey countered. "I need to clear my head."

Sean stayed quiet, probably sensing this was best left between mother and son. He was present but didn't hover. I was grateful for his tact. I had to make this decision.

"Okay," I said evenly. "Be careful. Text me if you change your mind."

For one fleeting moment, surprise softened Trey's features, but then he recovered, shrugged, and took off down the road.

"Good call," Sean said. "Teenagers aren't a whole lot of fun."

"I thought you didn't have children," I said dully.

He said something unintelligible into his radio, and then leaned against the car, right next to me. "I was a teenager once, and I was a mouthy, impulsive piece of crapola."

"Crapola?"

"I'm trying to be mindful of the presence of a lady."

In response to that, I snorted. "What did your mother do?"

"She smacked me upside the head."

"I'm not—"

He held up his hand. "I know you wouldn't. And I don't even know if that worked or if I grew out of it on my own."

"You were good at handling Trey. I have to ask this, did your father die? Because I've noticed that people who've lived through some type of trauma tend to be a lot better at recognizing it in others."

He went quiet a moment. "My parents were divorced, which is a whole different thing. I'm not comparing the two—"

"Because that would be insensitive." Someone came up to me after Jesse died and told me I was lucky because death was better than an acrimonious divorce. If I hadn't been so weak from lack of eating, I would have punched her into the following week.

Sean ran a hand over his face and took off his cap. In the sunlight, his red hair caught fire, all gold and orange and copper. "I'm not doing very well with this. What I'm trying to say is that the odds are with you with this one. A kid only needs one good parent to keep him anchored. He may float off and do goofy things, but you'll always pull him back."

I didn't know if I was heavy enough to be an anchor. I was missing 185 pounds. Jesse was simply better at parenting. He would've known what to say to Trey. He would've been able to get Trey behind the wheel without giving the poor kid a nervous breakdown. He would've known what to do. It was innate with him. It was learning by trial and error for me.

"Are you going to be okay?" Sean's face, full of concern, was closer to mine than it had been a moment ago.

"Yes," I said automatically. "Fine. I need to go home, though. I should start dinner." A meal likely to be eaten alone, if Trey went over to Colin's. As usual.

"Sure," he said. "Sorry I'm not much help."

He did look sorry. In fact, he appeared absolutely dejected. "All you've done is try to help," I told him, feeling a little spark when he perked up. "Can I ask one more favor of you?"

"Yes," he said. "Anything. Happy to do it."

"I'm throwing a garden party next Saturday night. Will you come?"

A slow grin. "A garden party? Do I have to drink tea?"

"Do you like tea?"

He laughed. "You know? I do. With lots of milk."

"I think I can provide that."

"Then yes," he said, and I instantly felt a mix of dread and anticipation. "I'll be there."

"Good," I said.

His eyes grew serious. "Is it really?"

"Yes," I said, and, to my surprise, it was.

CHAPTER 20

"Trey tells me you've been forcing him to get behind the wheel of a car. I don't think it's beneficial to force a child outside of his comfort zone."

Charlene, Colin's judgy mother, had called me out of the blue. Why couldn't she prefer texting? Everyone was a texter these days.

"How I parent my child is my business," I countered, trying to keep my tone mild. "Trey needs to complete driver's education, or he can't graduate. If he doesn't—"

"I don't think you're seeing the big picture," Charlene interrupted. "You are *traumatizing* him."

"His father's death traumatized him. I'm giving him a little necessary push to start living again."

She sniffed. "Putting undue pressure on a child will only strengthen his resolve to rebel."

"Does this work with Colin?"

"What?"

"When Colin's father died, did you take your own advice?"

A beat. "Colin's father is still alive."

"Exactly."

Another beat. "I guess you made a point."

"I did. A pointy one. I hope it hurt. If not, I can drive the sharp end in even further." Had I really just said that? My heart fluttered. I hated confrontation.

"Trey just seems depressed," Charlene said, softening her tone. "I'm trying to help. I'm sorry if . . . I'm sorry if I overstepped. Okay, I did overstep. My concern is real, though. Even if I might have chosen the wrong words to express it."

Whoa. Condescending Charlene's apology sounded real. "I'm sorry if I snapped at you. I'm doing the best I can. Can you please accept that I am?"

"I suppose."

"You suppose?"

"Okay, yes. But I can't ignore the fact that your son is hurting."

"I can't either. I live with it every day."

I could hear Charlene breathing on the other end, but her response took a little time. "I'm sure you do. Again, I'm very sorry. Will you accept my apology?"

"Yes," I said.

"Well."

"Well."

I could have hung up and put an end to all the awkwardness. Instead, I said, "I'm having a garden party next Saturday. Would you have any interest in coming?"

"You're too nice," Mykia said when I got off the phone. "I would have torn her a new one."

"I did a little damage, I think." I passed mugs of coffee to the girls around the table—Mykia, Jackie, and Glynnis. I thought about inviting Rhiannon, but Byron seemed pretty taken with her, and Glynnis was having a difficult time with it. It occurred to me that friendship should come above all that. Was Rhiannon a friend? I sensed she could be. I would invite her next time. Glynnis would just have to suck it up.

Mykia stirred some cream into her coffee. "Did you invite the jerk next door yet?"

"Nope. I'm waiting for the right opportunity."

Jackie snorted. "There is no right time with that guy. Just go over and ask. He's going to say no anyway."

"Probably," I admitted. "If I ask him, he'll be less likely to call the cops on us. Technically, I'm supposed to get a permit from the board to host a party larger than ten people."

"I don't understand suburban living," Mykia said. "Not one bit."

"But the police will already be here, right?" Glynnis said, her cheeks blooming pink.

I tried to hide my smile but couldn't. "You're right. That is, if Sean comes."

"Oh, he'll come," Mykia said. She in no way attempted to hide her grin. "I'd bet my truck on it."

I could feel my blush. Embarrassed, I collected some dishes and brought them to the sink. My garden, green and mostly healthy, was all I could see out of the small window above my sink. It resembled an Impressionistic painting—a wash of green, red, brown, and yellow, softened by the summer sun.

"Paige," Jackie said, pulling me from my reverie. "I think your neighbor is out, and he has company. This might be the right time you were looking for."

~

Mr. Eckhardt sat with military stiffness in his Adirondack chair, flanked by Miss Khaki and Label Lover. They each clutched a glass of lemonade. Label Lover had scooched her chair slightly closer to Mr. Eckhardt's, and she stretched out her leg so it nearly touched his. Miss Khaki couldn't stop staring at Label Lover's Michael Kors sandals and brightly painted toenails.

I called hello over the fence, and they all startled. Mr. Eckhardt slowly balanced his glass in the grass. Then—surprisingly—he helped both ladies to their feet in a gentlemanly fashion.

"Nice day, isn't it?" Oh, geez. I could come up with something better, couldn't I?

"It's too hot," Miss Khaki said. "Bill's lemonade is the only thing making it bearable."

"There's no such thing as too hot," Label Lover said, talking over her rival. "Right, Bill?"

Mr. Eckhardt squirmed. "I do like the heat, but the grass can't take too much of this sun."

Wow. The diplomat.

Label Lover leaned over the fence. "I'm sorry your garden isn't working out."

"What do you mean?"

She gestured grandly at my backyard. Her red fingernails matched her toes perfectly, the color of fresh blood. "This is a mess. We've been more than patient. I haven't filed a complaint with the board because Bill asked me not to, but my patience is wearing thin."

I looked at Mr. Eckhardt, but he wouldn't meet my eye. "Do you think my garden has promise?"

"I suppose everything deserves a chance. I still think the tomatoes won't make it, but the herbs look promising."

I beamed at him. Couldn't help it.

"Everything deserves a chance," echoed Miss Khaki. She gazed at Mr. Eckhardt with dreamy eyes.

"We need to be practical," Label Lover said, scowling. "This will be an absolute eyesore in a few months."

"Why don't we deal with that later?" I said. "Let's enjoy it for the moment. I'm having a party on Saturday. A garden party. I'm extending the invitation to the three of you."

For a moment, I relished the silence that fell over the group.

"I don't know," Miss Khaki said.

"Absolutely not," Label Lover said.

"I'll be there," Mr. Eckhardt said. "Haven't been to a party in a while."

Miracle of miracles, he looked happy to be invited. *Delighted*, even.

The two older women glanced at each other. "I'll be there, too," they said simultaneously.

Label Lover downed the rest of her lemonade. "Will you refresh my glass, Bill?"

Mr. Eckhardt took her glass, and the one Miss Khaki had quickly emptied, and headed into his mystery kitchen. When he was out of earshot, Label Lover leaned over the fence and said, "Your backyard project is putting undue stress on our Bill. All that man asks for in this life is a little peace. Why must you disrupt it?"

I opened my mouth to defend myself and realized I didn't quite know what to say. I didn't have a clue about what Mr. Eckhardt wanted out of life. I didn't know anything about him. "Maybe he'll learn to get some enjoyment out of watching it grow," I said lamely.

Label Lover raised one penciled eyebrow. "You think very highly of yourself, don't you?"

"She should be proud of herself," Mykia said, coming up behind me. "I'm sorry you can't see that."

Before Label Lover could hit back, Mr. Eckhardt returned with a tray of glasses filled to the brim with lemonade, enough for all of us. Simple as it was, I was touched by the gesture.

"Bill makes his lemonade *from scratch*," Miss Khaki crowed. "How long has it been since you've had homemade?"

I'd made some the day before. "A long time," I said, flashing a smile at an obviously embarrassed Mr. Eckhardt. "Too long. And this tastes great."

CHAPTER 21

Everything was set for the party.

But I couldn't entirely take responsibility for it. Mykia, Glynnis, and Jackie pitched in. Mykia brought food, more than I could possibly feed to the small group attending. Glynnis helped set up a few card tables in between the rows of plants, topping them with tablecloths made from vintage sheets she'd been collecting since childhood. Jackie dragged folding chairs from my basement, hung twinkly lights, and gave me general emotional support.

In addition to Mr. Eckhardt and his harem, I'd invited everyone from Guh, including Lukas, the few women I knew from the neighborhood, and, of course, Trey and Colin, who actually said they might attend. Charlene called to say she would bring a seven-layer salad. Sean also said he would be coming, which led me to . . .

"What are you wearing?" Jackie asked while I tore around my bedroom, slapping deodorant under my arms and generally trying to make myself look human. She wore a jean miniskirt with a tight, iridescent-pink tank top. It was wholly inappropriate for a fiftysomething woman and 100 percent Jackie. I loved it. The only articles of clothing I felt comfortable in were my new garden clothes—shredded jean shorts and dirt-stained T-shirts. I had very few casual ensembles. Everything else fell into the category of dated professional attire or clothes reserved for weddings and funerals. I had nothing that said *garden party*.

Jackie sifted through my closet. "I would have thought you'd have more clothes. This is pretty sparse pickings."

"I store my winter stuff away in the summer," I said. "But it would still be more of the same. Boring. Gray, black, or navy. Blah, blah, blah."

"What about this?" Jackie pulled a dry cleaning bag from where I'd half hidden it behind some of those gray-black-blue business suits. "Is this the one we found? You had it cleaned?"

On a whim, I'd brought the delicate shift dress we'd discovered to the cleaners with the rest of the previous week's work clothes. I'd told the cleaner to be very careful with it, and it looked great—the fabric seemed almost new.

"You should wear this," Jackie said, taking it out of the plastic covering. "It's gorgeous."

"You don't think it has memory ghosts? Couldn't it have bad vibes associated with it?" I was not one to talk about ghosts, or vibes for that matter, but the fact that the dress was white, and that we'd found it buried in the backyard, well, that added some unusual elements. Also, I was curious to see Mr. Eckhardt's reaction when he spotted it. Would he recognize it or have no clue? I couldn't wait to find out.

"Maybe it has some vibes," Jackie admitted. "But how do you know they're bad vibes? Maybe they're good ones. The woman who wore this could have been happy."

"Happy people don't bury the things that made them happy." After I'd said it, I realized that, yes, sometimes they did. I did.

Jackie went silent for a moment. She laid the dress out on the bed, and then rummaged through my closet until she found a pair of brown leather sandals with a wedge heel. I hadn't worn them since Jesse and I'd had date nights.

I shrugged out of my T-shirt and jeans and guided the delicate dress over my head and shoulders. It fell a little loosely around my hips, but otherwise, it fit perfectly and offset the tan I'd acquired from working outside so much.

"You look beautiful," Jackie said, and I could tell she meant it. "Don't take it off. Give it some of your own memories."

My own memories. For the past two years, I'd spent every waking hour trying to avoid making any. I'd pressed the "Pause" button on my life, and then lost the remote. "I don't know if I even remember how to make memories."

"Of course you do," Jackie said. "You do it all the time. You just need to let the special moments happening around you register in your brain." Her heavily mascaraed eyes filled with tears. "When you give something meaning, it's worth remembering. We filter out the stuff that doesn't touch our heart."

"Do you have those memories . . . about Big Frank?"

"I do," she said. "A treasure trove of them. He did so many good things worth remembering."

Had I done anything worth remembering over the past two years? I got up every morning and somehow got out of bed. I'd managed to keep a roof over our heads. I'd dug a garden that I marveled at more every day.

"I wasn't sure I could come up with a good enough reason to host a party, save for the fact that Mykia told me to," I said. "I worried it wouldn't mean anything. You know what? I shouldn't have worried. This garden does mean something."

"Then let's party," Jackie said, making a "rock-on" gesture with her hand.

"Yes," I agreed, mimicking her hand gesture. "Let's party. And let's make sure it registers."

~

I'd chosen some soft Spanish flamenco music to provide a soundtrack for the festivities, but Jackie had taken over DJ duties when we finally came downstairs, and Bon Jovi boomed through the speakers I'd set strategically throughout the garden. Not a single male had arrived yet, so the ladies, guzzling the strawberry margaritas I'd made, were loose and a little loud, giving Jon Bon some competition.

"I can't believe they let you get away with this," said Peggy, the dog walker from one block over. "I once accidentally left some poop on the sidewalk, and someone from the subdivision board showed up at my door, shitting a brick."

"Ha! That's kind of a pun," said the woman I ran into at the grocery store on a regular basis. She'd guzzled two margaritas in about ten minutes, and her consonants were beginning to slur. But what did I care? These were women I'd smiled at, chatted about harmless topics with, and never, ever bothered to invite into my home. If they wanted to get blotto, then good for them. I figured I owed it to them.

I turned away from them just as a small group walked into my yard. Charlene, carrying a huge bowl of salad, greeted me with a surprising kiss on the cheek, then Rhiannon and Byron arrived, joined by Seth, whom I'd invited but I did not think was going to come. I hugged them all warmly and sent them in the direction of our makeshift bar. Lukas sauntered in next, wearing skinny jeans and his omnipresent leather jacket, though it had to be at least ninety-five degrees in the shade. He kissed my cheek, and then studied the backyard garden with a mix of awe and confusion.

"What do you think Petra Polly would say about what I've done?" I teased him.

Lukas grew serious and thoughtful. I felt almost ashamed at my tone—he was truly attempting to answer honestly. "I think she'd say you were going for the brass ring." He smiled at me, a genuine grin that reminded me so much of Big Frank it nearly took my breath away. "I've got to say I hope this doesn't eat up all of your creative energy," he added. "But it might do the opposite. It might spark something that will rejuvenate you, Paige."

Disappointment gnawed at my gut. I needed refreshing? "Do you think I'm in a slump?"

"Look, I paid attention when my dad told stories about his employees. Do you remember what a great storyteller he was?"

I nodded, my eyes filling with tears. "You always felt like you were really there," I managed.

Lukas briefly touched my arm. I could tell that even casual warmth was difficult for him, and I appreciated the gesture. "The stories about you, well, my dad always got great joy out of telling them, because they always ended well. You came through. An impossible deadline, a difficult client, a technical apocalypse—you somehow managed to always get the job done. He had total faith in your abilities."

"And you don't share the same faith?"

"Things change. People change. And I haven't seen anything yet to confirm it." He smiled again to soften the blow. "I'm waiting until the day I have my own Paige stories to tell. I don't have the same performance skills as my father, but I think I'll be able to get the point across."

"I will take that as a challenge," I said, and I meant it. "I'm good at what I do, Lukas."

"You *were* very good," he said. "Now let's see if you can be again." He glanced at the relaxed, laughing group at the bar, generously helping themselves to drinks. "It's not just that they're young, you know. Talent needs energy. It needs life. They've got fire running through their veins."

And probably a few other things, I thought, but I nodded in agreement. "I've got some fire. It might not be roaring, but it's there."

"You've got embers," Lukas said before heading to the bar. "Find a way to reignite them."

~

162

Sean arrived at dusk. He wore khakis and a light blue polo shirt that enhanced everything—his coloring, his build, the fine dusting of hair on his strong forearms.

"He gets cuter every time I see him," Jackie whispered.

I felt like a teenager at her first dance. The fluttering in my stomach started the moment I saw him walking up the driveway, and it turned into a full-scale tsunami by the time he kissed my cheek and handed me a bunch of pink peonies. My flush was as bright as the flowers.

"You look nice," he said.

"Doesn't she?" interrupted Jackie. "I picked out the dress. Well, not in the store. We found it in the—"

"*Officer* Doherty doesn't need to know my shopping habits," I said, shooting Jackie a reminder of Sean's profession.

Her mouth made a small O, and she excused herself to get a drink.

"My coworker," I gave as an explanation. "But she's also my friend. I've worked with her for seventeen years."

"That's a long time," he said, stepping a little closer. "Some marriages don't last that long. Mine didn't."

The mention of his divorce must have slipped out, because I watched as his features closed up, one by one. His glance broke away from mine to the bar. "I'm going to get a drink, too. Would you like something?"

I shook my head. I noticed Trey watching our interaction, a stricken look on his face. *Shit.*

I followed Trey into the kitchen, calling his name in a low voice, as not to bring attention to the argument I was certain was brewing. I should have talked to him more about dating. I should have warned him that Sean was coming and that I considered him a new friend. Because that was what he was, right? But given Trey's reaction, I was sure the expression on my face told him so much more than I was willing to admit.

"Why is *he* here?" he said when I caught up with him. The anger in his voice I could take, but the hurt made me want to hurl myself off the roof.

"I invited him," I said lamely. "He's become a friend."

"Sure. A friend," Trey said, the sarcasm so heavy it put pressure on my chest.

"I can do that," I said. "Have friends. I'm allowed."

"What about Dad?"

"I would have loved your father until I took my own last breath. You know that. But I don't get that option anymore, as much as I want it. Be honest. Do you think he'd want me to be alone?"

Trey worked through that idea. I knew he hated the idea of me being with anyone else, but I also knew that he was old enough to recognize that he would soon be moving on to his adult life, and I'd be left behind, the years stretching out like one lonely, narrow road.

Trey lowered himself onto a kitchen stool. He hunched over, and I resisted the urge to rub his back like I did when he was a scared toddler who was afraid of the monsters under the bed. "You're different," he said. "You're changing."

"So are you," I said gently. "Tragedy makes permanent changes. Some good, some bad, I suppose." I placed my palm to his back, marveling at the fact that my hand looked so small against the broad expanse. I once held him in the crook of my arm. "Trey, I don't think there's anything wrong with seeking companionship. We're all built for it. No one likes to be alone."

"I guess." He glanced at the gathering outside. "Is that why you had this party? Do you think these people are going to help you feel less alone? Because they're not."

"I have to try."

"Colin's dad always talks about how important it is to decide where you're going to put your energy. I think you're putting your energy in the wrong places. You're being totally random."

164

I had to concede the possibility that he had a point. My decisions, previously so well thought out, seemed rash and made in an effort to push back the scary emotions rising to the surface. Was it all a Band-Aid? I wasn't sure. I wanted to think of the garden as an affirmation of life, as a new path toward fulfillment.

"I don't think that's true," I told Trey. "I really don't."

"You keep thinking that. I'm going to spend the night at Colin's."

"I wish you wouldn't."

"Why? Don't you want to have the house to yourself tonight?"

"That's not fair."

Trey shrugged and headed for the French doors. "Nothing is."

After composing myself, I checked on the status of food and drinks and, once satisfied everyone was happy, tried to enjoy myself. The sun had gently moved from dusk to darkness, and the twinkling lights Jackie hung looked magical. Someone cranked up the music, some old Van Morrison that seemed perfectly appropriate. The smells from the garden were not overpowering but subtle and soothing, a perfect mix from nature.

"Those tomatoes are going to be amazing," Sean said as he came up behind me. His words brushed against my ear, and I felt a shiver of anticipation. It was a foreign feeling, and I tried not to analyze it.

"I really hope so. I've been working pretty hard to keep them healthy."

"A garden is hard work." While he talked, he slipped one hand around my waist and took my hand in his other. "But dancing isn't. Want to give it a whirl?"

We got a few raised eyebrows, but more smiles, as he spun me around the patio. Rhiannon and Byron soon joined us, followed by Seth and Glynnis, a very serious expression on her face as they held an intense conversation while swaying to the music. Her gaze kept straying toward Byron, and I watched heartache dull her eyes.

"You're pretty good at this," Sean said, but it was he who knew how to move. I'd never been very good at following someone's lead, but he sensed that and effortlessly made adjustments. "There's something I've been meaning to ask you," he said softly as he brought me up close.

"Yes?"

I felt something cold on my shoulder. Sean's eyes widened, but he didn't step back, and held on as I turned to see . . .

Mr. Eckhardt. His face resembled one huge broken capillary—red, angry, expansive. He hooked one long finger under the strap of my dress.

"Hey," Sean said. "Take your hand off her, sir."

Mr. Eckhardt ignored him and tugged hard on the delicate material. "This isn't yours! You stole it!"

The other partygoers drew closer, like bees to the dramapot.

Mr. Eckhardt's glassy eyes held anger and confusion, but not the healthy dose of crazy I expected to find jumping up and down behind his irises. Instead, sadness put a film over them, tragedy's glaucoma.

"I found it," I said, voice shaky. "I found it in the backyard."

Mr. Eckhardt stepped back and nearly lost his footing on the edge of the concrete. He shook my hand off when I tried to steady him. "You're doing this on purpose. You want to torture me with it. Are you so angry with your lot in life that you have to make others feel badly? That's a pathetic trait in a person. I don't think much of you, but I did think you were better than that."

I blanched. "Can we talk about this inside?"

Mr. Eckhardt glanced around at the others. "Why? Because you don't want them to know that you're a thief? That you steal from good, solid people?"

I crossed my arms over my chest protectively. The dress suddenly felt too flimsy, too exposing. "I didn't steal anything from you."

"No," he spat. "But you did steal from someone."

"From who?"

"My wife."

~

"Let's sit down and have a talk," Sean said as he ushered us into the kitchen. "I'll get us some drinks, and we'll pretend we're all nice, civilized people."

"I'm not sitting," Mr. Eckhardt said as he leaned against my counter.

"But you'll stay?" Sean asked.

Mr. Eckhardt's eyes met Sean's, and a silent, masculine agreement transpired between them. "I'll stay for a few minutes."

That was good enough for Sean. He dashed out to the bar, leaving me with my very surly neighbor.

I plucked at the collar of the dress. "You know where I found this, don't you?"

"You should leave things as they are," Mr. Eckhardt said. "Why can't you do that? You've got some kind of sick obsession."

"Are you sure it's me who's got something sick going on?"

Sean came back with three strawberry margaritas. I thought Mr. Eckhardt would refuse his, but he accepted a glass and took a healthy sip. "This is good."

"Well, then we've found some common ground," Sean said with a forced smile.

Sean remained standing. I thought maybe I should get up as well, but then, suddenly, I was exhausted. "Could we talk about the dress?"

"You took it with no regard for my feelings," Mr. Eckhardt said. He sounded hurt. Was it an act?

"Took it from where?" Sean asked, confused. "Can we start at the beginning?"

Mr. Eckhardt didn't offer any additional information, and I didn't either. I tried to see how my digging up a dress and then actually wearing it might look to Sean. Would he find it charming or creepy?

Creepy. Definitely creepy.

"I would like it back," Mr. Eckhardt said. "Along with an apology, and a promise from Paige that she will no longer take what's not hers."

"I didn't steal it," I said, sounding a bit too much like Trey.

"It's my wife's dress," Mr. Eckhardt said, his voice pained.

"And where is your wife, sir?" Sean asked gently.

A thought pierced through my annoyance. What if she'd died, and he was still mourning her? How could I, of all people, have not thought of that possibility?

"She's gone," Mr. Eckhardt said, and my heart broke.

"Passed on?" Sean said.

Mr. Eckhardt rolled his eyes. "Nope. Just gone. Took off."

I don't blame her, I thought.

"Oh," Sean said.

Silence.

"I'm not going to get the whole story here, am I?" Sean asked.

More silence.

Sean sighed. "Okay. Will you give the dress back, Paige?"

"Yes. I don't want it anyway." I stood.

They both stared at me as though I'd strip down right there. Mr. Eckhardt was horrified. Sean . . . not so much.

"I'll be right down." I dashed upstairs and tore off the dress. Maybe it was bad luck. If so, I'd counter it with a soft T-shirt and the jean shorts I seemed unable to take off lately.

When I returned to the kitchen, Mr. Eckhardt and Sean were talking companionably.

"Will you stay and enjoy the party, Bill?" Sean said, and I kind of wanted to kill him.

Mr. Eckhardt caught my expression. "No." He snatched the dress from my arms. "I'll be going as soon as I get my apology and a promise that it won't happen again."

I didn't want to apologize. I didn't want to promise him anything.

"It's up to you," Sean said mildly. He wasn't coercing me in the least. It really was up to me. Perversely, that made me want to choose the safe route. Sean really was good at this cop thing. "I'm sorry," I said robotically. "It won't happen again."

Mr. Eckhardt nodded, and then he was gone.

Sean stepped closer to me and ran his index finger along the collar of my T-shirt. "You look great in this, too. Actually, almost better."

My heart lurched. "Yeah?"

"Yeah," he said. "Now that I've fully complimented you, are you going to tell me how you got your hands on that dress?"

"Am I under arrest, Officer?"

"Not yet."

"Should I hire a lawyer?"

"Not unless you've got something to hide."

I felt a blush spread from my chest to my hairline.

"Now I'm really curious," Sean said, grinning.

I explained how I'd found the dress, trying to make myself look as sane and innocent as possible.

Sean's grin turned into a belly-rumbling guffaw. "You are such a weirdo. Definitely a strange bird."

I'd spent my entire life trying to fit into the mold of a respectable, conventional citizen. His comment brought on a strange sense of panic. "I think anyone would have done the same," I said primly.

"No. Most women wouldn't have been digging in the first place." He drew me to him, and his strong arms felt good against my back. "I think you're phenomenal. I like that you're offbeat. I like even more that you have no clue that you are."

He held me for a moment, and then pulled back slightly. "I've got to admit I'm curious as to why Bill would bury his wife's dress in the backyard."

"Can you look into it?"

He nodded. "Something tells me we're going to be surprised by what we find out. That man is in pain." I ignored the look of recognition on Sean's face that told me he knew exactly what that was like.

"That might be true," I said, "but I'm more concerned with her whereabouts. I've lived next door to Mr. Eckhardt for over ten years, and I've never once seen a hint of a wife. He's got a nephew who comes to visit with his family, and some neighbors pause to talk to him every so often, but that's pretty much it."

"That's sad," Sean said.

"It is."

"Sometimes people never really learn to connect with other people."

I smiled at him. "You don't have that problem."

Sean took my hand. "I want to dance with you again. Under the stars. In your beautiful garden. With all those people staring at us."

I took a deep breath. I could connect, too. "I would like that," I said. "Very much."

CHAPTER 22

Excerpt from Petra Polly: Chapter 12—Managing the Expectations of Others: What to Do with a Difficult Client

So your dream client is no longer happy with your company's work. What to do? Remain calm. Remember that the organization should be seen as a person, body and soul, and what happens when a body needs to woo a wandering lover? Romance. The showering of gifts, both tangible and spiritual. A few mea culpas for not giving your undivided attention. Make the client feel cherished. Adored. Imply you have forsaken all others in order to make them happy.

And then work your ass off to make sure it doesn't happen again.

"We haven't lost any clients," Rhiannon said. "We've gained some. Why did he make us read this chapter?"

"Maybe because the wooing applies to signing the client as well?" Glynnis said, but she didn't sound sure. "Then again, that was covered in chapter 4."

We sat in the conference room, all of us save Lukas, arguing over what would attract a person like Petra Polly to a small advertising agency like ours. Lukas insisted the best route was to follow the instructions she'd laid out in her book to every detail, but I silently disagreed. Why would she need us if we could only provide her with what she already knew? We needed to add significant value to her investment. We needed a little flash and pizzazz. We needed a touch of Big Frank.

"She's the type to want infomercials," Byron said with a roll of his eyes. "Am I right? Tony Robbins, that *Rich Dad Poor Dad* guy, and . . . Petra Polly."

Rhiannon snorted. "We don't know what she sounds like. I couldn't find one podcast or YouTube video. No television or radio interview. Nothing. Why do you think that is?"

"Maybe she's been too busy?" Glynnis contributed. She'd been more talkative than usual, and a tad more assertive. I didn't know if she'd talked to Byron at the party, or if she'd spent the evening crying on Seth's shoulder. She, Jackie, and I attempted to get away at lunch to discuss the party drama, but it was impossible with Lukas monitoring our every move. Petra Polly would arrive in Willow Falls in exactly two weeks. We were anything but prepared, and Lukas was skirting a nervous breakdown. He was downing kombucha like a Brooklyn hipster on a bender and pacing the hallways endlessly.

"Maybe she's hiding something," I said, thinking of Mr. Eckhardt, fingering the earrings he forgot to take back. I wondered about his marriage. Had it been a happy one, like mine and Jesse's? Instinct told me it hadn't been. Bill Eckhardt was an angry, difficult man. I suddenly had compassion for this woman, this poor soul who married him.

Mr. Eckhardt's attitude toward other people essentially boiled down to this—*leave me alone because you are a lesser human who doesn't deserve to breathe my rarified air.* After a decade of it, I had difficulty finding a soft spot of compassion in my admittedly hardened heart. Still, I had to wonder why it was that a lonely man seemed so intent on ensuring his own loneliness.

"Paige!" Glynnis's voice brought me from my thoughts.

"What?"

"We haven't got an idea worthy of Petra. Stop being so distracted. This is serious," she said. "I talked to Seth at the party about his job search. He said he hasn't had a single call, and he's sent out dozens of résumés." Glynnis groaned. "I can't go back out there. I can't lose this job."

"None of us can afford to," I said. If Seth—young, hip, and full of energy—couldn't get a callback, then Jackie and I were destined for a temp agency. I didn't know how to make decent coffee. Starbucks wouldn't even hire me on as a barista.

"Then we have to be better than *them*," she whispered, nudging her head toward Rhiannon and Byron, who were talking excitedly about . . . something. Though we'd all been hanging out in the conference room, they'd been increasingly distant from the rest of us, sharing inside jokes with Lukas and generally acting like they were from a slightly different species than us. "I need you to focus," Glynnis stated primly.

"I am focused."

"No," she said, that newly minted assertiveness shining through. "You're not. You're thinking about your garden and that police officer who's into you, and—"

"Do you think he's into me?"

"Seriously, Paige. You are nearly twice my age. Grow up."

I was acting like a teenager. But then again, it wasn't exactly my choice. I was dating again, and what came with that was an avalanche of insecurities and second-guessing and forensic-scale analysis of every word or action. I even had acne, perimenopausal, hormone-induced acne, but still. For the second time in my life, I had to put an *Open House* sign on my heart. I had to accept the risk that no one might be interested. At Jesse's funeral, a neighbor said to me, "You won the lottery when you met Jesse." As time went on, I knew what he was implying. *This isn't going to happen again.* It might not. Knowing that—and accepting it—was the only thing that told me I was ready.

"You're spacing out again," Glynnis said. "Stop it!"

"Okay. Sorry." I dropped Petra's book onto the table with a thunk. "Let's start by focusing on what value we can bring to her organization."

"Seriously?"

"Okay," I said, conceding lameness. "How can we sell her better than she can sell herself?"

"She's not selling herself," Glynnis said. "Beyond what her publisher is doing for her. She doesn't have much of a Google presence. For someone who is expanding her company, Petra Polly doesn't seem to want to be seen."

That was odd. Maybe it meant she didn't understand the power of social media? How could it be that we were following her every dictum when she didn't understand how to use the Internet? It didn't make sense. Petra was choosing to stay mysterious. But why?

"Let's focus on the products," I said, going with a hunch. "Not Petra."

"But she's cute and hipstery," Glynnis said with a skeptical lift of her brow. "Don't we want to use that?"

It was an easy way to brand herself. If Petra wanted to use it, she would have. "I don't think that's what she wants."

"I disagree. I think you want the easy way out." Glynnis gathered her things angrily, and then stooped to whisper in my ear. "If I wanted someone lazy and old-fashioned, I would have gone to Jackie."

"That's not fair."

Glynnis's fair skin had grown ruddy with her frustration. "If you want to keep your job, you need to start thinking—"

"Don't say 'outside the box.'"

She shoved Petra's book into her messenger bag. "Make fun of it all you want, but, yes, that's exactly what we need to be doing."

"Giving her the expected response does not qualify as creative thinking."

"We'll make it special." To my horror, her eyes welled up. "We can offer her that."

"Of course we can," I said soothingly.

"You're the most talented, Paige. We all need you. I don't want to keep living with my parents and asking to borrow their car when I need to go somewhere. I have student loans bigger than a car payment. I—" She dissolved into tears.

"I'll try," I promised. "I'll really try."

~

"We should go over there."

Mykia sat on my counter a week after the party, popping blueberries into her mouth and staring out my kitchen window at Mr. Eckhardt's house. She brought the fruit with her because my bushes wouldn't produce enough blackberries to make a jar of jam for at least another year or two. *Patience will be rewarded,* the garden reminded me. Why was it so hard to listen sometimes?

"I'm trying not to obsess about my blackberry bushes making it next year."

Mykia told me not to worry. "That's the beauty of a garden," she said. "Some stuff works, some stuff doesn't, and some stuff you think isn't working ends up producing the following year. Keeps you living in a constant state of suspense, so whatever comes, you're grateful for it."

Grateful. That morning, when I got up early to water and weed and do all the caretaking things that had become second nature, I'd found my tomatoes had changed from the greenish-orange slightly tie-dyed look to orange, burgeoning on red, like a really beautiful sunrise. The plants looked healthy and strong, their leaves a deep green velvet. I couldn't disguise my pride when I showed Mykia as soon as she'd arrived.

"This is good," Mykia had said with a deep sense of satisfaction. "You did good, Paige."

No one had told me I'd done well at anything in so long that I'd teared up and hugged her.

She had a sharper expression on her face as she hopped off the counter and went to the window, taking in Mr. Eckhardt's perfect lawn. "You still have the earrings, right? You didn't give them back?"

When I wasn't wearing them, I set them on the small plate that held a few special pieces I'd gotten from Jesse over the years. Mr. Eckhardt's rage, along with Sean's presence and the party overall, had me flustered, and I'd forgotten to even think of returning them that night. Had he noticed? Would he show up at my door again, even angrier that I'd kept them to myself?

"Maybe I should give them back."

"You shouldn't just return them, no questions asked," Mykia said. "Don't you want to know why he buried the dress?"

I did and I didn't, but curiosity was one of my emotions I could never quite turn down. "Yes, I guess I do."

"Bring the earrings, but don't show him just yet. We'll go over and knock on his door. We need the element of surprise on our side."

Given that we had to cross the broad expanse of lawn in bright daylight and knock on the door, I didn't think we exactly had that going for us.

We didn't. Mr. Eckhardt had the door open before we reached it.

"What do you want?" he said, his tone unwelcoming.

I gathered up my courage. "I apologized to you at the party, but you didn't apologize to me."

"Thieves don't deserve apologies."

I tried to match his haughty expression. "It was half on my property."

"And half on mine," he said.

"I didn't give you everything in the box. If you tell me why it was buried, I'll give you the rest."

Mr. Eckhardt looked like he might be sick. "You are an evil woman."

"No, I'm not. Just curious about who I've been living next to for ten years."

"Okay," he said, which I should have realized was not really a promise of anything.

I opened my hand, and the earrings glistened in the sun.

"Where . . . ?" Mr. Eckhardt shot out of the house and stopped cold right in front of me. He took the earrings, cradling them in his palm, and closed his eyes. "You don't know what you're messing with."

"What happened?" I asked.

"You don't have a right to ask," he snapped.

"You promised," Mykia said, but her tone had lost its bite. She was softer, as if she wanted to offer Mr. Eckhardt a reason he could let his story loose. It obviously pained him greatly.

"You're talking about my things," he said tightly.

"Sometimes it helps to talk," I offered.

"Well," he said. He opened his eyes and fixed them on me. They were harder now, unyielding. "You have no respect for other people's property because you have no respect for your own."

"That's not fair."

"Isn't it? Look at what you've done. Do you think you're honoring your husband's memory? You're tarnishing it. Don't you understand that?"

"Enough," I said. "Enough."

Mr. Eckhardt tossed the earrings on his lawn. "Pick them up," he said.

"What?"

"Pick up the earrings!"

Stunned, I did as he asked.

"Now, take them away," he boomed.

"Are you sure?"

"TAKE THEM AWAY, PAIGE!"

Mykia and I left him standing there, a totem in the summer sun, casting a shadow over the fence.

CHAPTER 23

"It says you won't graduate." I held the letter from Willow Falls High School, the one that outlined why Trey would not be marching to "Pomp and Circumstance" with his fellow classmates unless he added driver's education to his schedule.

"It's fascism," he said. "Pure fascism."

"I don't care what kind of -*ism* you call it—you can't get a high school diploma without it."

"We could sue. We could call the ACLU."

"This isn't funny."

I busied myself making pancakes and scrambled eggs, Trey's favorite, minus the bacon, as he'd recently discovered the truth about industrialized pig farming. His passion made me smile—who could deny the devotion of the teenage activist?—and I could feel it rising in myself a bit thanks to the garden. There really was something to living a simpler, more natural life. I always knew that to be true, but the notion never sank deep.

Trey pushed back from the kitchen table and grabbed his backpack from the peg. "I'm going to Colin's."

"I'm making breakfast! We never eat together anymore. I thought we'd have a Saturday morning pancake fest, like we used to." I could hear in my voice all the things that acted as instant repellant to a teenager—disappointment, nagging, hurt, and anger.

"We've got a project to work on. Save it and I'll eat when I get back."

"Fine," I said. "But I'm driving you."

"I can take my bike. It'll be easier."

Trey had managed to avoid getting into a car with me since the attempted driving incident. He'd been surly and defensive any time I brought it up. Actually, surly and defensive seemed to be his primary personality traits overall. I alternated between being worried and annoyed with his behavior. Ultimately worry won out, as it always does with mothers, and I made an appointment with the therapist we used after Jesse's death. He went once, about three weeks after the car accident, and then refused to go back.

"We're going to have to talk about this again. It's not going to go away."

"I need to go away," he said. "Far away."

He was trying to hurt me, and with the precision of a teenage assassin, he did. "Please don't say that, Trey. We have each other. Can't we be nice?"

"Sean's coming up the driveway," he said, effectively dodging the question.

Once upon a time, I didn't mind unexpected visitors. But that was when I showered every morning and kept myself as well maintained as Mr. Eckhardt's BMW. A quick scan of my person told me I was not only unshowered but not wearing a bra. "Are you sure it's him?"

My son shot me a look that said he was less than impressed with me, but for other reasons. "Yeah, it's definitely the cop you're trying to hook up with," he said before stepping out. "I'll let him know you made pancakes."

179

Sean wore his uniform, so I was briefly uneasy. "Is there a problem, Officer?"

He smiled shyly. Occasional hesitance in a confident man could make a woman forget she wasn't wearing a bra.

"I just got off my shift," he explained. "I was driving past and thought I'd stop in."

"Really?"

"Well, I did have something to talk to you about." He grew serious, more professional, and my stomach dropped.

"Trey?"

"Oh, no," he said quickly. "Not him. Your next door neighbor, Bill Eckhardt."

"Did he off his wife?"

He laughed, dug a Post-it note from his pocket, and stuck it to my kitchen table. On it he'd scrawled an address. Somewhere in New Mexico. "Nope, he did nothing of the sort. Noreen Eckhardt did disappear from Willow Falls sometime in the early seventies, but she lives in Santa Fe now. Definitely breathing."

"Disappeared?"

"That might be overstating it. Left? Got outta Dodge?"

"She just left him?"

"Looks like it. I couldn't find any record of divorce."

"So he's still married?"

"It's not uncommon."

"Oh. Yeah. I guess you're right."

"You sound disappointed."

It was my turn to laugh. "No, I just thought the story would be more interesting."

"You don't know the story," Sean said. "It might be *very* interesting."

I wondered if I would ever hear it. Would it change my impression of Mr. Eckhardt or reinforce it? "Thanks for looking into it."

"All part of the job."

Silence. The kind that felt like it could preface something important.

Sean took a deep breath. "I didn't just come over to discuss Mr. Eckhardt's failed love life. I felt an overwhelming need to see your garden."

"That sounds slightly inappropriate."

That got a laugh. "Seriously. It's peaceful, and my night was anything but. Can we go sit out there for a while?"

"Could you give me a minute to freshen up?"

"You look fine."

I shrugged. "Okay. Let me grab you a cup of coffee first."

"Paige," he said, taking my hand. "I just want to see the garden. You don't need to keep adding things to keep me interested. I *am* interested."

"Okay," I managed. Interest. I'd forgotten what it felt like to be on the receiving end of that. The scrutiny was uncomfortable and wonderful all at the same time. How much did he see? Just the surface or down deep? I'd never been someone to allow too much emotion to reach the surface, but the past two years had painfully carved new pathways through my brain and heart.

That gave me pause. The unfairness of it all.

Jesse's death was making me a better person. As he'd done throughout our life together, he was still making sacrifices on my behalf. Sean would get a different Paige—slightly more empathetic, definitely more relaxed and open, and possibly more likeable. It just wasn't fair.

We walked outside, and the morning sun caught the red in Sean's hair, and I thought, *I could get used to looking at that.* He inhaled deeply and took in my haphazard mix of plants, all barely contained in their spaces, growing with an untamed wildness I'd come to truly appreciate.

"I like it out here," was all he said. "Sometimes I feel like the older I get, the more I chase down moments like these."

"Peaceful ones?"

"I guess that's it," he said with a slight shrug. "Growing up, I was the youngest of eight. My house was loud. My parents yelled all the time. If we wanted to be heard, we had to shriek above the rest. Do you have siblings?"

"I was an only child," I said quietly. "My mom wasn't equipped to have me, much less anyone else."

Sean took my hand in his. "That sounds like a sad story. I see a lot of those, even in Willow Falls."

"And how do you handle the sad stories?" I got flashes of my mom, cops at the door, my grandmother crying, bruises on my legs and arms, screaming, dirty fingernails, and blood. It wasn't a way any child should grow up, and I was glad for a moment that Trey's biggest problem, save losing his father, was getting up the courage to get behind the wheel of a car.

"I try to be kind," he said after a moment. "But firm. Given the way I grew up, I'm pretty good at defusing problematic situations."

I thought of how he'd handled Mr. Eckhardt's fury. He was firm, but also respectful and even-keeled. "I can see that. You're very good at what you do."

The compliment made him obviously uncomfortable, and he shifted away, losing himself to the garden again.

"What does this mean to you, Paige? Have you worked it out yet, or are you acting on instinct?"

I wasn't sure if he was talking about the garden or our possible coupledom. I decided my answer would be the same. "If I say instinct, would you think less of it? Of me?"

"Of course not. Some of the best choices in my life I made not because I carefully thought through the potential outcomes but because I trusted my gut. It's okay to do that when that small part of your brain that you trust implicitly tells you to go for it." He turned to me, the intensity in his eyes telling me what was coming. He put one strong hand on my shoulder, gave me a moment to stop him, and when I didn't, leaned over and touched his lips to mine.

He moved slowly, conscious of my shyness. Jesse's kiss had been the kiss of long-term love, of familiarity, of confidence in the future, of a comfort born of many years together. Sean's touch was unfamiliar and . . . different. The differences kept me from telling him to stop. The strangeness of it offset some of the guilt. But then I thought about what Trey would think, and potential disappointment if it didn't work out, and the sheer terror if it did. I could lose someone again. I could be left alone. I could—

And then I heard Jesse's voice in my head. He told me that it was okay to be new with someone and that growth was the natural by-product of change. He said I shouldn't fight it or taint it with guilt or wish I'd been more like this new self with him, because it would discount the beauty of what we'd had. He said I should be open not only to life but also to love.

"Okay," I whispered.

"What?" Sean said, a quizzical look on his face. "Did I say something?"

"No, I did. I wanted to know if you'd be interested in having dinner with me this week."

The shy smile returned. "I was going to ask you. You beat me to it."

"Is that a yes?"

"It is," he said. "Unequivocally."

"Good," I said.

"Are you sure it is?"

"Yes," I said. "Unequivocally."

"Can I sit here for a while and watch your garden grow, Mary, Mary?"

"I'm not the least bit contrary."

Sean laughed. "You might want to reevaluate that statement."

He settled onto the cement porch, took my hand, and pulled me down next to him. "You know, I'm like those beneficial bugs Mykia was talking about at the party."

"She's obsessed," I said, smiling at the memory of her talking animatedly about soldier bugs, lacewings, and beneficial nematodes.

"They might not look all that good, and you might mistake them for a pest, but they end up helping things along and keeping the bad stuff at bay. They move quickly and take care of the lesser business so the plants can take care of the big stuff."

I squeezed his hand. "I'm grateful for them," I said. "I really am."

CHAPTER 24

"So are we just going to ambush her?" Byron sat at the conference table in the spot normally held by Lukas, who was out, supposedly at a lunch meeting, though we suspected he was yet again shopping for the perfect outfit for his upcoming audience with Petra Polly.

Rhiannon sighed. "This doesn't make any sense. You all realize that, right? We're going to embarrass ourselves."

Lukas's plan was very simple. Lukas, Byron, Rhiannon, and I would get in line at different points. When it was our turn to approach Petra, we'd give her an elevator pitch. Hopefully, by the time the last of us reached her, she'd be so charmed she'd be willing to stop by Gossamer Space for a full presentation. Jackie and Glynnis were to stay in the office and get things ready, a job both grumbled at, and both suspected was the lesser position.

"I don't see why I can't go," Glynnis whined to me. "Why do you get to go?"

"Maybe he wants one old person there. The voice of authority."

She shot me a dubious look. "You're not that old. You know the real reason."

The stress of possibly losing her job had made Glynnis a touch cynical. Cynicism was a natural by-product of being in a corporate atmosphere, but Glynnis wore it awkwardly, like an ill-fitting shirt.

"Will you talk to Lukas about letting me go to the bookshop?" she pleaded. "Maybe if you say something . . ."

She didn't finish her sentence. Passive-aggressiveness was one of my pet peeves. "What would happen if I said something? When has Lukas listened to me? The only thing you can control is the job you have to do." That gave me pause. Was that advice I wasn't heeding myself? I wanted to control Trey and Lukas and even Mr. Eckhardt. Perhaps I had to let go of those feelings and focus only on what my brain and two hands could do.

"You know there's more to it," she said. "I'm learning that, so I suspect you've known it for a long time. Office politics. The balance of power."

"Aren't you being a little dramatic?"

Tears sprang to her eyes, and I immediately felt like a villain. We were all stressed and worried, but was there something else going on I didn't know about? Was this about Byron and Rhiannon?

"Are you okay?" I asked gently. "Is something else bothering you?"

She glanced at Byron, who was punching something on his keyboard. "No," she said dully. "I just don't understand why there needs to be a competition. We all add something to this company, don't we?"

"We do."

"Even Seth did. He shouldn't have been fired." She fiddled with her phone. "I don't like change, especially when it happens because of stupid reasons, because then the outcome is just as stupid."

"That's something I can understand." Jesse's death was stupid. "I don't think many people ask for change on a regular basis," I said. "But it happens. You have to learn to react to it. To take action." The garden flashed through my head. Mykia. Sean. Was I finally breaking a pattern?

"I take action all the time," Glynnis said, sadness in her voice. "It doesn't matter if no one is paying attention. People pay attention to you, Paige. I could come up with the greatest ad in a hundred years, and no one would pay attention to me in the slightest. I wasn't lucky enough to get . . . what is it? Charisma."

"That's not true," I soothed. But . . . maybe she was right. I followed Byron's lead, punching on my own keyboard, because this conversation was getting uncomfortable.

I'd always felt success was won by hard work—I lived my life by it. But what role did luck play? I didn't like to think luck had much to do with it, because that would mean life was mostly random. To think of the major happenings in my life as flukes belittled them. To say Jesse was merely unlucky didn't sit right with me. Why would the death of a healthy, larger-than-life forty-two-year-old father and husband result from a small, random occurrence? How would I get meaning from it if I bought into the notion that shit just happened, and I had to buck up and accept it? Maybe life just unfolded like those ash snakes on the Fourth of July—messy and moving in unpredictable directions, sometimes longer and sometimes snuffing out before things really got started. If that were so, where would I find meaning in something that was so fundamentally unfair?

By living as if what I did while I was on the planet did have meaning, even if I secretly feared it was all one big nothing.

Maybe Glynnis was born unlucky. Maybe not. And in the end, how much did it matter? Life would still unfold unpredictably.

"You know what, Glynnis? Lucky or unlucky, you do what you can," I said, wishing I could erase her sad expression. "I wish I could tell you something more profound, but that's all I've got. Just do what you can."

~

It was just a meal. Dinner. Two people sitting down, ordering, laughing, trying to eat without making chewing noises or burping. Easy, right?

Nooooo. Not right. Not right at all.

Sean's text said fifteen minutes to arrival.

I was *not* ready.

Clothes. Makeup. Hair. Three things I normally did on autopilot were as foreign to me as driving on the wrong side of the road. My hand slipped, sending my eyeliner off into Catwoman-like wings. My clothes had somehow wrinkled, even in dry cleaning bags. My underwear could be worn proudly by a nun . . . my underwear? Why was I even thinking about that? No one but me was going to see my underwear tonight.

No one.

Thinking about intimacy unleashed too many conflicting feelings, so at odds my brain could've been having a tug-of-war with my heart. Except for some brief, fumbling hookups in high school, I'd only been with Jesse. We were partners in the bedroom, truly in sync, and thinking about sharing more than a kiss with Sean vaporized any courage I'd mustered.

Ten minutes. I would shove that thought to the back of the line. I swabbed lip gloss on with a heavy hand and then dabbed most of it off with a tissue, determined not to look like a Real Housewife. I fluffed my hair and patted it back down. I yanked off the gray blouse that suddenly seemed too dingy and replaced it with a black silk tank. But my pants were black, too. I looked like a ninja.

Five minutes.

I found a soft pink linen skirt and managed to squeeze into it, and added some black strappy sandals. Three minutes. Jewelry! I rummaged through my jewelry tray, determined to find something that didn't remind me of Jesse. I'd taken off my wedding ring almost immediately after the funeral—the shock of pain I felt whenever I glanced at my hand was too much to bear—but everything else I owned was somehow tied to a memory. With thirty seconds to spare, I found Mr. Eckhardt's wife's earrings and put them on.

The doorbell chimed. Sean was right on time.

~

Jesse got his driver's license before me. Neither of us had any hopes to own a car, so we were well into college before we ever headed to the DMV. An elderly neighbor told Jesse he could occasionally use her '78 Buick if he mowed her small, postage-stamp-sized front yard. It was she who drove us to the DMV that morning, a good ten miles under the speed limit the entire time, and complaining incessantly about the inconvenience. When we dropped her off afterward, she sent Jesse to fill the tank at a local gas station.

We'd never gotten gas before. Nerves rattling, we looked at each other with big eyes. Did we pay first? How did the pump work? Was the window-washer thing gross or not gross?

We managed to fill the tank without spraying gasoline everywhere. We cleaned the windows, and they sparkled. Smiling and satisfied, we drove home, pulling up to our block at a crawl, wanting to be seen. Then Jesse stopped the car just in front of a tight spot and parallel parked with surprising finesse.

When he shut the engine off, neither of us moved. We'd been friends, such good friends. I fiddled with my seat belt, wondering why the silence suddenly felt so heavy when it was usually such a comfortable respite between the two of us, a shared ability to just be.

"Congratulations," I said, my voice unsteady. "You're a good driver."

"I don't have insurance," he said, but he sounded distracted. "I don't know how much I'm going to be able to drive us around. It's too risky."

"I don't care about that. You have your license if you need it. That's enough."

He removed the key from the ignition and placed it between us on the leather seats. "I wish this was our car, and we could go anywhere we wanted."

"We don't need a car for that," I said. "We do okay on the bus and the 'L.'"

"But it's not ours," he insisted. "I just want something to be mine."

"I could be yours," I blurted, instantly mortified that I'd shoved a truth I'd sheltered for so long into the cold, open air.

"Could you?" he asked softly, so softly. He picked up the car keys and placed them in my palm, closing my fingers over them. "Someday, I'm going to give you everything you want."

One honest comment made another come easier. "I just want you."

He lifted my chin, and I caught his gaze with mine. I knew those eyes as well as I knew my own, but for the first time I saw something different in them, a longing I'd since realized was desire.

Jesse kissed me. Our first real kiss. I held tightly on to his broad shoulder with one hand and the keys with the other, their sharp ridges burrowing into my hand.

~

Sean was a confident driver, cruising steadily through the streets of Willow Falls, heading to the center of our village.

"Where are we going?"

"It's a surprise," he said.

"I've lived in this town for almost twenty years. I doubt anything could be a surprise." It hit me, the ambiguous thing I'd been fearing. He could take me somewhere familiar. He could take me somewhere packed with memories. He could take me somewhere Jesse, at some point, had been.

"Stop," I said.

"What?"

"Pull over. Please!"

I knew it was simple panic, but my chest tightened from fear, the muscles bunching to protect my heart. I couldn't catch my breath.

Sean swerved into a parking spot. "What is it?"

"I'm—" I focused on breathing. *In. Out. In. Out.*

"You're what? You can tell me, if you want to." His voice was gentle.

"It's just that . . . I'm afraid."

Sean nodded, settling back in his seat. "Yeah. That's probably normal, though, right?"

"I guess."

"Let me ask you. Are you afraid of me, or of something else?"

"I'm not afraid of you at all. I just thought about all of the places we could go in downtown Willow Falls, and nearly every one of them has memories attached."

"Good memories?"

"Yes."

Sean thought for a moment. I just sat there, breathing.

He finally said, "If we're going to date, we can go to other suburbs if we need to, no problem. We could drive an hour away if you need to, but I'm not quite sure that's the solution to this problem."

"I think that sounds like a good solution."

"Part of me thinks I don't have a right to tell you how to grieve, but the other part of me is gonna tell you anyway."

"Go ahead and say it."

"Tonight, I think you should pick a restaurant that has good memories. It doesn't have to be one that was very special to you two, but one that has memories you can deal with. Pick out one of those good memories, and tell me about it. I didn't know Jesse. Maybe it's about time I did."

"I don't know." I really didn't. Would it hurt too much? Would it hurt too little? I didn't know which one was worse. I would have no problem telling stories about how wonderful Jesse was, even to this man.

"I'm not looking to replace him," I said. "He was irreplaceable. I hope that doesn't make you feel weird."

"Not at all. People can't be replaced. Anyone with half a brain knows that." He took my hand, lacing his fingers with mine. "Especially someone who caught your heart. He had to have been pretty special."

"He was."

My awareness returned, and I realized we were parked on the main strip, right outside one of our favorite Italian restaurants. We'd celebrated Jesse's promotion there, and Trey's eighth-grade graduation. Big Frank spent his last minutes there, spooning ravioli on everyone's plate and chomping on his cigar.

"Let's eat here."

Sean got out of the car and dashed around to open my door. I took his arm, and we walked into Marinetti's Chop House. "This one time," I began, "Jesse mistakenly ordered the squid-ink pasta . . ."

~

When Sean pulled up to my house, it was dark save for the front porch light. I was used to a dark house—the past two years had me coming home to one more often than not—but in the stillness of late summer, it looked particularly lonely, like an old photograph.

"I'll walk you to the door," Sean said.

I paused. Dinner had gone well, but there were stages here, stages I'd long forgotten. And there were choices. Did I go with propriety, or did I chuck the rules into my new compost bin?

Into the bin they went. "Do you want to come in for a cup of coffee?"

He smiled to himself, a satisfied grin that told me he'd hoped I'd ask but didn't expect it.

"Yeah," he said. "I'd like that."

He got out of the car in a hurry so he could dash over to my side to open the passenger door. *He's nice,* I thought. *And thoughtful. This is okay.*

We walked to my front door, and I thought about how many times I'd done that while married, taking for granted that I would always have Jesse with me or waiting on the other side of the door, a presence I realized I had taken for granted.

I glanced at the man next to me. He was shorter than my husband, sunrise-colored hair instead of Jesse's dark, rich brown, broad instead of thin, rougher around the edges . . . different. But different was good. Different was necessary. I felt drawn to this man. He was not my husband, and that was fine. He was Sean, and I liked Sean. The rules could disintegrate under a pile of old eggshells.

"Do you think you'll kiss me tonight?" I asked, my voice loud enough for a nosy neighbor to hear.

He laughed. "Would you like that?"

"Yes."

"I was hoping you might kiss me."

"You like a woman who takes charge?" I was flirting. Oh, God, I was *flirting.*

"I like a woman who knows her own mind."

Sean stopped at the bottom of my porch. He didn't reach for me, just smiled. A dare.

I took a breath. Stepped forward.

He still didn't move.

"Are you going to give me a little something here?" I asked, nerves getting the better of me. "Meet me halfway?"

He grinned. "Nope."

"Fine." I stood directly in front of him. I curled one hand over his shoulder to steady myself.

"That's a good start," he said.

I leaned forward. I could see his beard had already made a return appearance, the scruff a burnt-orange color. Sean's lips were full and lush for a man. I licked mine and then slowly pressed them to his. He let me, but he didn't take charge. He let me lead myself to a place of comfort. His mouth, soft and accessible, didn't demand, it just accepted.

He was giving me a chance to get myself together. And I needed it. I pulled back, surprised my breath had left me. I could feel the goose bumps rise on my skin, though it must have been ninety degrees.

"Was that okay?" he asked, his features etched with concern.

"Yeah, it was—" A bright orange sticker affixed to the front door grabbed my attention. I had a feeling I knew what it was. "Son of a bitch!"

"What?"

It was stuck at the top like a Post-it note. I tore it down, reading quickly in the glow of the porch light. "It's a cease and desist command. From the village."

He ran a hand over his face. "They don't mess around, but they usually have a pretty sound reason for taking action."

"It says that using my private residential property as a profit-seeking business is against the bylaws. I have to shut down the garden. How would they know that I intend to sell anything?"

Sean stuffed his hands in the pockets of his jeans. "I might have said something about your salsa to Mr. Eckhardt."

"You didn't."

"I kind of did."

I took the letter in both hands and slowly ripped it in two. "I'm allowed to have a garden. They're going to have to dig it all up if they want me to stop." I tore it again and again, until it was reduced to bright orange confetti.

"I don't know if that's wise," Sean said.

"Wisdom hasn't done all that much for me," I said before tossing the shredded papers onto Mr. Eckhardt's pristine lawn.

And then I pulled Sean to me, and kissed him with the force of a woman on a mission.

CHAPTER 25

Excerpt from Petra Polly: Chapter 6—The Personality of a Successful Business

Your company has a personality. Like every living, breathing being, its personality is made up of traits both positive and negative. You must assess these traits objectively—is the company stodgy and rigid? Passionate and creative? Adventurous and impulsive? Once you've composed a personality portrait, determine whether it's working to boost the company. If it isn't, then it's time for some reshaping. Reward the positive attributes, and squelch the negative. Remember that bubbly, effervescent, high-energy cheerleader? That's what you're shooting for. Minus the hair product and domineering quarterback boyfriend.

"Do you notice that Petra gets a little weirder toward the end of the book?" Rhiannon mused from the floor of the conference room. Convinced her vertebrae were out of alignment, thereby fracturing her train of thought, she'd taken to stretching out on the hard floor with a tennis ball under her lower back.

"The tone shifts," Byron contributed. "She seems snarkier."

"I don't mind it," Glynnis said, shooting daggers at Byron. Rhiannon and Byron were officially a scandalous office romance. Everyone knew and no one talked about it, though I sensed both Rhiannon and Byron couldn't wait for the gossip to reach a fervor. Jackie and I refused to give them the satisfaction. Glynnis couldn't help herself. She seethed.

"I like her better this way," I said. "She's got a little something to her."

Lukas burst into the room, a trick he'd overused. None of us flinched. "Tonight," he said with a healthy dollop of drama. "To-*night* is the night!"

None of us was to leave the office until it was time to head over to the bookshop. Instead of dashing home for a quick dinner with Trey, as I'd planned, I would practice my script for when I, lowly ad gal, had an audience with the illustrious Petra Polly.

Lukas would place himself first in line to introduce the company and our plans to turn her into a superstar. Rhiannon and Byron would follow, and I, loitering at the end of the line, would try to seal the deal. Frankly, I was surprised Lukas would trust me with such an important part of the mission, but he seemed to think I could be an authoritative presence.

In other words, I was *old*.

If Petra hadn't called for security by the time I made it to the front of the line, she might be amenable to listening to a middle-aged woman in a dated power suit, sporting a farmer's tan. We'd kept the script simple, direct, and professional. The advertisements already lined the walls of the conference room, blown up to poster size and somewhat intimidating. Lukas decided to play all bases—some featured the photo of Petra from her book cover, wide-eyed and dewy skinned, and others featured the products, the aesthetic and design heavily borrowed from the kitschy-hipster style of Anthropologie with the clean, inviting lines of Restoration Hardware. It felt derivative to me. Too safe.

As a general rule, I liked safe. Or, I used to. But then my safe life betrayed me. Jesse and I built our lives around cultivating security. We took risks far fewer times than other couples our age, and when we did, like canceling one life insurance policy before taking up with another, it not only bit us in the ass, but it chewed and chewed until we couldn't sit down.

A woman like Petra Polly needed something so far outside the box that the box could no longer be seen. This wasn't it. But then Lukas seemed to understand Petra on a deeper level than the rest of us. I kept my mouth shut.

"What are you wearing tonight?" Lukas had come up behind me while I mused.

"What? I thought I'd wear this," I said. I had on a gray linen suit, with a coral shell underneath for a pop of color. I'd even scrubbed out under my fingernails and painted them to match. When I left the house in the morning, I'd thought I looked pretty good.

"No," Lukas said with a moan. "No, no, no. We do not want Petra Polly thinking we're suburban. Suburban equals slow. You look like an advertisement for the LOFT."

The shell I was wearing came from that very store. "What's wrong with the LOFT?"

"Nothing. That is, if you're selling Tupperware." Lukas glanced over at Glynnis, who wore a mustard-colored shift dress with a crazy pattern at the hem. Then Rhiannon walked by sporting loose-knit, almost too-revealing leggings, a T-shirt with an iron-on unicorn emblazoned on the front, and a bright blue beret. Rhiannon was surely over thirty—weren't there rules?

"Jackie's look is so dated it actually almost works," Lukas said. "But you? You need to change."

I mentally itemized my closet. Did I have anything remotely hip? "It'll take me at least a half hour to get home and back. Maybe more."

"You don't have that kind of time. We need to be at the bookstore an hour before Petra arrives. You're creative, Paige. Figure it out."

~

"I look ridiculous."

I stood inside Mykia's truck, wearing her ratty overalls, grubby tank top, and floral Doc Martens.

"How do you think I feel? I'm the one who looks like somebody's mother," she said.

"That is not a bad thing," I sniffed. Mykia looked good. The gray suit softened the hard lines of her body, and the coral shell complemented her dark skin. "You look better in my clothes than I do. That's not fair."

"Life's not fair," Mykia said. There was a catch to her voice, a sadness that I had to explore, whether she was open to it or not.

I lowered myself to the flat edge of her truck. Some people nearly passed her stall, struck by the oddness of her appearance, but then stopped when they noticed the scarlet tomatoes, deep green cucumbers, and glossy black eggplants. Mykia might've looked like she sold insurance, but her produce was anything but boring. She attended to them, working slowly, as if she wanted to eat up my available time.

"What is it you don't want to talk about?" I asked when the last customer walked away.

Mykia avoided my eyes. "Nothing. Let's talk about what you're going to say to that Petra person."

"Mykia . . ."

"Paige . . ."

This mother type knew how to work this one. I didn't say anything else, letting silence do its job.

"Oh, okay," she said after a moment. "I made an agreement with my father. I'm going back to dental school in the fall."

To a parent, news of a child returning back to school should elicit a thrill. I felt anything but. "What about the farm?"

She shrugged. "Maybe I can work it part-time."

"Aren't you the one who told me part-time and farming don't ever go together?"

When Mykia finally met my gaze, tears sparkled in her large brown eyes. "I am twenty-five years old, and I'm still being semisupported by my father. He will need to continue to do so if I keep doing what I'm doing."

"If he's okay with that, I don't see the problem."

"But *I* see the problem, Paige. All he's asking is that I be practical. I'm trying to do that. Going back to dental school assures my future."

"If there's anything I've learned, it's that our futures are *never* assured. You need to do what you love. You'll be miserable otherwise."

The side of her mouth quirked up. "That's pretty good advice. Has it worked with Trey?"

She had me there. I'd fought Trey's pursuit of photography with every tooth and every ragged nail. "Touché. But it doesn't mean I'm wrong. It might just mean I've been stubborn and obstinate."

She laughed. "With you, those aren't necessarily bad qualities."

"Will you at least give it a little more thought?" I said softly. "Please, Mykia."

"All right," she said.

"And anyway, who's going to go to a dentist with a missing tooth?"

"All part of my charm," she said with a smile. "People will love it."

~

I walked back into the office, bracing myself for a flurry of comments, but everyone was so nervous and distracted they barely noticed me.

Lukas offered a quick nod, which told me he approved. In T minus twenty minutes we were heading to Tomson's, the cute indie bookstore in the center of our town.

"Can I speak with you a minute, Paige?" Jackie lifted one heavily penciled eyebrow. *"In private?"*

I followed her into the hallway. She fidgeted, moving her phone from hand to hand, and picked at a stray hair caught in her lip gloss. "I need you to do something for me," she said. "Please."

"Of course."

"When you bring Petra to the office, I want you to steer her in my direction so I can make the first impression. You know I like Glynnis, but I think you understand how difficult it would be for me to find another job at my age." For the second time today, a woman teared up in my presence. "Please," she said. "I'm desperate for this to go well."

I wanted to tell her that I thought the chances of Petra Polly stepping foot in the offices of Guh were slim to none. I wanted to tell her that I thought one of the two of us was definitely going to be let go. But I couldn't. Her hope, frantic as it was, shimmered as brightly as her frosted lip gloss.

"I'll try," I promised. "I really will. But I won't purposefully block Glynnis. I hope you understand."

Jackie touched my shoulder. "I just need a chance. I'm really good at what I do."

"You don't need to tell me that. I know."

She pulled a smoke from her purse but didn't light it. "At this point in my career, I didn't think I'd still need to prove myself. Did you?"

"No," I admitted. "I thought by now I'd at least have my own office."

"With a window," Jackie added. "I thought I'd have a window."

"I never thought that was too much to ask."

Jackie lit her cigarette and took a long drag. "It wasn't. That's the sad part of it all. These kids want everything and want it now. Byron doesn't want one window, he wants a floor-to-ceiling panoramic view. Rhiannon doesn't just want her own office, she wants the whole floor."

"Do you think they'll get it?" I asked.

"Hell if I know," Jackie said. "The only thing I do know is *we* aren't."

CHAPTER 26

"Take a chance. The corporate body becomes invigorated by risk—adrenaline pumps, neurons fire, energy surges—the end result might not match the original plan, but the zeal with which the employees embrace the risk can add vibrancy to the entire organization. Find a way to make use of it."

—*Petra Polly*

Tomson's Bookshop in downtown Willow Falls was indie in all the right ways, the perfect venue for Ms. Petra Polly. Her photo—blonde, kitschy, vaguely Icelandic—hung prominently in the window, copies of *The Petra Polly Workbook for the New, New Creative Workplace* stacked precariously high underneath. If they intended for all of those books to sell, then we were not only in for a long wait in line, but we also had a lot of competition for her attention.

So far as I could see, we had arrived before anyone else. Employees meandered through the aisles, apparently not as excited as we were about Petra's pending arrival. Lukas, in contrast, was beside himself. He carefully readjusted the collar of his light blue button-down shirt, which was halfway untucked from his tattered black skinny jeans. He wore a black sport coat, also ripped strategically, and a scarf made from leather and some material I assumed came directly from Mars, as I'd never seen anything so metallic that wasn't a product of NASA. Just looking at him made me break into a sweat.

"We need to strategize," he murmured unnecessarily. "She'll be sitting right there."

He pointed to a rectangular table and forlorn-looking folding chair. One young bookseller slowly began to stack copies of Petra's book on the table. With a sigh, she aligned three Sharpie markers and a generic bottle of water.

Lukas kept glancing at the door, his nerves giving him a slight twitch. He fluffed his hair over his bald spot and checked his phone. "One half hour," he announced. "She'll be here in thirty minutes."

Byron smirked. "Thanks for the clarification."

"I'll speak to her first, as planned," Lukas said, ignoring him. "But then I'm not leaving. I'll browse until I see Paige lock her in."

My stomach flipped like a gymnast. Even though I had a difficult time taking Lukas seriously at times, he was counting on me. So were my coworkers. So was Big Frank, in a way. I didn't want to let anyone down.

So I wouldn't. Petra Polly was toast.

But she had to show up first. People began to filter into the bookstore, congregating in small groups, until it became difficult to maneuver in the aisles. Petra's Chicago-area fan base was representing.

Lukas came up beside me. "There is a possibility . . ."

"What?" Either his outfit or the crush of bodies was getting to him. Small beads of sweat dotted his upper lip and the small protuberance of his brow.

"I might lose my shit. I feel . . . very connected to Petra. In a way I've never felt with anyone."

This is getting way too weird, I thought, but then Lukas being vulnerable was such a rarity I let him keep talking.

"How do you convey that to someone?" he asked, clearly struggling. "When someone's voice is in your head for months, when her words dictate your thoughts and actions . . . it's very intimate, isn't it?"

"Maybe it's important to remember our purpose here," I said gently. "This might not be the right venue for spilling the contents of your heart."

"Of course not!" he said, retreating, as I'd hoped. "I was simply thinking out loud." He dabbed gently at his upper lip with one perfectly ironed cuff. "You really aren't a romantic person, are you, Paige?"

"Too practical. Those things are diametrically opposed."

"Your thinking is too limited." Lukas and I both started at the sound of Rhiannon's voice. How long had she been standing behind us? The outfit I'd thought looked ridiculous in the office fit perfectly with the indie spirit of the bookstore. Rhiannon managed to achieve an odd balance between *Girls* cast member and seasoned professional.

"Romance can serve a practical purpose," she continued. "You should use it, Lukas, if you think it would work. We should use anything we think will work."

"That seems cynical," I said.

Rhiannon smiled. "I thought you said you were a practical kind of person. Don't you want to get Petra into our offices?"

"It's time!" called a bookstore employee. She seemed irritated by the haphazard way the customers formed a line. People doubled up, cut, and wove in and out. Petra's fans were an eclectic bunch, everything from hipster to *Wolf of Wall Street*. The only thing they had in common was the inability to organize.

"We need to spring into action," Lukas murmured.

"Just push your way in," Rhiannon said. "That's what Byron did."

As if on cue, Byron waved from his spot in the middle of the line.

"He's quick," Lukas said, with admiration. "That's good. We need to get in there. Paige, get to the back of the line. Keep letting people in front of you so you lock in your position. Rhiannon, find a place ten or twelve people down from me."

I sauntered over to the end of the line, behind a madly texting woman and her college-age look-alike daughter, also madly texting. No one paid me the least bit of attention. I watched Lukas authoritatively march to the front. He stood in front of the small table until people made room for him. Surprisingly, he had that effect on people. Rhiannon slithered into the line somewhere between Lukas and Byron. I lost sight of her.

A few minutes to the hour and still no Petra. According to Tomson's Bookshop, there would be no speech, no reading, no Q&A, just Petra scrawling her John Hancock on the inside of the book cover. I'd only been to a few of these author things, but even I recognized this as unusual. No online interviews, no podcasts, no public speaking—what was Petra hiding? Her book had hit the *Times* list, with mentions in *Entertainment Weekly* and *Vanity Fair*. Petra qualified as big-time. Why wasn't she acting like it?

A few minutes after the hour. Petra's fans grew antsy. The girl next to me stopped texting and started swiping, probably on Tinder. "This isn't worth it," she muttered to her mother. "She isn't even going to talk."

"Who cares?" said the older woman. "The photo will look good on Instagram."

The younger one subtly rolled her eyes.

"There she is," someone shouted.

Petra Polly appeared, hair braided, multicolored knee socks matched to an expensive-looking robin's egg–blue silk dress, Buddy Holly glasses, and a messenger bag made out of what resembled aluminum foil—like a manic pixie dream girl for people who actually had jobs and should know better. A Tomson's employee guided her to the table and made an announcement about the rules: Petra would only sign copies of her book; she wouldn't pose for photos—at this the two in front of me sighed—and engaging Petra in conversation was a no-no, as there were too many of us. That didn't throw me. We'd have to work quickly in the time it took to write the inscription, but a lot could be said in thirty-second increments.

Petra smiled wanly and nodded at Lukas. It was difficult to gauge from my vantage point, but I thought I saw him swoon. After a moment, a couple of Tomson's employees glanced at each other and walked over to the table. I couldn't see Petra's response, but Lukas was gesticulating wildly. Another employee scurried over. He put a beefy hand on Lukas's shoulder and physically pulled my boss from the line. Lukas began to animatedly plead his case, but the guy's face went cold.

"Great," I muttered. "Just great."

Lukas was escorted out by the literary bouncer.

Even with Petra's lack of engagement, the line moved at a dinosaur's pace. Lukas was gone, hopefully helping Glynnis and Jackie back at the office. Rhiannon's and Byron's exchanges with the illustrious Petra happened way out of my earshot. I did know one thing—they didn't last very long.

I practiced the script in my head, wiped my sweaty palms against Mykia's overalls, and cupped my hand over my mouth to check my breath. The phone-obsessed mom and her daughter approached the table. Up close, Petra was tiny and delicate, with bright blue, inquisitive eyes. She smiled up at the duo but said nothing. She did take her time writing an inscription in each book. A good sign. The bookshop employees, bored and happy the line had reached its end, wandered to other parts of the store. A better sign. There wouldn't be anyone around to stop me.

"Thank you," Petra Polly said to the women in front of me. It was a modulated voice, the phrase coming out a little strange.

"Can we get a quick photo?" the mother said, already shoving her phone in my hand. "It'll only take a second."

"No," said Petra Polly. Very calmly. Very firmly.

"It'll just take a second," the daughter whined.

"No," Petra said.

Undaunted, the two women sandwiched Petra anyway. "Take it," the mother said to me. "Quickly."

Petra winced. No matter if she was a public figure, this was a violation. I tossed the phone in their general direction. "She said no. Have some respect."

"You're both bitches," the daughter said as they walked toward the exit.

Petra and I stared at each other. "Thank you," she finally said. The woman's face drooped with exhaustion. I felt sorry for her, and more than a bit maternal. I had a job to do, but the job could wait a minute or two. Petra needed some coffee and a jelly donut.

"Can I get you something?" I asked. "Coffee? There's a café next door."

Petra stood and stretched. She leaned over the table, and I had to bend my knees to make eye contact. "These people are fucking awful," she said, in the broadest, cockneyist Oliver Twist accent. "There's a guy earlier, right? My number one fan? Scared the fucking bejesus out of me." She gestured to the lethargic bookstore employees. "None of these twats'll save my ass if he's waiting outside, and I don't want to wait for a cab with creepers like him around. Have you got a car? I'm staying at some hellhole right outside of town. Can I get a lift?"

Sometimes, when in shock, the brain takes a while to catch up with the mouth. "Sure," I said after a beat. "I'll pull around the back."

CHAPTER 27

I had to remind Petra to use her seat belt. She frowned and clicked it with a huff, then immediately dug through her bag and pulled out a pack of cigarettes.

"You don't mind if I smoke, right? I'll blow it out the window. There won't be a trace."

She lit up before I could answer.

Petra sat in what my grandmother would call an "unladylike" fashion. She stuck one foot on the dash, like Trey often did, and hunched toward the passenger door.

"Where am I going?"

"Oh, I don't know," she said. "I don't feel like sitting in that hotel room, that's for sure. It's all beige. Everything—carpet, bed, furniture. It's like a doctor's waiting room for the NHS."

"So you really are from England . . ."

"Do ya think?"

I let that comment pass. I drove through town slowly, figuring I should let her finish smoking before I brought up stopping at Guh. Would they still be there? I regretted not texting Jackie when I got the car. Since I hadn't shown up yet, maybe they thought I was still convincing Petra? I had to try.

"So that man who was talking to you?"

She snorted. "There's one in every city. This one was going off about helping me advertise my business. What kind of idiot presents a business plan at an author signing?"

"He's my boss."

"Really?" She cackled. "Lucky you."

On impulse, I decided to go with honesty. "I was also on a mission to talk to you. I'm supposed to convince you to come back to our offices for a presentation of our services."

"That's weird."

"You got that right."

I cruised past the municipal building, McAllister's Café, and O'Malley's Pub.

"God, I just want to get soused," Petra said, her voice growing sad.

"We can stop at the bar if you want." *And I can text Jackie from the bathroom.* Maybe the crew could move all the posters to O'Malley's. We could wow Petra after she'd had a few American beers . . .

"I'm in recovery. Been to rehab twice. I'll always *want* to get soused, but I don't think I'll actually ever do it again. I'm fucking twenty-nine years old. Could be a long life, you know? That's just a pisser." She tossed the cigarette butt out the window, which made me wince.

"Your book made it to the *New York Times* bestseller list. That is an incredible accomplishment. You've managed to persevere."

"Fuck yeah," she said, ear-piercingly loud.

That was the response of the woman who wrote so eloquently about the emotional life of an idea? I glanced at her out of the corner of my eye. She held another cig in one hand while she chomped on the nails of the other.

"Where do you live?" she asked. "Are you close?"

"Not too far."

"Let's go to your house."

"I don't know if that's a good idea. Why not stop by our offices and see what we have to offer? It'll only take ten minutes."

She put one small hand on my arm, lightly, so as not to affect my driving. "What's your name?"

"Paige."

"Paige, I don't know how to say this without sounding mad, but Petra Polly doesn't really speak to people. I don't match my own image. People don't want to hear someone like me give advice. And it's fucking exhausting to be silent. For some reason I like you—you've got a face that tells me you've been through some shit. Let's go sit on your sofa and watch the telly."

"Okay," I said, against my better judgment.

~

"You did all this yourself? It's brilliant! Messy as all hell, but brilliant!"

Petra walked the haphazard rows of my garden. She couldn't see much under the light of the moon, but she touched everything, gently, reverently.

"You're growing a miracle here! You know that, right?"

Petra's hair had come out of its braid and stuck out in all directions. Her silk dress had rumpled, and she'd peeled off the knee socks the minute we got to my house. She seemed lighter. Happier.

"I guess it is a miracle I've managed to grow something," I said. "The tomatoes are almost ready. I feel like they're my children, in a way. Isn't that crazy?"

"Not if you cared for them." She looked at me cockeyedly. "Have you read my book? I gave human qualities to corporations! I'm not going to question your feelings for your tomatoes."

"Do you believe everything you wrote about?"

She shrugged. "Yeah. I think I do. I change my mind about things sometimes, but more often than not I stick to my crazy thoughts like mashed potatoes to a person's ribs. My mum always said I was a stubborn cow, and she's right."

"Are you close?"

"We were. She's passed on. Didn't know my dad."

"I'm sorry."

"For what?"

"For all of it."

"No need to be. I'm living a life, you know? If people went around apologizing for every bad thing that happened to everyone, we'd be bored out of our fucking skulls."

I thought about all of the people who said they were sorry when Jesse died. I knew they meant it, and I appreciated it, but I wondered if there was something else I would have rather heard. "What do you think people should say to someone who's just lost a loved one? I don't think there are many options."

Petra thought for a moment. "If you knew the person who died, I think you should share a memory, something you don't think they'd know about. The wilder the better."

"And if you didn't know the person who died?"

"Then you should ask for a good memory that best describes him or her. Let the grieving person have a moment with that person again."

"Couldn't that be too painful?" I asked.

"It's all painful. Listening to a hundred people apologize for something they had nothing to do with is excruciating, isn't it? They can't reverse anything with their apologies."

I wasn't sure I agreed with her, but it was a fresh perspective. Petra was rough around the edges, but she had wisdom I suspected was hard-won.

We walked back inside. I sat Petra in my living room while I put a tray together—lemonade, some zucchini bread I'd made myself, and the last of Mykia's blueberries. I could hear my phone blowing up in my purse, but I didn't text Jackie. I didn't check my texts. I just made my way back to my guest.

"So, forgive me if this seems rude," I said, not worrying about it all that much, "but how in the world did you decide to write a book about business? You seem so, I don't know . . . earthy."

"I really did write the damn thing, if you're thinking I cribbed it," Petra said, though she didn't seem offended. She settled into the soft cushions of my couch and scooped up some blueberries.

"Sorry if I implied that it wasn't yours," I said, trying to be sincere. The thought had crossed my mind that she'd at least gotten help. "I guess the better question is how did you come up with the idea?"

Her smile was sardonic. "Never finished university. My family needed me working, so I got a job fronting the office of the head of a public relations firm. I was busy, but not that busy. No one paid me much mind, so I could pay them all the mind I wanted. I watched as the company slowly went under. I saw all the fuckups and petty, avoidable disasters. I was bored out of my ever-loving mind, so I took notes. Eventually, I typed them up at the lunch hour.

"When things were really getting bad, my boss started showing the effects of the strain. He looked a mess. I got to thinking how the way the company fell apart was quite like how he was unraveling. That started the whole thing. I got up at five in the morning to work on the book every day. I've always been good with words on paper, so I knew it wasn't a total nightmare. When I was done, I shared it with a friend who knew some literary agents. One agreed to take me on before having met me. He'd already sold the book before he realized I was from Birmingham and talked like a Brummie."

"That seems a little archaic. Is it really such a big deal you don't speak the Queen's English?"

She shrugged. "It's all about branding. I'm this ethereal, spiritual presence, or something like that. Not someone who curses like a sailor and smokes two packs a day." She pointed a finger at me. "Don't lecture. I know it's unhealthy."

"I wouldn't lecture." At least I wouldn't now. "But I have to ask, you obviously want to expand your business and brand. How do you expect to do that without being a physical presence at things like trade shows and interviews?"

She drummed her fingers on the armrest, and I knew she was itching for a smoke. "I dunno. I've been working on some sort of solution, but nothing's come yet."

My mind reeled. "We could help you rebrand yourself," I said, wondering if I actually believed it. "You could be the voice of common sense. And in America, we're fascinated by British accents but not all that interested in your class system. So if you can ditch the f-bombs, you'll be in good shape."

"That's a habit even my mother couldn't break." Petra smiled. "Is this what your company does?"

"We're a boutique advertising firm, but we like to help our clients establish an overall presence. If you'd come with me to the office tonight, we could have shown you. Of course, the work we did was fairly generic, as it was completed before we got to know your lovely personality."

Petra snorted.

"But it's solid work."

She nodded. "I don't want to go back to that empty hotel and stare at the minibar all night. Tell ya what, if you let me sleep on this comfy couch here, I'll stop by your office in the morning."

Everything inside me jumped for joy. Everything outside remained calm. "That sounds like a deal."

"But now I need a fucking smoke. Is it okay if I go out back?"

"Only if you stand at the fence and exhale toward my neighbor's house."

She smiled. "He a wanker?"

"That is an incredibly apt description."

She stood up and held out her hand. "Come with me. Let's go stand in your garden for a while. Maybe all that Zen will curb my need for nicotine."

I decided at that moment that I liked Petra Polly, very much.

We made it to the sliding glass door before I noticed the figure in the garden. I flicked on the porch light and saw him, hunched over the tomato plants. The plants, the ones I so lovingly, painstakingly cared for, lay on the ground in tangled heaps. They'd been yanked violently from the ground, roots exposed and pathetically reaching in the wrong direction. The crimson tomatoes, some crushed, others split, but all . . . ruined.

Petra screamed.

Trey shuddered.

"What have you done?" My voice shook with the energy required to keep control of my anger. "Trey!"

He turned to me, face stained with tears. "I'm so sorry, Mom. So sorry. I didn't mean it. I didn't mean any of it."

The vision of him crouched over the dead plants tugged fiercely at my heart but, unlike the plants, not enough to rip it from the roots. I heard the sorrow in his voice. It was enough to bring me back, and I took in the scene more carefully. Trey wasn't pulling the last plant out—he was trying to pack the ground around it.

He was trying to save it.

"You just wanted one thing," he sobbed. "That's it. You deserved for this to work out. I'm sorry, Mom. I'm so, so sorry. I gave you a hard time about it because you found something you loved. I thought you didn't need me anymore."

I knelt beside him and wrapped my arms around his substantial shoulders. "You are everything I ever wanted. I need you more than I need air. Don't ever forget that."

We both lost ourselves to tears, until I heard Petra say, "Well, that fucking plant is going to live if I've got anything to do with it. Let your mom baby it a bit. Come on, get a bucket for these tomatoes, and let's see what we can salvage."

"Who the fuck is she?" Trey said.

"Language," I said automatically.

"I'm fucking Tinker Bell," Petra said. "Stop crying. When life gives you tomatoes, you make tomato sauce."

Trey stared at Petra for a moment before silently leaving in search of a bucket. Before he walked away, he squeezed my shoulder, a loving gesture that brought a surge of emotion.

"Why are you crying?"

A male voice.

Mr. Eckhardt leaned over the fence, taking in the mayhem that was once my lovely garden. "Well," he said. "Well."

The anger rose swiftly and mercilessly. I launched myself at him. "You! You did this! Do you hate me so much? Do you hate seeing people happy?"

"But you're not happy," he said.

"How would you know?" I spat. "How the hell would you know?"

"Is this the wanker?" Petra asked.

"Yes," I said. "This is exactly the wanker."

"You think I did this," Mr. Eckhardt said dully. He squinted at the destroyed tomato plants, eerily lit by the porch light. "Why would I do a thing like that?"

"Are you kidding me?" I screeched. "You'd uproot this whole garden if you could!"

Mr. Eckhardt calmly walked around the fence to my side. "Does your water line have a filter?"

I nodded.

He turned to Petra. "You. Get a pitcher of room-temperature water and a glass."

"Excuse me?" Petra said. "Are you fucking ordering me around?"

"Yes," Mr. Eckhardt said. "I am. If you want this plant to have a chance, you'll do it."

With a frown, Petra retreated to the kitchen.

Mr. Eckhardt knelt in the dirt, gently patting the earth surrounding the remaining plant. "If the main stem wasn't injured, this one should be fine. We'll give it a careful watering so as not to disturb it further."

I joined him on the ground. "Why are you being nice? Do you feel guilty? Did you psychotically rip these from the ground in a fit of rage? Remember, I found your wife's dress buried in this backyard. Did you bury other dresses in this backyard? Are you looking to dig up all the evidence?"

Mr. Eckhardt stiffened beside me. "You're embarrassing yourself. I'm just trying to help."

"We don't need your help," Trey said. He carried a large blue bucket that had seen better days. "This is what I could find, Mom."

"Let's gather as many intact tomatoes as we can see," I said, fighting the urge to lie down and sob until my tears soaked the ground. "I think you should leave, Mr. Eckhardt."

Petra returned, and Mr. Eckhardt reached for the water. He poured some into a glass and slowly fed it to the survivor. "You need to do this again in the morning. I can manage it if you don't have the time."

"I think I can water one plant. I've been watering twenty-five all summer."

He sat back on his heels. Trey watched him, still holding the bucket in one hand, the other curled into a fist.

I nudged Mr. Eckhardt with my elbow. "I think you should go. It would be best."

"I don't . . ." He paused. Whatever he had to say took great effort. He glanced at Trey's angry face and Petra's puzzled one, and then finally locked eyes with me. "I don't want to go. I'll help you pick up the tomatoes. I'd really like to do that. Or I can work on making a nice tomato sauce. I cook for myself all the time."

In the strangely bright porch light, the deeply etched lines in Mr. Eckhardt's skin mapped his face like rivers leading to the tributaries at the corners of his tired, sad eyes. What had this man been through? There was a story, and part of me wanted to hear it.

"Tell you what," Petra said. "Young Ponyboy here will help me pick up the tomatoes. Paige, why don't you and the wanker go into the kitchen and prep it for some major cooking. Have you got some dried pasta?"

I nodded.

"Then pasta with tomato sauce it is."

Mr. Eckhardt had only stepped foot in my house once before, yet he got up and walked in like it was his own. I followed the man into my own kitchen.

CHAPTER 28

"Are you going to tell me the story?" I asked as Mr. Eckhardt and I worked companionably to prep the meal. He definitely wasn't new to cooking, and we achieved a natural split in duties as Petra and Trey alternately ran in with bucketfuls of tomatoes. Some were salvageable, some weren't, but we'd do what we could.

"We're going to be eating at midnight," he said in response. "I'm usually asleep at that hour."

"Oh, live dangerously," I joked.

"I have done that," he said. "It didn't work out very well for me."

"If you're going to make tomato sauce with me in my kitchen, then you're going to need to spill some secrets. Why did you bury your wife's dress?"

"It was her wedding dress," he said while deseeding a Roma tomato. "Those earrings you're wearing were my bridal gift to her."

I guiltily fingered my earlobes. "I . . . I didn't know."

"It doesn't matter. She's not coming back for them."

Because she lives in New Mexico, I wanted to say. But then I didn't want him to know my stalker proclivities, or Sean's for that matter.

"What happened between you two?"

Mr. Eckhardt didn't answer, but his military-straight shoulders drooped ever so slightly, and his hand stopped working the knife.

I had never, in the ten years we'd lived beside him, touched Mr. Eckhardt. I decided it was time for that to change. I carefully placed my hand on his upper arm. "It's okay if you don't want to talk about it. It really isn't any of my business anyway. I promise not to be judgmental if you do want to talk, though."

"You are a very judgmental person, Paige. Don't try to be otherwise. It's who you are."

"I am not," I said, incensed. Was I? I thought about judgy Charlene. Was I like that?

"Maybe not outwardly," he said, "but you judged my behavior."

"Your behavior was begging to be judged. The pope would have a difficult time not judging your behavior. Would it have cost you much to smile sometimes? To say hello? To invite us over for a burger? We lived next to you for ten years. Why were you so resistant to making any kind of a connection?"

He resumed chopping the onions, a slight smile on his face. "My wife lived in this house," he said quietly. "And I lived next door while she did. It was the only way we could manage to stay together, to be separated. Then that wasn't enough, and she took off in the middle of the night. This was before Google. I didn't know where she went."

Wait . . . what? "Your wife lived here? And you lived right next door?"

"We were two people who didn't know how to live closely with another, so we came up with a solution. It worked until she wanted to move back in with me. I refused."

"Why?" I asked, flabbergasted. I couldn't imagine spending my married life without Jesse in my bed.

"Because I was certain it wouldn't work."

"Oh. Again, *why?*"

He shrugged. "It sounds impossible, but we fought over everything and still loved each other. If I said the day was cloudy, she'd say it was sunny. If I wanted to paint the living room beige, she wanted blue. I wanted children, and . . ."

"She didn't."

"No. Our differences were nearly irreconcilable. I loved her madly, though, and I was certain she loved me with the same fervor. My heart shattered when she moved away.

"She left her wedding dress and those earrings behind, and the rest of this house empty as the day we bought it. I was so furious I put her things in that metal box and buried it in the backyard. There wasn't a fence then. She called once, about fifteen years ago, and wondered if we could get together to talk. I told her about the buried wedding dress and set my condition—if she could figure out where it was, I would talk to her. She hung up on me."

"I would have, too. You're kind of a jerk, Bill." I'd never called Mr. Eckhardt by his first name either. He rolled with it.

"She hurt me. I lost her and learned to live a good life even with the pain. That's what strong people do."

I thought for a moment. "Is that why you got so mad about the garden? You thought I wasn't being strong?"

"In a way, yes."

"With all due respect, *Bill*, even though I'm still not sure if you deserve any, I don't think you've lived a good life without her. Definitely not as a strong person."

"I disagree," he said.

"You've been a miserable neighbor. Rude. Haughty. You've never once invited us over, even though we extended invitations until we got tired of hearing you say no. You didn't even offer an excuse. I see those biddies from the village coming by to discuss whatever evil amendments you're making to village bylaws, but other than that? No one walks up to your door unless he's delivering the mail. Shutting down is not strong. I tried it, and it doesn't work. Jesse's dead. Acting like I am, too, isn't going to bring him back."

"That's the wisdom you're offering me?" he said angrily.

"It is." Like Petra's, my wisdom was hard-won, but I didn't know how to explain that to Bill. His misery was hard-won, too.

He tossed the onions into the oiled pan with more violence than the vegetable deserved.

"You know I'm right," I said. "It takes a *strong* man to admit it."

"My wife had a garden," he said. "It was smaller than yours. Neater. *She* knew what she was doing."

"I'm learning. I've realized that's what I should be doing at this stage in my life."

"And what should I be doing at my stage?"

I paused and took in this hardheaded, heartbroken man. "You should start healing. It's not too late."

He didn't fight me on that one but said nothing, losing himself to cooking once again. We made the sauce together and let it bubble. I found a couple of boxes of spaghetti in the pantry, and he wordlessly filled the pot with water and salted it. Petra and Trey stopped bringing tomatoes in at some point but didn't come back inside. I could see their figures standing in the garden, talking.

"The rest of the tomatoes are ruined," Bill said. He set the pot to boil and sat down heavily in a kitchen chair. "Who would do such a thing?"

Yes, who? I'd been so distracted by the events of the evening that I hadn't been able to analyze the situation. With Trey and Bill off the suspect list, who else would commit such an act of violence?

"I don't know," I said.

"As much as I dislike you personally, I'm getting a sense that I'm in the minority. You don't have any enemies, do you?"

"I didn't think so."

"So you really have no idea?"

"I'm sure I'll figure it out."

I wasn't quite sure I'd actually ever heard someone harrumph, but the sound Bill Eckhardt made was pretty close to what I'd imagined.

I joined him at the table. The kitchen resembled a crime scene, a description that made me think of Sean. I'd call him in the morning to get his take on things. There weren't enough tomatoes left to make canning worth our while, I sadly realized. I'd make some more pasta sauce and give jars to Mykia, Jackie, and Glynnis. It was something I could do.

"I still suspect you don't know what you're talking about," Bill said, "but do you really think a man my age can heal an old wound?"

"I don't think it's all that old. Sounds pretty fresh to me."

"Maybe."

I tried to be respectful when I asked, "Why did you give your wife such a hard time when she called? Why didn't you welcome her back? Was it all anger? Revenge? Something else?"

"I couldn't let her come back into my life, so I gave her that impossible task."

"Why couldn't you let her back? Oh, Bill. Was it your ego? Were you too proud?"

"No, nothing like that. I just knew, with certainty, that she didn't love me. She never did. You can feel love in a touch, can you not? A look. A way of caring for someone. I saw it every day with you and Jesse. Noreen didn't communicate love with any of these things, and she didn't find any other ways, that's for sure. I'm sure she had good reasons for wanting to live as a married couple again, but they didn't have anything to do with love."

I opened my mouth to contradict him, but I could tell this was his truth. Whether she'd ever loved him or not was irrelevant. He didn't *feel* loved.

Bill's blue eyes, which I suddenly realized were a deep, clear shade of cornflower, filled with tears. "It's not easy for me to admit this, but I don't know how to heal. I haven't the first clue."

I had at least one clue. "Go get the dress."

"Pardon me?"

"Go home and get the wedding dress. I have an idea."

He did what I asked without any more questions. By the time he got back, I had the bubble envelope waiting on the kitchen table. On it, I wrote *Noreen Eckhardt*. "Do you know her address in Santa Fe?"

"How do you know she lives in Santa Fe?" His brow furrowed, but there was humor in his voice.

"I thought you might be a serial killer. I had to look out for myself."

"With the help of a certain Willow Falls police officer, I presume."

"We'll discuss that later. Give me the dress." I carefully folded it into the envelope. I put the earrings in a baggie and dropped them in as well. "Do you want to write a note?"

He took the pen and paper I offered, thought for a moment, and then wrote, *We no longer have any ties, so I am no longer bound.*

"Wow. You're kind of a poet." I watched as he sealed the envelope.

"I will write my own future," he said, a grin taking up most of the real estate on his narrow face. "So being good with words might be beneficial."

"I can't believe I'm saying this, but I might actually like you, Bill Eckhardt."

"And it completely shocks me to say that I might almost tolerate you, Paige Moresco."

"Well, if that's true, will you call off the village dogs? I've got a citation with my name on it."

"Seems to me that citation somehow ended up on my lawn, in pieces."

"I might have found my temper."

He blushed. Mr. Eckhardt blushed! "It wasn't real," he admitted. "I stole the form from the village hall. The terrible twosome was breathing down my neck. I had to do something."

"Well, I won't tell. You didn't press charges for my thievery, so I'll conveniently forget you stole government property."

"I think that's fair," he said.

"Oh, nothing's fair, Bill, but sometimes things work out all right."

~

We ate with gusto. The dinner wasn't the somber affair it should have been, given the circumstances. Bill Eckhardt, to Trey's and my great shock, had a sense of humor and regaled Petra with stories of visiting London in the swinging '60s. The tomato sauce was rich and savory, and we all had second helpings. I made up the couch for Petra before she slipped into a food coma, and then I kissed Trey before he trudged up to his room.

"You grew some good tomatoes, Mom," he whispered before kissing my cheek. "You did it, even if it didn't work out like you thought it would."

"I allowed myself to take a risk," I said. "I've been thinking maybe I should allow you to do the same. Let's carve out some time to discuss colleges that have good fine arts programs."

Trey's mouth opened in shock. "Really?"

"Really. I mean, I still want you to go to a good school and keep your mind open to all the opportunities that will come your way. But I don't think I should discount your passion." I pulled him into a hug. "You're a good kid, Trey. I'm so happy to be your mom."

Trey held me just as tightly. "I don't always show it, but I'm happy, too, Mom."

CHAPTER 29

I'd texted both Lukas and Jackie before going to bed the night before, so the employees of Guh were not surprised to get a visit from Petra Polly, but they were absolutely shocked by the woman who walked into the office.

"Fuck, this place looks like IKEA vomited a metric ton of plastic. I can smoke in here, right?" she asked, first thing. "There's nothing to soak up the smell. It's all impermeable. Haven't you ever heard of non-synthetic furniture?"

Lukas smiled tightly. "Of course."

Jackie's mouth fell open. "What? *She gets to smoke in here?*"

"Go ahead and have a smoke, if it sets yourself right," Petra said. "I've got spares if you need one."

"Maybe later," Jackie mumbled when she caught Lukas's stricken expression.

The room went silent as she lit up and took a nice, long drag. "Well, are you gonna show me something or what?"

I was hardly an Instagram-loving, "let's document everything" type of person, but at that moment I would have given a body part to have a photograph of the reaction to Petra-in-person. Byron smirked.

Rhiannon seemed impressed. Glynnis, her cheeks blotchy with embarrassment, wouldn't make eye contact with anyone. Lukas, stunned that his idol stood only feet away, swayed on his feet. Jackie gazed longingly at the cigarette dangling from Petra's lipsticked mouth. The blue-red color bled into the lines bracketing her mouth, the wrinkles common to chain-smokers everywhere. I'd suggested a softer color, but she'd found the bright lipstick in my makeup drawer and declared it "dishy." It was the only thing she'd agreed to borrow from me. She wanted to look like her real self, she'd said, adding, "It's important I establish the right message. If you think I'm good to go just the way I am, then I want them all to see me the way I am in the day-to-day, you know?"

"Which is?" I'd asked.

"I'm a right hot mess."

After getting over their initial shock, the employees of Guh scurried around the conference room in a tizzy, frantically getting their act together. They presented the mock-ups in a perfectly professional manner and discussed our well-planned, if generic, strategy for putting her ahead of the pack of millennial self-help experts. They offered ideas for a website redesign and talked product placement.

Petra blew smoke in perfect rings, her face a stony, expressionless mask.

"We believe you're special," Lukas said passionately. "No one else can touch your wisdom and wit. Your beauty and class—"

"Stop right there," Petra said. "There's a problem."

"Whatever it is, we'll fix it," Lukas insisted.

Petra lit a new cigarette with the dying remains of another. "That's the thing. It can't be fixed."

"Could you be a little more specific?" Byron asked, earning a withering side-eye from Lukas.

Petra gestured to her heavily creased, tomato-stained silk dress, her tattered stockings, and her horrific bedhead. "What you see here," she began, her accent hitting us all like a sledgehammer, "is the real me, in fucking person. How the hell am I supposed to talk to people and get them to listen? Those pictures look nice, but if I'm taking this business to the next level, I need to be a fucking spokesperson. You get that? Me. A spokesperson."

Lukas nodded like a bobblehead. "I understand what you're saying." He didn't continue, which meant he couldn't. He had no idea how to handle the situation. Wild-eyed, he said, "Could you give us a few minutes, Ms. Polly? There's a lovely farmers' market in the parking lot. Paige, would you mind taking our guest to get some fresh coffee? It's on us, of course."

"It sure as fuck better be," Petra said, but she winked at him to lessen the harshness of her comment. "Get your ideas together. We'll be back in the shake of a lamb's tail."

~

Mykia's laugh could probably be heard on a distant planet.

"*You're* Petra Polly? I thought you were supposed to be some uptight hipster bitch!"

Petra laughed. "I am a hipster bitch, bitch." She leaped up on the back of Mykia's truck and plopped herself down at the edge. "I'm not uptight, though. Not in the fucking least."

"I thought we were curbing the f-bombs," I pleaded. "At least try."

Petra shrugged. "Okay. How about every time I curse, I give you a fiver. You'll have enough money to repair your garden in no time."

Mykia grew serious in a flash. "What is she talking about? What needs to be repaired?"

With a sigh, I pulled my phone from my purse. While Petra got ready, I'd documented the damage. I'd practically had to shove my phone in a bag of rice it was so soaked with my tears. "This happened sometime last night. I don't know who did it."

"That creepy neighbor," Mykia said, incensed. "I will rip every tooth out of his skull."

"She's violent," Petra said with more admiration than was proper. "I like her."

"It's not him." I paused. "It isn't Trey either."

Mykia's face softened. "Did you think it was him?"

"For a few seconds, yes."

Mykia hugged me fiercely. "Oh, Paige. I don't know what to say. You worked so hard."

Maybe I'd become efficient at grieving, because while what Mykia was saying struck me as undeniably sad, it didn't throw me over the edge. Caring for those tomatoes gave me great pleasure. Cultivating them sustained my soul over the summer, but when Bill Eckhardt and I managed to make such a delicious sauce with them, I felt like I'd honored their life cycle, as hippie earth mama as that sounds. They were ripped from the soil prematurely, but their life cycle was complete. Applying this to Jesse wasn't beyond me. I'd mourn him every day until I drew my last breath, but I had to stop obsessing over the unfairness that he was taken and focus on the wonders he'd given us. He'd spent his life sustaining me, but now I had to let him rest.

"I'm okay," I said into Mykia's shoulder. "Really, I am."

"I know," she murmured back. "That fact was never in question."

~

"Whatcha got for me?"

Petra and I rejoined the group after hanging out with Mykia for an hour. It was work to get Petra back inside, but once in the conference room, she took her place at the head of the table. By the way Lukas and the others were smiling, I knew they had something. Whether it was any good or not was yet to be seen.

Lukas stood.

And then he knelt. Right next to Petra, as if asking for her hand in marriage. By the horrified look on her face, I could tell that was exactly what she was thinking.

He placed his palm on her chair and curled his fingers over her armrest. Much too close for comfort.

Jackie and I both squirmed, trying to hold in our laughter. Glynnis's eyes were close to popping out of her head. Byron's mouth curled in disgust, and Rhiannon's eyes sparkled with anticipation.

"Ms. Polly," Lukas began. "Petra. Your words have meant more to me—to us—than I can ever successfully express. You've guided our organizational philosophy. You've offered us hope when it was in short supply. You've been my North Star, my guru, my teacher. You've helped me turn Guh into the powerhouse it is today—"

At this, Jackie coughed to mask her hysterics.

"We love you as you are," Lukas continued. "And if we do, America will love you, too. Our ad campaigns will focus not only on what you can offer corporate America, but your sense of style, your infectious joie de vivre, your ability to relate to the everyman . . . or woman. We will turn what you see as a detriment into an asset. I promise you that."

Lukas's eyes shone with emotion. Up until that point, his passion had given me a fit of giggles, but watching him bare his hipstery soul to Petra, well, I saw shades of Big Frank in his presentation. I started a slow clap, and everyone joined in. Lukas blushed. "I meant every word," he told Petra.

She was more difficult to read. After the applause died down, she tapped Lukas's shoulder. "You can stand up now. I'm not the fucking Queen."

"Of course," Lukas said, practically bowing in response.

She was going to make us wait. Petra drew yet another cigarette from her purse and slowly lit it. She inhaled deeply and blew the smoke into the air. We watched, mesmerized. Petra had a presence. *We could figure out how to use it effectively,* I thought. We could do that for her. She held one hand up. We held our collective breath.

"I'm going to give you people a chance," Petra said, and flashed me a quick smile. "But I want to make sure of something. I want a full team behind me." She addressed Lukas. "Can you guarantee that everyone in this room will be working in some capacity on Team Petra?"

Oh, you dear girl, I thought. On the way over, I'd revealed the competition and my worries about one of us being let go. Petra Polly was one smart—and kind—cookie.

Lukas cleared his throat. "Of course. Guh is a family. Every person in here is important to that dynamic."

"Would you be willing to put that into the contract?" She batted her eyelashes coquettishly.

Lukas nearly fell over. "Of course. That won't be the least bit of a problem."

"Well, then I guess we have a deal," Petra said, and stuck out her small hand. Lukas smiled dreamily while he shook it.

"We have," he said. "And you won't regret it."

"I know I won't," she said. "But you might."

~

Lukas insisted on bringing Petra back to her hotel himself. I hugged her goodbye and promised to call her regularly about non-work-related things.

"You fucking better," she whispered in my ear. "And you better keep boss man on a leash for me. I think he'd shine my shoes with his tongue if I asked."

"Ew. That's an image I'll have to scrub from my brain."

She laughed, hopped into Lukas's BMW, and immediately lit up. He didn't tell her no.

The tents were coming down as I made my way through the office parking lot. Big, voluminous white tents puffed up into the summer sky before collapsing in on themselves. I spotted Jackie helping Mykia fold hers into the back of the truck. A hint of fall hit my nose, and I noticed some vendors already hawking early apples and cider.

As I approached, I saw Glynnis sitting on the edge of the truck bed, where Petra had sat only hours before. The contrast between the women couldn't have been more clear—Petra, brash and Technicolor, had stuck out like a fuchsia rose against the white-painted metal, whereas pale Glynnis became lost in it.

Mykia's mouth was grim. "Glynnis needs to talk to you."

"About what?" But something inside me clicked, and I knew.

I motioned for her to come to me. She did, slowly, fearfully. Her eyes were puffy and swollen.

"You'll keep your job," I said. "Aren't you happy?"

"I didn't think I would," she said miserably. Her eyes skipped from Mykia to an equally solemn-faced Jackie and then back to me. "I was angry at you, Paige. I thought you'd abandoned us . . . abandoned me."

"What are you telling me, Glynnis?"

Her face scrunched up into a red ball. "I came over to your house last night. I saw the lights were on in your house. You never came back to the office! Lukas was so mad—he was going on about how he was going to fire half the staff!"

"So you pulled up my tomatoes." It wasn't a question.

"Yes," she sobbed. "I'm so, so sorry."

I wanted to strangle her. I wanted to pull every fine strawberry-blonde hair from her head. But I wasn't like Mykia. I could replace my rage with pity. Glynnis let her anger get in the way of her respect for me, and for the life in the garden. I walked away from her, to the small patch of grass where we ate lunch sometimes. She followed, a sobbing, hiccuping puppy, full of remorse but not understanding.

"Are you mad?" she asked.

I used the best tool a mother had. "I'm disappointed in you, Glynnis. Sorely and devastatingly disappointed."

Her shoulders fell, and she continued to cry softly. I let her suffer for a while.

"I'll make it up to you," she said after catching her breath. "I promise."

"Do you think that's something that can be made up? It's a pretty dramatic imbalance, isn't it?"

She nodded fiercely, all agreeableness.

"How do you make something right that can't be fixed?"

"I don't know. I guess you can't," Glynnis said, renewing her sobs.

I scooted over and put my arm around her thin shoulders. "I can't replace those tomato plants, but I still have plenty of herbs and vegetables in the garden. You can't work with what's gone, but you can work with what's left. And you will. Every day after work until the end of the season."

"Okay," she said, breathless and grateful. "I can do that."

I gave her a side-hug. "So can I."

CHAPTER 30

Petra Polly Epilogue: A Note on Success

Some say success, like love, comes when you least expect it. I don't believe this to be true. If one works hard, both singly and in tandem with others, success is always a presence. It's like the sun on an overcast summer's day—you may not be able to see it, but you will be drawn to its warmth. When it envelops the body, true change occurs. Success gives one a solid base from which to grow, and just as the individual mind requires continued growth in learning to stay healthy into old age, so does the collective. The most simple definition is this: success is increased opportunity. So explore. Take educated risks. Stride confidently into the unknown. But . . . make choices with the long-term health of your organization in mind. Keep a steady pace, and adhere to a stable, ethical framework. There are a few certainties about the business world. Competition will always increase. The future keeps changing. The bar keeps being reset, higher and higher. A company that follows the Petra Principles won't have to rise to meet these goals, because it will already be there, wondering what to conquer next.

> *Best of luck,*
> *Petra Polly*

It seemed like a good idea when I called Sean and talked it over with him, but now, as we stood in the empty parking lot of an abandoned distribution center, I wasn't so sure.

"I require payment for this service," he said. "Did you bring it?"

I handed him a paper bag containing one perfect tomato, still warm from the plant. The lone survivor had thrived, bearing fruit bigger than my fist. I'd already eaten one with Trey, sliced and salted and better than the steak it was named for, and it was perfect. I gave another to Mykia, one to Jackie, and one to Mr. Eckhardt just this morning.

Sean gazed into the bag and smiled, and then glanced up at Trey. "Is he going to get out of your car? It sure doesn't look like it."

Trey sat in the passenger seat of my SUV, feet up on the dash.

I waved at my son, and he ignored me. "Let me go talk to him."

I slid into my car and immediately popped the earbuds from Trey's ears. "Well?"

"I don't know," he said. "I just don't know. Doesn't Sean have to be at work?"

"Not for an hour."

"Can't he get into trouble for this?"

"He's willing to take the risk, but just this once. He trusts you."

"Why?"

"Because he knows you're afraid, so he also knows you'll be careful."

"I'm not sure I follow his logic," Trey said with a sigh. "Maybe we should just go home."

I pointed at Sean's squad car. "Police cars are very durable. They're a thousand pounds heavier than a civilian car, and they have stronger brakes. They're built to sustain a lot of impact and keep the driver safe."

When Trey spoke, I could hear the tears in his voice. "Could it sustain crashing into a median?"

I placed my palm on the back of his head, like I did when he was little and needed comforting. "There aren't any medians here, my sweet boy. It's all open space, perfect for practicing. There are a few telephone poles, and a dumpster or two, but those are easy to avoid because you'll be driving slowly and in total control."

"Dad always had control. It was one time he didn't. One time, Mom. And he died because of it."

I took a breath. "Okay," I began. "You could die behind the wheel of a car. I'm not going to lie and tell you the thought of that won't keep me up some nights, staring at the ceiling, imagining all kinds of horrible scenarios. But the more likely scenario is you drive yourself to school, to Colin's house, to your favorite Thai restaurant, to anywhere you want to go. You might have a fender bender or scrape the paint off trying to get into a tight parking space, but the likelihood of something truly catastrophic happening is slim."

"But it could happen."

"It could."

"And you're okay with that."

I mussed his hair. "I'll never be okay with it. But that doesn't mean I should stop living my life, or you should stop living yours."

He spent a long moment staring at the squad car. I was asking a lot of Sean, but we both agreed that this was an important milestone for Trey, and maybe for me, too. I wondered if I should say more to tip the balance, but then Trey unclicked his seat belt and hopped out of the car. I quickly followed.

"I'm going to do it," Trey said to Sean. "But only if you and my mom will be in the car with me."

"I have to be," Sean said. "This solution has its legal limits. Paige?"

"Of course. But can I be a back-seat driver through the glass partition?"

Sean laughed. "Just knock once for slow down, and twice for speed up."

"What if he needs to brake?"

"Scream?"

I glanced at Trey, fearing our banter would increase his nerves, but he laughed. It was a shaky one, but definitely sincere.

Sean helped him adjust to the unique position of being the driver of an official police vehicle. After giving Trey a lecture about not touching anything that wasn't absolutely essential, he opened the door for me, and I slid into the back seat, wishing I had some antibacterial wipes as I wondered who'd last sat there. I tried not to touch anything, straining to resist the urge to wipe away the smudges on the glass partition.

I felt, rather than heard, the engine roar to life. I wished I could see Trey's face, that I could hear what he said to Sean before cranking it into gear. The car moved slowly forward, then climbed to a comfortable speed.

We approached the first telephone pole. Sean said something to Trey, and he turned the wheel, avoiding the pole by driving in a slightly jerky half circle. Then he righted the wheel, and the car picked up speed again, this time more smoothly.

"Good job, Trey," I whispered, fighting tears. He was doing it. Driving. Without any help from me. It should have been a bittersweet moment, but it wasn't, just triumphant. This was yet another step toward healing, and those were nothing less than magical.

We reached the end of the parking lot. Trey came to a jerky halt at a stop sign. If he didn't back up, he'd have to turn onto the main road. I rapped on the glass partition. Trey turned for just a second and flashed me a smile.

Then he took his foot off the brake and drove us into the future.

ACKNOWLEDGMENTS

On a sunny morning in May 2016, Tom, my husband of nearly two decades, left to play a round of golf. The next time I saw him was in the hospital, but he was already gone. Sudden heart attack. He was forty-five years old.

I'd finished a third of *Digging In* when Tom died. For months afterward, paralyzed by grief, I couldn't write a word. Jodi Warshaw, my patient editor at Lake Union, and Patricia Nelson, my agent at Marsal Lyon, kindly supported me through this difficult time. I will always be grateful. When I finally finished the book, Jenna Free, my developmental editor, expertly pushed me to bring the story where it needed to be. Thanks, Jenna.

Paige's experience with loss in *Digging In* is completely different from mine. She didn't have the welcoming arms of a community to fall into, but I did. Parts of her story arose from the question I constantly asked myself—how would I have managed the loss of my husband without the incredible people I'm so lucky to have in my life? My family, both biological and in-law, set aside their own grief to lift me up. My friends fed me and my two sons for six months, using something entirely lovely called a "meal train" (fantastic meals would magically appear on my doorstep, often including chocolate and wine!). Friends, family, and, occasionally, total strangers dropped off cards, some containing a handwritten memory of Tom, some containing money for my sons' education fund, others just saying, "I'm sorry." A simple "thank-you" doesn't seem sufficient to cover my gratitude, but that's all I have. So thanks to every one of you. Your outpouring of love gave me the strength to get back to writing. This book is for you.

I wish I could thank everyone by name, but if I did, these acknowledgments would run longer than the novel. Still, I'd like to mention a few folks in particular.

To all my La Grange Park friends and neighbors, your kindness is unparalleled. You are the true definition of "community," especially Scott and Robin Reimer, Bill and Libby Black, Rachel Reid, Paul and Renee Brizz, Dan and Jen Stirrat, Matt Chadesh, Matt and Carolyn Beumer, Mike and Lisa O'Malley, Steve and Suzie Tullis, Tiffin and Mike Bolger, Chrissy and Jay Cmelo, Kelly and Rich Vaicuilis, Karyn and Matt Denten, Maureen Houston, Jeff and Colleen Olsen, Maura and Mike Webster, Kara and Padraig Brophy, Ashley and Brian Long, Phil and Anna D'Amico, Jim and Megan McCarthy, Donna and Brad Dodge, the ladies of Baby's Got Paperback, and countless others from the LGP.

To Jenny Kales, I think you baked me forty-eight dozen cookies over a twelve-month period. Not one went to waste! Thank you, my friend.

To Erica O'Rourke, thank you for listening and never judging, for advising but never dictating.

To Zen and the gang at The HIT Locker in La Grange, thank you for balancing out my crazy grief brain by encouraging me to keep my body strong and healthy and giving me the tools to do so. Special thanks to Rachel, my yoga guru at Real Yoga, who taught me to find peace within myself. And to those who practice with me—Carry, Amy, Carolyn, and many others—thank you for your positive energy!

To the old neighborhood crew—John and Alexa Frangos, Tim and Erin Powell, John and Teri Nosek, Mike and Michelle Callero, and Joe and Lori Gillespie—to paraphrase Fleetwood Mac, we will never break the chain.

To Gus Richter, sometimes miracles come in six-foot-six packages. Thank you for being so wonderfully you. And special thanks to Sophia and Hannah, who've brightened my life immeasurably.

To my dad and mom, Henry and Maxine, and my siblings, Joyce and Brent, Steven and Lori, you always have my back, no matter what. Thank you for your loving support.

To my mother-in-law and father-in-law, Maureen and Tom, and my siblings-in-law, Mike, Erin, Alex, Ann, and Dan, your first words after Tom died were, "How can we help?" even though you were all dealing with horrific loss. Thank you for showing me that the only way to deal with grief is to continue loving life and one another.

To my boys, Dan and Jack, you are the strongest, most loving and resilient boys I know. I love you both so much and am so proud of the men you are becoming.

And, finally, to Tom, who offered me such an incredible amount of unconditional love and support in life that I still feel it, even in death. Thanks, Bub.

ABOUT THE AUTHOR

Loretta Nyhan was a reader before she was a writer, devouring everything she could get her hands on, including the backs of cereal boxes and the instruction booklet for building the Barbie Dreamhouse. Later, her obsession with reading evolved into an absolute need to write. After college, she wrote for national trade magazines, taught writing to college freshmen, and eventually found the guts to try fiction. Nyhan has cowritten two historical novels with Suzanne Hayes, *Empire Girls* and the Kirkus-starred *I'll Be Seeing You*. Her solo work includes *All the Good Parts* and the teen paranormal thrillers *The Witch Collector Part I* and *The Witch Collector Part II*. When she's not writing, Nyhan is knitting, baking, and doing all kinds of things her high school self would have found hilarious. Find her online at www.lorettanyhan.com.